IT WAS HER LAST NIGHT

at Totum Air Base. She was saying good-bye to Lieutenant Bill Mason. As she turned from him, he caught her in his arms.

"Do you realize I have the right to keep you here . . . right here, in this house!"

Relief flooded her. "You mean . . . you mean you don't want me to go?"

"This will show you how much I want you to go."
He crushed her close, kissing her eyes, her lips, her throat.

And Dee's pounding, exultant heart drowned out the cautious voice which whispered that this man had failed her once, that he must not be trusted again . . .

Bantam Books by Emilie Loring
Ask your bookseller for the books you have missed

    1 FOR ALL YOUR LIFE
    2 WHAT THEN IS LOVE
    3 I TAKE THIS MAN
    4 MY DEAREST LOVE
    5 LOOK TO THE STARS
    6 BEHIND THE CLOUD
    7 THE SHADOW OF SUSPICION
    8 WITH THIS RING
    9 BEYOND THE SOUND OF GUNS
   10 HOW CAN THE HEART FORGET
   11 TO LOVE AND TO HONOR
   12 LOVE CAME LAUGHING BY
   13 I HEAR ADVENTURE CALLING
   14 THROW WIDE THE DOOR
   15 BECKONING TRAILS
   16 BRIGHT SKIES
   17 THERE IS ALWAYS LOVE
   18 STARS IN YOUR EYES
   19 KEEPERS OF THE FAITH
   20 WHERE BEAUTY DWELLS
   21 FOLLOW YOUR HEART
   22 RAINBOW AT DUSK
   23 WHEN HEARTS ARE LIGHT AGAIN
   24 TODAY IS YOURS
   25 ACROSS THE YEARS
   26 A CANDLE IN HER HEART
   27 WE RIDE THE GALE!
   28 IT'S A GREAT WORLD!
   29 GIVE ME ONE SUMMER
   30 HIGH OF HEART
   31 UNCHARTED SEAS
   32 WITH BANNERS
   33 AS LONG AS I LIVE
   34 FOREVER AND A DAY
   35 LIGHTED WINDOWS
   36 HILLTOPS CLEAR
   37 FAIR TOMORROW
   38 GAY COURAGE
   39 SWIFT WATER
   40 THE SOLITARY HORSEMAN
   41 A CERTAIN CROSSROAD
   42 THE TRAIL OF CONFLICT
   43 SPRING ALWAYS COMES
   44 HERE COMES THE SUN

Rita

EMILIE LORING

BEHIND
THE CLOUD

BANTAM BOOKS · TORONTO · NEW YORK · LONDON

A NATIONAL GENERAL COMPANY

*This low-priced Bantam Book
has been completely reset in a type face
designed for easy reading, and was printed
from new plates. It contains the complete
text of the original hard-cover edition.*
NOT ONE WORD HAS BEEN OMITTED.

BEHIND THE CLOUD

*A Bantam Book / published by arrangement with
Little, Brown and Company, Inc.*

PRINTING HISTORY

Little, Brown edition published April 1958
Grosset and Dunlap edition published September 1959
Bantam edition published December 1960

2nd printing ..... January 1963	10th printing ... November 1966
3rd printing .... June 1964	11th printing ... December 1967
4th printing .... June 1964	12th printing ... February 1968
5th printing ...... August 1964	13th printing .... June 1968
6th printing ...... August 1964	14th printing ..... October 1968
7th printing .... April 1965	15th printing ..... August 1969
8th printing ... November 1965	16th printing ... November 1969
9th printing .... July 1966	17th printing .... June 1970

*Bantam Books are published by Bantam Books, Inc., a National
General company. Its trade-mark, consisting of the words "Bantam
Books" and the portrayal of a bantam, is registered in the United
States Patent Office and in other countries. Marca Registrada.
Bantam Books, Inc., 666 Fifth Avenue, New York, N.Y. 10019.*

PRINTED IN THE UNITED STATES OF AMERICA

BEHIND THE CLOUD

I

DELIGHT TREMAINE studied her reflection in the narrow bedroom mirror, weighing the appropriateness of the pink linen sheath for her first formal dinner in Totum. Sunlight touched the satiny waves of her fair hair and gilded the dark brows arched in speculation as she turned from side to side.

The dress was versatile, she thought; its bolero could be quickly slipped off should the affair turn out to be more formal than she anticipated. Although her brother, Major Tremaine, had neglected to brief her on social customs when he asked her to join him at this remote Army post in Alaska, she had a strong hunch that they would prove rather free and easy.

A dinner party! She felt the tingle of excitement which such an event always gave her, the anticipation of meeting new people, making new friendships. With the thrill, it seemed momentarily that she was back in her aunt's quietly luxurious home in California, not here in these almost pioneer surroundings.

That fancy evaporated when she saw, reflected behind her shoulder, the anxious expression in the tawny face and black eyes of Tamara, the Indian maid-of-all-work, who waited breathlessly for the important decision.

"Will I pass inspection, Tamara?" she demanded gaily. "Remember, as the post commander's sister I must make a good impression on his officers."

The dark eyes glittered in admiration.

"You'll give 'em goose pimples, Miss Delight! Some of them been here so long they'd whistle at a sea cow," the maid added with a grin.

"They must absolutely deafen *you*, then," Delight said, as she turned around and considered Tamara's dusky beauty, her slim figure and glistening black hair.

"Not the officers." Tamara shrugged. "They've got some rule against it, maybe? And the soldiers don't whistle—much —since I got a man. He'd murder 'em if he caught 'em."

Her brows drew together and the black eyes were suddenly hard as flint.

"Same way I'd kill any woman that looked at my Jed!" she added.

It was not said humorously. Delight was disturbed, and not for the first time, at the undercurrent of savagery in the muttered words. Tamara was a creature of varied moods, it appeared, and some of them almost frightening.

With another lightning change, the Indian girl skipped across the room to lift a white evening wrap from its hanger behind the faded denim curtain which served as a closet door.

"You wear this, maybe?" she asked in a thrilled whisper as she stroked the rhinestone embroidery with loving fingers. "It's awful pretty!"

"Heavens, no!" Delight laughed. "And I was crazy to bring it up here. In just these few days I'm beginning to think I should have filled my trunk with slacks and dungarees. Anyway, July here in Alaska seems as warm as California and the sun won't set for hours, so I'll hardly need a wrap."

"California," Tamara sighed wistfully as she replaced the cloak. "If you were living there why'd you ever come here?"

"The call of Adventure—with a capital 'A'!" That was true enough, thought Delight, and a more suitable answer for the Indian girl than the long and involved explanation of why she felt that her place was at her brother's side.

"Living a life of leisure as the unpaid—although very much loved—companion to an elderly aunt, who has absolutely no need for a companion, was a dull existence," she continued. "Even driving for the Red Cross never became exciting, and that constituted my entire contribution to life as a useful human being. So I snatched at the chance to fare forth into the wilderness."

Tamara blinked, apparently having difficulty with such a succession of unfamiliar words, and by childlike frankness reduced the conversation to essentials.

"You had a man back there," she wondered, glancing at the ring on Delight's left hand, "but you came here just the same?" She shook her head reprovingly.

"That had nothing to do with it," Delight said firmly. Turning to the mirror, she gave a last touch to her hair and picked up the evening bag on the bare little bureau. "You run along now, Tamara, and thank you for all your help. I'll see you in the morning."

On the front steps of Major Tremaine's quarters she stood for a moment taking in the scene which was still so new and strange to her. This was hardly the frozen waste of perpetual ice and snow the name "Alaska" had once conjured up in her youthful mind. The northern country's all too short summer was at its height, with every living thing enjoying it to the full.

Cormorants circled slowly high overhead as though flying air cover for the innumerable swans, geese, ravens and sandpipers which thronged the shoreline. Out over the bay a dagger-winged jaeger made a sudden swoop and snatched a fish from a careless tern, leaving the complaining bird to flap disconsolately away for further hunting. Swarms of dragonflies formed shimmering clouds above the long, irregular windrows of yellow kelp and brown seaweed rolled high up the beach by the twenty-foot tides of the Pacific.

Offshore, as far as the eye could see, the sparkling sapphire water was dotted with small and large green-forested islands. On the horizon their green faded to mingle with misty blue where sea met sky, and to the north a volcano reared its serrated crater top through a filmy scarf of cloud.

Delight found less beauty in the immediate neighborhood. Her brother's house and the others which made up Officers Row, a series of square, unadorned clapboard boxes, ranged along the top of a rolling slope of straggling grass. Below them spread the dusty parade ground of the post, with its weather-beaten barracks and administration buildings—the Stars and Stripes atop an unpainted pole the one touch of color in the drab encampment.

A barbed wire barrier surrounded the camp—a relic of wartime occupation, Major Jim had smilingly assured her, and not preparation for expected attack. It was noticeable, however, that an armed sentry paced before its gate at all hours of the day and night, proof that the detachment was not stationed here for a rest cure.

On one side of the parade ground a muddy river, widened by the myriad shallow pools dug by each winter's ice, wound away to disappear among the steep-flanked mountains which seemed threatening to crowd the post into the bay. The river separated the camp, and the airfield upstream which it was guarding, from the old Russian-founded town of Totum—a clutter of frame houses and larger buildings which sprawled along the steep hillside above the single wharf and trailed dwindling down to the river, where it degenerated into the even less pretentious native village.

That at least was interesting, if not lovely. From a distance it appeared thickly settled, but Delight had discovered this to be an illusion caused by the universal Indian custom of building a cache for supplies near a dwelling. These miniature, windowless log cabins, lifted on tin-coated stilts to discourage marauding mice and moles, doubled the number of houses visible among the scraggly pines and spruces.

Her destination was the only comfortable-looking house in Totum, perched on a cleared knoll at the beginning of the town's street and a short distance beyond the bridge over the river, and she started down the hill. Before she had taken a dozen steps a jeep pulled up beside her.

"Can I take you somewheres, ma'am?" asked its grizzled driver with hoarse politeness.

"I'm only going to Dr. Bentley's, thank you."

"That's clean across the river!" he protested. "You'll get them pretty slippers awful dusty." He sketched a salute. "Sergeant Hogan, ma'am, Baker Company."

"I'm happy to meet you, Sergeant." Delight capitulated and took the seat beside him. "I am Miss Tremaine."

"Sure, the C.O.'s sister." Hogan grinned. "I don't stop for every dame—uh, *lady,* I mean." He stepped on the throttle and the jeep bounded into and out of a hole with a force which shook a gasp from the girl.

"Sorry, ma'am!" The sergeant reduced speed to a cautious crawl. "Forgot I had a passenger. I'm due to stand retreat with Lieutenant Mason and it don't pay to keep him waiting."

"Then you most certainly are not going out of your way to save my shoes," Delight announced positively. "You will debark me at the gate, and from there I'll navigate on my own. That's an order, Sergeant."

"Yes, *ma'am!* Darned if you don't sound like your brother —or Lieutenant Mason."

"You seem to have that lieutenant on your mind."

"Why not?" grunted Hogan. "He commands Baker Company. And I *mean* commands it. Ma'am, I've been twenty-two years in the service an' seen a lot of 'em come and go, but I never seen a young feller with more on the ball than him."

"Isn't it unusual for a lieutenant to command a company?"

"Well, by rights a captain commands, yes, but we don't need one with Lieutenant Mason on the job. He ain't been here long, but long enough to turn the company from a bunch of goldbricking bums into the making of soldiers. You met him yet?"

"The day I arrived I met all the officers, I think. And your Lieutenant Mason," she admitted ruefully, "made a distinct impression—by paying as little attention to me as possible."

As the machine approached the gate of the parade ground she ordered:

"Let me out here, please. I won't begin our acquaintance by exposing you to the wrath of your superior."

Obediently, if reluctantly, the sergeant stopped at the entrance. Delight attempted to toss him a grateful smile while she dismounted airily from the jeep, but the two actions failed to mesh smoothly. She caught one heel on the car's side, staggered sideways with embarrassing awkwardness, and would have fallen flat but for a man's arm which swung her upright.

Pink with chagrin, she looked up—and was startled to identify her rescuer as the officer they had been discussing. A face brown as tanned leather, a smiling mouth and gray eyes, black close-cropped hair below his tilted cap. The smile lit a responsive glow in her as she inventoried the broad shoulders, the lean waist—and the heavy automatic pistol holstered on one hip. What a perfect lead for one of Hollywood's epics, she thought. Lieutenant William Mason had piqued her curiosity at the reception; now he awakened admiration.

She combined an old-fashioned curtsy with a demure upward glance.

"Thanks, kind sir, for the timely help of your good right arm."

There was a flicker of amusement in the gray eyes as he returned a courtly bow.

"Ever at the service of a lady in distress, Miss Tremaine. I'm sure that when you've been with us longer you will become better acquainted with our jeeps—and act accordingly."

"I hope to become better acquainted with the personnel also, Lieutenant." She could not resist adding, "You scarcely spoke to me at Jim's—Major Tremaine's welcoming party for me."

He looked down at her soberly, realizing that his distant manner that day must have hurt her feelings. Lucky she hadn't known how constantly he watched her, admired the grace of every movement, envied the captivating friendliness with which she met one officer after another. That same warm charm was engulfing him now.

"Sorry if I was rude," he said, and offered the first excuse which occurred to him. "I'm no use at social gatherings."

"Then it wasn't my fault?" Delight exclaimed with theatrical relief. "Oh, *good!* The way you avoided me gave me an inferiority complex."

"Perish such a thought!" Against his will Mason found himself responding to her gaiety. "For once in my life I honestly regretted having no supply of small talk to interest you."

"An *Army* man—and not a fledgling second lieutenant, either—with no polite chatter for the C.O.'s sister?" Delight teased. "I find that incredible, sir! Didn't you receive Emily Post indoctrination at your various assignments?"

"Never had the chance," he confessed with a grin. Outwardly amused, inwardly Mason was regretting all he had missed, as exemplified by this alluring girl. "My tours of duty have been in foreign territory, ranging from Germany to the Far East, where the social graces are unknown."

"*Unknown,* in Berlin and Tokyo?" she demanded.

"That I wouldn't know about. Somehow I was always assigned to the back-country districts. You don't meet Emily Post in the Korean mountains, for instance."

"Sounds exciting, anyway. Brushes with fiendish enemy agents at every turn, I suppose?"

"Occasional only, but that was often enough!"

Delight gave him an approving smile.

"Now, you see you can do the polite conversational act quite nicely when you try. Either you were born with a natural talent or you're concealing your past." At a disquieting change in his expression she explained hastily, "I mean, concealing past experience in the art of conversation, of course." Then she rushed on eagerly, "I'd love to hear some of your adventures—if you'll talk of them. Shall I see you at the Bentleys'?"

Mason's smile was gone, his face an expressionless mask.

"No, I'm on duty." He swung on his heel to the jeep and his voice cracked. "Sergeant! Were you detailed to drive Miss Tremaine to Dr. Bentley's?"

"No, sir! I only picked her up—" Hogan gulped and his mahogany cheeks glowed. "I mean, I was just giving her a lift!"

"Even so, why dump her off at this gate? You don't expect her to *walk* over there, do you?"

Before Hogan could justify himself, Delight, annoyed at the officer's obvious attempt to be rid of her, plunged into heated defense of the sergeant.

"He *dumped* me here—as you so elegantly phrase it—at my explicit request, Lieutenant Mason!" Again she detected laughter in his eyes, but this time it added to her indignation. "I'm quite capable of walking the rest of the way. I wouldn't think of interfering with important official ceremonies, so you may proceed with your retreat. Good evening!"

She went past the jeep with a smiling, "Thanks for the lift, Sergeant," and started along the road to town.

Hogan jumped from the machine and stared at the frowning officer.

"Shall I follow her and try again, sir? Don't guess she'll give in, though."

"Neither do I." Mentally Mason added, Not with that delightfully feminine version of the major's forceful jaw. Lord, what a girl!

6

Neither he nor Hogan were aware that Delight had paused a little way from the gate to watch the ceremony. But a soldier posted high on the camp's observation platform took note of the fact. Eagerly he rolled the brass mouthpiece of his bugle back and forth across his lips while he waited for a signal from the orderly outside Headquarters building. If that snappy dame wanted to hear retreat really blown, he'd give her something to curl her honey-blond hair. Sure seemed a dog's age since he'd had so pretty an audience.

Although Lieutenant Mason's attention was not occupied like the bugler's, his thoughts followed a similar path. He scowled around at the post, the stained olive-drab barracks, the hard-packed brown desert of parade ground, the glowering rusty brown and green of the rocky hillsides beyond. It took a girl like Delight Tremaine to awaken a man to the dullness of this outpost and the loneliness of Army life for a bachelor officer. Resolutely he shook himself out of that depression to concentrate on his job.

"I'll eat with the company tonight, Sergeant," he said. "Time I checked our mess again. Any idea what Baker Company's Waldorf Astoria is dishing out?"

"Steak—with some of them canned mushrooms they flew in yesterday," Hogan answered with satisfaction.

"Oh, good deal! Cook turns out steaks the way we had them at our ranch when I was a kid. Not much like some cooks I've chummed around with—they'd leave the hair on. Uh! What else?"

"Chocolate cream pie with—" Hogan broke off at a reverberating crash from the nearby mess hall.

A furious voice roared imprecations; a black and white Husky dashed out the door and fled around a corner of the building.

"That's what we'll have," the sergeant amended sourly, "if that overgrown mutt left any for us. That's Captain Kent's dog an' cook's soft on him. I'd as soon have a moose in my kitchen! And now that I think of it, we're sure eating better since you took over the company, Lieutenant."

At Headquarters the orderly looked up from his watch to wave an arm. On the observation platform the soldier straightened with clicking heels, the bugle flashed with machinelike precision to his lips. Ruddy cheeks quivered as the piercing notes of retreat echoed from the hills. The Stars and Stripes descended fluttering on its pole to the waiting arms of a brown figure.

Lieutenant Mason dropped his hand from his cap.

"Corporal Simmons never blew a sweeter horn!" he complimented. "Put him down for another stripe, Sergeant. We ought to ante up for perfection when we find it!"

So ended another day at the wilderness outpost, with the sun still high and no evening shadows yet softening the harsh outlines of parade and barracks. Only the clock and the hunger of the personnel suggested that mess call was soon to blow.

II

SHE WAS twenty-four, radiantly alive, with wit, pride and a hint of daring in her lovely face. Beside that Delight Tremaine happened to be the post commander's sister. Small wonder, then, that the officers gathered for dinner at the Bentleys' forgot that they were detailed to a remote garrison in Alaska while they basked in the sunshine of her charm.

Their open admiration flattered Delight, although she modestly credited a good part of it to the lack of competition. Mrs. Bentley and one young captain's wife were the only other ladies present. And credit some more, she decided, to the unaccustomed graciousness of the surroundings. The Bentley house was a far cry indeed from the Spartan quarters in Officers Row, those models of what the Army considered adequate shelter for its members.

Major Bentley, several years retired from the Medical Corps, had settled in Totum and dedicated the remainder of his life to the study of diseases among the Indians and Eskimos in hope of bettering their dismal existence. Faithful as the Biblical Ruth, his wife accompanied him, and devoted her life to making him comfortable. Delight marveled at the miracles worked by a woman's urge for homemaking in this barren village.

The doctor, a stocky, graying man with pink cheeks and lively green eyes, stood beside her in the living room, where the others were already breaking the conversational ice with cocktails. He was obviously proud of his wife's achievements and pleased when Delight enthused over the outstanding features of the room.

There was a broad picture window looking out on the river valley and the purple hills. At the bay end tall glass doors allowed the room to extend onto a flagstone terrace bordered by masses of deep blue monkshood and shoulder-high lances of giant lupine in a paler hue. The apple-green walls were suffused, even at this hour, with slanting sunlight; a Tyrian purple carpet and armchairs of opal-gray broadcloth seemed to float in the same golden haze.

The girl's eye was finally caught and held by a painting above the long bookcase which nearly filled one end of the room. Once glimpsed, the flaming swirl of grays, magenta and luminous green could hardly be ignored. Dr. Bentley noticed her absorbed look, pushed his glasses down long enough to identify the object which seemed to fascinate her and nodded complacently.

"Recognize it?" He had the quiet, persuasive voice of the born doctor.

"The aurora borealis?"

"Good for you! It is. You're to be congratulated that you didn't think it was a modernistic atrocity. But I meant did you recognize the artist. Alaska is proud of Sydney Laurence. I consider that one of his best efforts at pinning an impossible subject on prosaic canvas."

"Imagine!" Mrs. Bentley flung the exclamatory word into their conversation and herself with it. She was a small bouncy woman in a gorgeous powder-blue dress. Her chic haircut had been allowed to go slightly to seed, but there was nothing seedy about the lustrous pearls at her throat, Delight noticed. Evidently a woman of means, and a non-stop talker, as she proceeded to demonstrate.

"I saw that painting on one of my trips to Seattle," she chattered. "Fell in love with it—bought it on the spot."

"No wonder," Delight agreed. "It's breath-taking."

"It took George's breath away—my extravagance, I mean." She gave her husband a twinkling smile. "He was simply furious."

"Not after I saw the picture, my dear."

"That's true. But what I started to say was that it became the inspiration for the color scheme of this room. Unusual, don't you agree?"

"But beautiful," Delight amended. "I hope you won't object if I filch a few ideas to adopt—or rather adapt—for Jim's house. I'm trying so hard to make it pleasanter for him."

"And getting some practice for the future?" Bertha Bentley directed a significant glance at the diamond ring on the girl's left hand. "Tell me, is your intended the appreciative type?"

Delight smilingly ignored the question and pursued her own subject.

"All my efforts are concentrated on Jim's quarters for the present. I'm in no hurry to rush into the future."

"Very wise of you, my dear," the doctor approved. "Why try to anticipate what Marcus Aurelius called 'the yawning void of the future'?"

His wife brushed the ancient wisdom aside to launch a

voluble description of her herculean labors in obtaining the desired fabrics and furniture for the room—by mail order, naturally, since Totum's interior decorating supplies were limited to oilcloth and gingham.

Delight had difficulty in keeping her interest on the story. From the other side of the room a tall blond officer was regarding her with evident concentration. She shifted her attention back to Mrs. Bentley long enough for a few disconnected phrases to register. When she looked again the man was drinking. He set his empty glass on the mantel, propped an elbow beside it and listened to a discussion between two officers nearby. But a moment later, she saw from under lowered lids that his eyes were on her again, a thoughtful crease wrinkling the blond brows.

When her hostess was forced to pause for breath Delight murmured, "Don't look now, but who is the blond at the fireplace?"

"No need to look." The other's smile was of just-as-I-expected satisfaction. "So he has made an impression already? But then, he would be completely crushed if he failed to, my dear. That is Captain Steele, Warner Steele. Considerable reputation as a Romeo."

The girl nodded soberly.

"Now I remember meeting him at Jim's party." She took perverse pleasure in squelching the older woman's romantic supposition. "Perhaps he would be slightly crushed, anyway, to learn that the *impression* is not too favorable."

Dr. Bentley, who had grown increasingly restive during his wife's extended discourse on decorating, now took her arm.

"Come along, B.B.," he ordered, "we must circulate among our guests, you know."

"But I want to talk to Delight."

"So do others." With a sidewise shift of twinkling eyes he indicated a young man hovering near them, and firmly propelled her away.

Promptly the boy with carefully slicked down wavy brown hair and a single gold bar on his shoulder advanced and offered to refill Delight's glass before he noticed that it was still brimming.

"Don't give me away, Lieutenant," she begged with a conspiratorial smile. "I only took this to be polite, not to imbibe."

"Gosh, what will power! Wait till you've been in this hole for months, you'll drink like the rest of us and like it."

Dr. Bentley was still close enough to overhear the exchange and spoke over his shoulder.

"Disregard the ominous warning, Miss Tremaine. Lieutenant Peck is one of our young lions who like to consider themselves abandoned characters, driven to drink by the boredum of Totum. They must have read Kipling. Remember his 'Gentlemen Rankers'?" And the doctor, an inveterate quoter, intoned, " 'To the legion of the lost ones, to the cohort of the damned—' "

The lieutenant grinned.

"I surrender, Miss Tremaine. Nobody can put on an act with our good doctor around. Actually this is a very interesting assignment."

"I should think it would be," Delight agreed, "with the Air Force depending on you to help guard its secrets." She saw his smooth face assume an instant expression of studied incomprehension and bit her lip. "Oh, I shouldn't have breathed *that,* should I, Lieutenant Peck!"

"For Pete's sake, call me Dick!"

"Okay, Dick, but I'm ashamed to have violated one of the rules and regulations the major laid down for me."

"Forget you said it, I have. You follow Major Tremaine's orders and you won't go wrong, lady."

As always, Delight basked in praise of her brother. "You like him, then, Dick?"

"*Like* isn't exactly the word to describe a young shavetail's feeling for his commanding officer, but it'll do," he admitted. "The captain who commanded here was removed— for good reasons—and Major Tremaine and Kent were shipped in to reorganize us. They're experts at that, I understand. The day your brother took over he made a speech— about two minutes long—that sold us on him right down the line to the lowest private in the rear rank."

"Tell me what he said," Delight urged.

"I couldn't possibly give you the charge that we got from his words because I'm not the major, but—" Peck rubbed his chin for inspiration. "Well, he listed the objectives of this task force: first, to assist the Air Force in maintaining this station." He gave Delight a meaningful wink. "That covers what you just wished you hadn't mentioned.

"Second, to see that no—er—unfriendly element muscles in on this territory. Third, to show the natives that the Army is a bunch of friendly people who intend to get along with everybody, without imposing on them or being a nuisance."

Dick chuckled at a memory. "Then he talked about *us*— the different units—and what was wrong with us. And did he know! Maybe you heard the bugler blowing retreat just before we came here?"

"I did, never heard any better. I watched the ceremony, too."

Another lieutenant, who looked even younger than Dick, edged into the conversation. He stroked the pale mustache which was intended to add maturity—and would in time.

"Talking about 'Tremaine's Treatment for Sick Soldiers'?" he chuckled. "That's a quote from Sergeant Hogan—an old Army man. When the major found a lad who could *blow* a horn, he really went to town. You're going to hear every regulation bugle call every day, ma'am, and see more saluting than in the Pentagon."

"I was just telling her," said Peck, "how her brother cleaned the place up." He lowered his voice confidentially. "It's no secret that our last commander lost his grip and let things slide disgracefully. In a camp like this, with no entertainment for off-duty hours, no place for the men to go to relax, they can get dangerously low on morale. Even go to pieces, sometimes."

"We call it cabin fever," explained the other. "And the cure for it is to keep 'em too busy to get bored. The major sure goes along with that theory and has our tongues hanging out."

"He certainly lost no time in prescribing," Peck agreed. "I told you part of his speech. Dee—" he blushed slightly at his boldness and was relieved when it went unrebuked—"the finale was really good!" He repeated it with a reminiscent smile in his eyes and an imitative snap in the words:

" 'I think you are good men who have been allowed to run to seed. That's over! I intend to make this a *military* post, run under Army rules and regulations. You all know them, and you're going to operate by them from now on, if it kills you. I am in sole command of this post, and until I am relieved my word is law. So watch your step! *Dismissed!* ' "

The lieutenant stood twirling his cocktail glass and smiling at Delight. He shook his head in regret.

"Your brother's words put that sparkle in your big blue eyes, not my humble self, worse luck. But I'll keep trying." He stepped back politely when Dr. Bentley offered his arm to escort the guest of honor to dinner.

III

IN THE dining room Delight awarded an additional palm to Bertha Bentley for distinguished decoration. The room, paneled in waxed cedar planks and made octagon by four corner cupboards, showed only one concession to modernity, a copper and bronze ceiling light which she guessed was seldom used except during the long winter nights. This evening, tall yellow candles filled the room with their wavering glow, mingling with the late sunlight.

A Chilkat blanket of goat's hair in geometric designs of black, yellow and blue-green covered one wall, with similar figures echoing the colors in rug and hangings. The wide fireplace was of alternating bands of rough and smooth cement in which were set fossil ferns, strange fish and shells which Mrs. Bentley had collected from the local beaches.

As a focal point for the room a weird Tlingit ceremonial mask hung over the mantel against a cape of what were evidently hummingbird feathers to judge from their metallic luster in the candlelight.

A black trestle table, so old that it might have been used in the first Russian trading post in Alaska, was flanked by cushioned chairs too comfortable to be quitted in unseemly haste. Every detail gave welcome encouragement to Delight by proving what could be accomplished, even in Totum, with determination and imagination. Bertha Bentley might chatter idiotically at times, but she did have the decorator's equivalent of a gardener's green thumb.

Nor was her imaginative power confined to the manipulation of colors and fabrics, for she proved equally adept at concocting a menu, and on a magic carpet of cookery wafted the company far from their semi-Arctic base. The dinner was Mexican from soup to dessert, each successive dish greeted with laughter and subdued cheers as the beaming Indian woman bore it in steaming from the kitchen. As the meal progressed it became a contest in happy memories evoked by "the last time I tasted *this*—"

From beginning to end the officers resolutely ignored the sparkling ring on the third finger of Delight's left hand, as though by refusing to notice it they could cause it to disappear. Not so Bertha. Since the girl's arrival four days ago Mrs. Bentley's superdetective skill at ferreting out facts—and quite often fiction—had failed to uncover either the fiancé's name or anything about him. To her the ring had become an obsession, more goading with every setback.

Now she leaned forward, throwing discretion to the winds, and with a meaningful glance at the glittering diamonds commanded archly, "Give us the name of the fortunate man, my dear, that we may congratulate you." She settled back in her chair with a satisfied smirk at the guests.

For the fraction of a moment Delight sat hesitant, twisting her fork between her fingers, while she wondered how to answer the demand. Then, as she came to a decision, her

13

eyes darkened and gleamed with secret amusement, and an elusive dimple dented her cheek.

The level sunlight through the windows turned her dress to salmon-colored flame as she rose and lifted the coffee cup from beside her plate. Her smile drifted impartially from one pair of watching eyes to another; dramatically she proclaimed:

"A toast! I give you *himself*—the man I left behind me."

For a second her eyes widened and a tint of excitement colored her face. With a stifled exclamation she dropped into her chair. Why in the world, she wondered, should a tall dark-haired soldierly figure flash before her mind's eye as she offered that joking pledge? In her confusion she looked toward her brother, found his keenly questioning gaze riveted on her and flushed more deeply.

Fortunately the other guests were completely oblivious to her embarrassment. Being well acquainted with the prying proclivities of their hostess, they greeted the girl's evasion with shouts of laughter.

Dr. Bentley rocked in his chair with delight as his eyes flicked from face to face around the table. His pink face assumed the leer of an elderly satyr as he observed dryly, " 'Himself,' eh? Well, men, if that's all she'll admit, go to it, and see if you can put one over on the absent beau. Remember how we've twisted that old saying of the Russians here in Alaska? 'God's in His Heaven and the Czar is far away' has become 'Washington is far away.' "

He winked at Delight, surveyed the group over his glasses again, then turned his probing gaze on his wife.

"Where's Bill Mason tonight, B.B.?" he inquired. "Is he AWOL again?"

Delight felt her face burn still more at the question. Did everyone here have the heroic-looking officer in mind? Was it possible that her brother and the doctor had intercepted the wave length of her thoughts when she had proposed the toast? She covertly examined the doctor's smiling face, but could see no indication that it was more than idle conversation.

Bertha Bentley frowned as she considered her husband's question.

"William Hamilton Mason is the most unsociable officer on the post," she criticized. "He pleaded duty when I invited him. Major, why do you keep that handsome boy so busy?"

"My dear Mrs. Bentley." Jim Tremaine smilingly lifted a reproving hand. "Allow me a slight correction. Lieutenant Mason is no *boy,* although," he added with a wry grimace, "he may appear young to some of us. If I'm not revealing

14

any secret, he is twenty-eight. And because he has spent most of his time since West Point in our Intelligence and Military Police, both in Europe and Asia, where life is no bed of roses, he appears even older than his years.

"Mason," he murmured thoughtfully, "is what I call experienced and *rugged*, a splendid officer to have on hand if anything should get—well, shall we say, out of line?" He sipped his coffee, watching his hostess with a faint smile.

"And now to answer your question," he continued. "The lieutenant actually is on duty tonight. Although at present there seems little need for an Army detachment in this remote district, as long as we are here we must guard against any form of infiltration or surprise attack."

He paused thoughtfully and looked down at his plate. Delight noted a tensing of the officers about the table, as though they shared some secret knowledge.

"To guard effectively," the major resumed quickly, looking at his hostess again, "requires discipline and constant alertness. Lieutenant Mason is Officer of the Day, seeing to it that we are ready for anything, and I am sure that even you, Mrs. Bentley, will admit that *one* of my official family should be on duty while the rest of us relax."

The lady shrugged off his gentle reprimand.

"You make it sound so portentous, Major! And all I'm asking is a little of your prize policeman's time. But he's always 'too busy'!"

Tremaine grinned. "Sorry, ma'am, that's his affair. But give him a break. Remember, if my 'prize policeman'—and I'll go along with that 'prize'—isn't as socially inclined as you would like, lay it up to his long experience with the seamier side of our allies—and others—overseas. Experience which it will take him some time to get over, I'm afraid."

At this point Dr. Bentley pushed back his chair and stood up.

"That ought to hold you, B.B.," he told his wife with a chuckle. "Let's have some more coffee and smokes on the terrace. Candles in a country where it's daylight most of the night seem an awful waste of wax!"

Bertha glared in resigned endurance as he forgot his ladies-first training and strolled from the room.

With a sigh of utter content Delight settled into one of the wicker chairs arranged on the terrace. Mrs. Bentley was serving fresh coffee, ably assisted by Captain Kent and his wife. Two lieutenants were discussing the latest crack-up at the airstrip with their host. From the record player, which another officer switched on with a languishing look at Delight, drifted an old song, with new lyrics and a new tenor: "If you were the only girl . . ."

Susan Kent, the lovely gray-haired wife of Tremaine's executive officer, came to sit beside her.

"We're all so glad that you have come to be with your brother, Miss Tremaine," she said. "He seems such a lonely man."

"I hope I can help Jim!" The fervor in Delight's voice made it a prayer. "When I feel settled myself, that is."

"You're too modest," Mrs. Kent chided, sipping her coffee. "You've done wonders already; the major looks years younger tonight."

"While I feel years older!" Delight laughed. "Truly, it does seem years instead of days since I stepped aboard the plane in San Francisco and flew over that labyrinth of straits and islands and snowy mountains to Totum. Everything here still seems so strange. Have you been here long, Mrs. Kent?"

"Please call me Susan—Sue would be better still if you can manage it on such brief acquaintance. Mrs. Kent reminds me of my prematurely gray hair and wrinkles."

With all honesty Delight protested, "I think your hair is beautiful, and there isn't the faintest trace of a wrinkle!"

"They must be in my mind, then," the matron sighed. "Wait until you've trailed a soldier wherever the Army assigns him for ten years, my dear!"

Her eyes dropped to the girl's ring. "But perhaps you haven't picked a soldier husband—" She stopped short and set down her cup with an agitated clatter. "Heavenly day! I'm getting worse than Bertha Bentley! Scratch that last prying remark quickly, and tell me how you happen to be in this forsaken hole in the ground."

"I hardly know myself." Delight was glad to veer away from the delicate subject of her romantic ties. "Ever since Jim's wife died, six years ago, I have begged him to take me along on his varied assignments, but always he was adamant. Then, incredibly, following his tour of duty in Hawaii—which would surely have been Heaven!" she interpolated wistfully—"he seemed to weaken a little under my arguments.

"But just the same I'd about given up any hope of ever going with him, when he was ordered to this Alaskan outpost and wrote a long letter asking me to pack up and come. Asking me?" she repeated mockingly. "He practically *ordered* me to come! Quite took my breath away—with joy, of course. Jim is much older than I am, you know, and as a small girl I simply adored him. And still do, for that matter," she added with a catch in her throat.

"I hope," was Mrs. Kent's dry suggestion, "that you'll be able to transfer some of that affection to 'Himself.' Oh, dear!" she interrupted her own speech in disgust. "There I go again! I'd better round up *my* Adored One and have him take me home to meditate on my unbridled tongue." With a friendly pat on Delight's shoulder she wandered away.

Thoughtfully the girl looked down on the shanties of the Indian village which sprawled across the meadow near town. Drab and impoverished as they were, they faced on beauty, the azure bay sparkling with a million diamonds, and beyond it the black-seamed slopes of the cratered mountain thrust up from green wilderness. It was a glorious world, rough and frightening in places, but always awe-inspiring. What would it be like, she wondered, when snow and ice cut off the post from civilization, when the long Arctic night blacked out everything? She shivered uncontrollably.

"Homesick?" challenged a voice.

Delight's thoughts swung back from their wandering in the frozen future to concentrate on the officer who dropped into the chair beside her. Captain Steele had deep, cautious blue eyes narrowed by sleepy, drooping lids. Flawless features. Too flawless, she decided promptly with a recurrence of her initial dislike.

During dinner she had noted the uniform that was perfection in fit and finish, the manners—suave, sophisticated, almost ridiculously out of line with the boisterous younger men. But she suspended final judgment while she answered, "Homesick here with Jim, Captain Steele? I should say not! Wherever he is, is home for me."

"Where is—where was your home, Delight? Do you know, you worry me? I have the feeling that I've seen you somewhere before. Something about your lips—your rather determined but very attractive chin jogs my memory. It's nothing definite, nothing tangible, just a teasing, elusive impression," he mused.

"Doubtless in some previous incarnation you were a conquering Roman and I your shivering slave," she suggested dryly. "To answer your question about my home—for a number of years I have lived with an aunt in California. But how could I be homesick in any case when you are all so nice to me? I am in grave danger of being hopelessly spoiled."

The captain smiled. "You must remember that a girl, an outstandingly attractive person like you, is a rarity in this neck of the woods. After even a short tour of duty in this god-forsaken place most of us would lay down our lives for one of your charming smiles. Lacking that opportunity, we lay our hearts at your feet and try to outdo each other with our attentions—attentions which you would attract in any part of the world where you happened to be, I'll be the first to admit. If ours are a little more fervid than you have encountered before, just credit it to the fact that *we* are home-sick for 'outside.' "

Delight sat silent, nonplused by the storm of feeling evinced in the other's words. She tried to think of something to say which would change the conversation to a more conventional subject.

"Have you heard of the trip which Mrs. Bentley is planning?" she asked in desperation. "She has chartered one of the coast steamers, and next week some of us are going to sail up to see the ice fields and the glacier. Perhaps do some fishing, too, weather permitting.

"But the ice fields sound the most fascinating. They tell me that if you are lucky, once in a while you get a look at a polar bear marooned on an iceberg. Um—maybe not a *polar* bear, but some kind of bear. I'm so thrilled at the prospect that I shan't be able to eat or sleep," she prophesied with gay exaggeration.

"I mean to get in on that trip, if I may?" Steele's tone invested the question with significant tenderness.

Under the intense regard of his blue eyes Delight regretted her choice of subject. Why had she brought up the Bentley expedition with this man whom she half disliked, half distrusted?

"It isn't my party," she reminded him shortly. "You'll have to smile your sweetest on Mrs. Bentley to win a bid."

"Then I'm as good as aboard the boat; I'm in strong with Babbling Bertha." At her exclamation of protest he defended, "Everyone calls her that, although not to her face, of course. Really, did you ever know such a talker? A lady of excessive adjectives and unbridled curiosity. How two people of such widely different personalities and tastes as she and the doctor have lived together so long without a murder is one of the unsolved mysteries of this age."

"I think they are both delightful—" she began indignantly.

"But in slightly different ways." Smoothly the captain avoided an argument by reverting to the proposed trip. "How long are you going to be prospecting for ice and bears?"

"We start at daylight, I understand, or whatever they consider daybreak here. Not two in the morning, I hope! And we return sometime after supper."

Steele slapped the arm of his chair in disgust.

"Just my luck!" he growled. "A whole day with you—and look where I stand. I'd have to ask for time off, and I was down the coast on leave less than a week ago."

He turned on his charming smile full strength. "Your brother is the one I hate like—like the dickens to tackle. But if you'll be the angel you look and put in a good word for me with the major—"

"*I?*" It was an indignant gasp, tinged with relief. "I, not even a lowly private in the rear rank, interfere in affairs military? Nothing doing, thank you! You wouldn't make such a suggestion if you knew the long list of Major Jim's 'Don'ts!' to which I subscribed before he allowed me to leave my native land. They are indelibly branded on my memory, sir!"

A hand fell on her shoulder.

"Say good night to our host and hostess, will you, Dee?" asked Tremaine with a nod to Steele. "Too bad to tear you away, but there's a little emergency paper work you can help me with."

Obediently, not at all reluctantly, Delight went in search of the Bentleys.

The major lowered his voice. "What was the trouble in town this afternoon, Captain? Did you settle it?"

"Yes, sir," with a bored smile. "I returned too late to turn in a report; I'll take care of it first thing in the morning. There was nothing to it, though. A strange ship showed up offshore early today."

"Another of those Japanese floating canneries?"

Steele shrugged. "That's what the local fishermen thought when one of the boats reported her. You know they claim such ships break up the salmon runs and ruin their business, so a few hotheads grabbed guns and tried to recruit a riot squad to go out and do battle with her. They were really steamed up by the time I got there."

"Then there was some trouble?"

"No, sir. I know how to handle those loudmouths. It only took me five minutes to make them admit that they didn't know whether she's a Jap or Russian or in the Swiss Navy— or even a canning boat. Besides, she's clear outside the twelve mile limit and the consensus of opinion seemed to be that that's still the legal distance in the international agreement. It was just a case of jitters, complicated with a little heavy drinking. I talked them out of it without bloodshed."

"That's fine work, Captain." Tremaine nodded. "Anything we can do to help keep the peace around here is all to the good, you know. I'll ask the Navy to check on that ship."

"You don't think it has any connection," Steele jerked a thumb over his shoulder, "with the fly-boys' secret project at the airstrip?"

Tremaine's face froze. "Of all people, Captain, I would expect you to keep your mouth shut about that!"

"Yes, sir. Sorry!" Flushed at the rebuke, Steele hastily shifted his ground. "Major, when I got back to my quarters I learned that Mason had thrown my orderly, Jed Crane, into the guardhouse. A piece of unwarranted interference that I want to talk to you about." The glitter in his eyes spelled trouble for any inferior in rank so rash as to cross him. "That guy is taking himself too seriously."

Tremaine was not impressed by the threatening manner.

"Lieutenant Mason is Officer of the Day," he reminded caustically. "What was specified in the order confining Crane?"

"I don't know, Major. I reached my quarters only in time to come here for this party. But——"

"It is quite probable that Lieutenant Mason had a good reason," Tremaine interrupted. "He knows his business. He makes few mistakes. I wish," he added coldly, "that I could say as much for the rest of us. Good night, Captain!"

The major moved away to retrieve his sister from a group of laughing, protesting officers.

IV

"JIM, is there a mystery about Lieutenant Mason?" Delight asked as they walked slowly homeward through the evening twilight. Her brother turned his head so quickly to stare at her that she explained, "Whenever I talk with him, which apparently is just as seldom as he can diplomatically manage, I feel as though I were battling against an impenetrable reserve."

She felt her cheeks glow as she remembered how the officer's face flashed on the screen of her mind when she was offering that absurd toast. Why, she had only spoken to the man on two occasions, and each time he appeared so anxious to be rid of her that it was mortifying.

In spite of that, quite possibly because of that, her contrary self liked him, liked his very aloofness that was so maddeningly—and therefore so intriguingly—difficult to fathom. She admired his clean-cut face, the direct look of the gray eyes and inflexible decision of the handsome mouth, even the obstinate kink in his dark hair. His hands fascinated her, their strength felt when he saved her from falling, their look of dependability. Good hands to cling to in an emergency.

She laughed under her breath. That was a curious attribute to attract Delight Tremaine, who was definitely not of the clinging-vine variety. On the contrary, some of the boys back home had been known to complain that she was "too darned independent."

She had forgotten her question to Jim while she mused

over its subject, so that his voice recalled her with a start.

"A mystery about Mason?" His laugh sounded forced. "I wouldn't say that, Dee, unless you want to make one of the bitter tension between him and Captain Steele. The lieutenant was already here when Steele arrived and I'll never forget Mason's expression when they came face to face in Headquarters. As though someone had stuck a knife in him."

"They knew each other before?"

"Classmates at West Point, graduated six years ago. But somewhere along the line Mason missed out on a promotion."

"Then he might resent Steele's ranking him."

Jim shrugged that off. "He's too much of a man; those things happen, we all know it. Remember, he's been overseas continuously since he left the Point, on various assignments —extremely important but not spectacular. And all of them a long, long way from Washington."

"If he did good work, and it wasn't rewarded—"

"Promotion isn't a reward for past services, my innocent child. It's a prediction that a man is qualified to handle the duties of the higher grade. And everyone doesn't always win it when he should. A biased commanding officer, for instance, could drop a word or two into a man's service record that might cost him the step upward."

"I wonder if Captain Steele did that to Mason," the girl muttered resentfully.

"Impossible," Jim stated flatly. "The two have never been in the same area, let alone the same command. Until now."

"Are you sure of that?" Delight persisted, reluctant to abandon a possibility which would explain so much.

"Certainly. I've checked Mason's record thoroughly and—" Jim bit off the sentence, cleared his throat and veered away from that thought with a sharp question. "Delight, is it possible that you have seen Mason before you came here? Could —could you and—and Gerry have met him in the States?" His words came hesitantly, his face gray and drawn.

A shadow clouded the girl's face, the troubled look which any mention of her life with her sister-in-law brought on. Her eyes filled with sympathetic tears. What a tragedy it must be to have the memory of one's wife hurt unbearably, she thought. She patted her brother's arm.

"No, Jimmy, I've never seen Lieutenant Mason before— that I can remember." Her breath caught in a little frightened gasp at the last word. "Of course, there was that blank stretch of days when I was so ill—but unless he was one of the doctors you surrounded me with," she suggested with determined lightness, "which hardly seems likely—"

"Mason has never practiced medicine, I'm sure." Jim

21

matched her whimsical tone. "At that time he was en route to Europe for his first assignment."

"Count him out then. But Captain Steele thinks *he* has met me somewhere, Jimmy. I'm not sure whether it's a usual line with him or he really means it. Whenever we are in the same room, if I look in his direction I encounter those sharp blue eyes fixed on me in what seems to be baffled scrutiny. It's always a shock, like Alice in Wonderland suddenly finding the Cheshire Cat grinning from a most unexpected place."

With a ripple of laughter she confessed, "You know me, Jim! Every time it happens I'm gripped by an almost irresistible, naughty, small-girl desire to stick out my tongue and say, '*Yah!*' "

"He does seem strongly interested in you, I've noticed."

"And I dislike it, Jim. I'm not at ease with him. He is as keen and ruthless as his name, or I miss my guess," she added belligerently. "Didn't I hear him complaining about Lieutenant Mason back there on the terrace?"

Tremaine frowned. "Yes, he's burned up because Mason had his orderly, Jed Crane, thrown in the jug."

"Crane—Jed Crane? Oh, he's the man Tamara talks about!"

"You'll put it stronger than that when you've been here a little longer, Dee." Jim laughed. "You'll become thoroughly fed up with your maid and her Great Lover. Yes, Tamara Rostov is Crane's current heart-throb, the latest of many, I judge."

"She seems very much in love with him."

"They're two of a kind," was Jim's disapproving comment. "A pair of firebrands. And now Crane's under arrest. I don't know what it's all about, but I'm sure Mason was justified. He has an unusually good working knowledge of human nature—and inhuman, too—after his overseas work. As I told Steele, he makes few mistakes. None, as a matter of fact. And his men swear by him—also unusual when he's been in command so short a time."

They reached the bridge over the river and halted to watch the play of sunset on the flats and shallows below.

"You say you don't like Steele?" Jim muttered.

"I don't think I do, Jimmy, but I'm not sure why. Why should a man with his good looks and personal charm give me a feeling of—of distrust?"

"Far be it from me to attempt to read a woman's mind. But that knocks out my plan for your trip to the glacier," he admitted.

"Oh?" Delight allowed only polite interest in the word, although she remembered the captain's plea for assistance. "So you had picked him for my adoring escort?"

"I intended to send him along to keep you out of trouble," Jim corrected dryly. "I want one of my officers on that boat. Of course, Bertha Bentley would like to have them all go, along with those friends of the doctor's who live in town. You'd think we were stationed here solely for her entertainment," he growled.

"Steele seemed the logical choice for your trip. He is liaison officer with the airfield and could be spared for the day. But," he sighed, "if you don't go for the captain, who will you have?"

Delight walked in silence, as though weighing the question. After the lapse of what she considered a decent interval for reflection she casually—almost too casually—suggested, "Could you spare Lieutenant Mason? I'd—I think I might like to have him, since you feel that I require someone to tag along. But, Jimmy," she begged, "for Heaven's sake use finesse for once in your dear, blunt life, *please?* Don't stuff me down the gentleman's throat. Just impress him with the tragic fact that, although you hate to inflict him with the job, you really can't spare anyone else to do the ice fields with your troublesome sister. Will you, huh?"

Tremaine looked down at her with a gruff laugh.

"Finesse, is it? Great Scott! Delight, if you knew how much—" He checked the words as he met her surprised glance and continued in a lighter tone, "Why in the world pull Mason into your stagline? Aren't there enough lovesick officers hanging around you?

"Look here, young lady," he continued sternly. "Don't make me sorry that I sent for you. You ought to know better than to try and stir up my officers. For the most part they are a fine straight lot of men, simply starving for the society of an attractive girl. So far from home and with these wild surroundings, they'd fall in love at the drop of a hat, and it's cruelty to animals to lead them on just for a brush-off. And what's more—"

The girl indignantly broke in. "I think it's poisonous of you to—"

"Never mind that!" he ordered. "When so rudely interrupted, I was about to point out that your job as sister and official hostess of the commander of this post is to be friendly with them all. Not to break anyone's heart by singling him out for special attention and then bouncing him. I've counted a lot on having you here; don't make me regret that you came."

"There are no indications that Lieutenant William Hamilton Mason is starving for my society, as you so bluntly put it!" she retorted. She shook his arm for emphasis as she continued, "Don't worry about me, Jim. You know I'll do whatever you wish. I came with the idea of helping you. I mean really and truly to be a help. I'll try to be the best friend I can to every one of the officers, and nothing more. I rather suspected that the men up here would be susceptible to feminine charm, would go overboard for anything in skirts, whether or not it measured up to their at-home standards. So I thought that perhaps arriving equipped with *this* would make matters a little less torrid." She stopped and faced him, holding up her left hand.

"Sort of a keep-off-the-grass sign?" The major's lips tightened, his eyes narrowed, as he studied the ring. "You haven't forgotten, Dee, you promised faithfully, no matter how great the temptation, not to marry until you have talked it over with me? Much as I trusted your word, I've had some uneasy moments these last few years when I thought of you on the loose back home with only easygoing Aunt Alice to hold you down.

"You see, I—well, there are some shellholes I want to warn you against when the proper time comes. Don't for a minute be afraid that I'm going to dictate to you the choice of a husband. But, I've seen, and had dealings with, a lot more men than you. So, I would like to give the lucky fellow you pick out the once-over before things get too serious."

He was silent while he proffered his cigarette case and snapped the lighter to their cigarettes. Then his voice tense he asked, "Did he—is this the only ring he gave you? Have you ever accepted a ring from anyone before?"

"Another ring! Good grief, no! How many rings do you think it takes for an option on me? Of course, I admit that I'm a terrific charmer and have left rows and rows of broken hearts behind me," she teased with a laugh. "But I have my limitations. As to your question, I now get what you were driving at in your roundabout way. You may calm your hysterical fears.

"I have never been engaged or married and I'm not now. This ring is what you Army people call camouflage. It doesn't even mean that I have a boy friend. The stones were Mother's, Aunt Alice had them set as a birthday surprise. You know I'm nothing if not spectacular in my taste in jewelry and she certainly went to town when she ordered this trinket! She frankly admitted that it was a bribe to get me to stay on with her instead of coming up here."

Delight wiggled her fingers and the ring flashed brilliant sparks of light.

"I never intended to wear it here; it's too theatrical for the mere sister of a post commander. But you gave me such a going over the day I arrived, with so many regulations to follow in regard to your precious young men, that I was fairly terrified into wearing it. I thought it would reassure you, but apparently it has quite the opposite effect. You seem more worried than ever."

As they reached their house the notes of a bugle sounding taps floated from the parade ground. The sweet, hushed call rose and fell in cadence to die away at last as a whispering echo from the hills. The girl choked and brushed a hand across her eyes.

"Every time I hear that," she confessed, "it does something to me."

The major nodded soberly. "It does something to most of us, especially in an out-of-the-way spot like this, and especially, too, when it is so well done. Seems strange, doesn't it, that a man as rough and irresponsible as Corporal Simmons can produce such music from a brass pipe?"

He followed Delight into the house, switched on lights, and then stood sniffing the air.

"Flowers!" he announced, and located the pink fireweed in an Indian bowl on the mantel. He looked from them to the pink hangings at the windows, the rose-shaded lamps, and his voice was gruffly unsteady when he said gently, "It's a crime you weren't born twins, Dee, then you could have made *two* men happy. You have the homemaking instinct developed to the *n*th degree."

"Thank you, kind brother, for your ovation," she mocked with a laugh. "Just the same, all evening I've been wishing for a touch of Mrs. Bentley's decorative genius."

"Bertha has more money to indulge her taste than a major's pay affords. You're doing fine, Dee, even with the inadequate resources of Totum's general store. Believe me, my dear, already you have turned this house into a real home. More of a home than I've had since I left the Point."

He cleared his throat of huskiness. "Well, I dragged you away from the party to help me with some papers, but I think I'll let them go over till tomorrow. I'm going to take a turn through camp, maybe find out why Mason has Crane in the guardhouse. Good night, and pleasant dreams!"

Delight watched him swing down the hill toward the barracks with his springy, military step. Shaking her head she soberly addressed his back.

"Captain Steele's orderly is Jed Crane, and Jed is Tamara's boy friend, and Tamara is still a savage from the tips of her loafers to the ribbon in her glossy black hair. In spite of her civilized front I don't think she is a safe person to antagonize. I'm much afraid, my beloved Jimmy, that at last your perfect lieutenant has made an error in judgment."

V

"TODAY," Delight announced after breakfast, "I start being more efficient. I shall *not* spend so much time admiring your Alaskan scenery, impressive though it is, and I'll whip through the housework and try to finish my marketing in Totum *before* lunch. It will be a record, if I do."

Jim Tremaine grinned at her valiant determination. "You're entitled to shop at the post exchange, you know—such as it is," he qualified.

"I know, and I'd probably save you money—"

"That wasn't a consideration, Dee," he hastened to assure her.

"But it's so much more fun in Totum," she continued, disregarding his interruption. "The Indian woman who helps tend the general store hardly ever understands what I ask for, so she lets me rummage until I find it for myself. And they have the oddest things tucked away there, it's really a very interesting place."

"Go to it, then." Jim went off to Headquarters and left her to the announced program.

She carried it out successfully to the point of leaving for town. Armed with a Tlingit basket large enough to hold a medium-sized grocery order, she took a white cardigan from the hall closet and opened the front door. To her consternation Warner Steele was mounting the steps.

"Good morning, Delight!" He clicked heels and snapped a salute in an exaggerated manner. "Going shopping, it appears. What luck I came in time to go with you." With a confident smile he added, "Perfect timing, I call it!"

Delight bit her lip in indecision. Whatever *his* feeling might be, the prospect of an hour with a man she couldn't like held no attraction. Yet it seemed unpardonably rude to refuse point-blank. Then inspiration flashed and she walked composedly across the porch to place the basket near the steps.

"Your timing is slightly off, Captain Steele." Her smile was disarmingly innocent. "I'm not ready yet. You catch me red-handed, displaying what a scatterbrain I am. I have to put the basket where I'll practically fall over it or I may forget it."

His frown was suspicious. "You're really not going now?"

"Not for some time. I have a dozen things to do in the house."

She felt no qualms at making the statement because it was true at any time, particularly today, when Tamara was not to come until afternoon. As the frigid blue eyes continued to stare at her, she assumed the offensive.

"Did you come to see the major? He's left for Headquarters."

"I came to see you!" The arrogant tilt of Warner Steele's chin, while it indubitably added to his handsomeness, merely increased her annoyance. "As you seem so busy I'll make it short. I've spoken to Babbling—to Mrs. Bentley—about going on the sail with you. Only a hint, you know; I'll follow up with a little pressure and I'm sure she'll put in a word for me with the major. I just wanted you to know that I'm working on it."

Delight resisted an impulse to laugh in his pompous face. Not only did the man behave as though he were conferring a royal favor, but he actually seemed convinced that her eagerness for the proposed twosome equaled his. Suppose she did laugh at him, would he collapse like a pricked balloon, or react with the menacing enmity which seemed always smoldering beneath a suave exterior? No matter which, she had her orders from Jim to treat every man of his command with equal friendliness—and no more.

"It was thoughtful of you to alert me, Captain Steele," she said, tongue in cheek, and retreated to the doorway. "If you'll excuse me now——" She shut the door and stood listening while his boots clumped on the steps and thudded on the path. He even *walks* like a conquering hero, she thought with a suppressed giggle.

Then it was necessary to consume an hour with indoor tasks before she dared to appear in the open, lest the rejected escort be lurking in wait for her. Even so, when she had crossed the river and entered the town, it gave her a shock to round a corner and come on a tall figure in uniform.

To her intense relief it was Lieutenant Mason and not the captain who greeted her.

This meeting, unlike the other, was pure chance. Mason, on his way to inspect the Army warehouse at the town's wharf, had halted, as he often did, to admire the picturesque old Russian trading post which stood, a huge building of square-hewn logs, at the beginning of the main street.

A question about it from Delight, an answer from him, and before he realized what was happening they were in agreeable conversation. At once they discovered a common

27

interest in the ancient building, and to the girl's pleased surprise Mason seemed to forget his coldness while he answered her questions with all that he knew of its history.

It was a matter of wonder to both of them that it could have survived such a series of battles and sieges and so many generations of use which had left their marks without bringing the old building down in ruins. But the Totum folk prized the trading post and cared for it as best they could. In many places the rotted, sagging timbers were shored up with new unweathered braces; the roof had been patched and repatched with progressively newer shingles.

"Doesn't that roof look like some of the geometric designs the Indians used in their basket work!" Delight marveled.

"Or like a stained and tattered old manuscript," was Mason's suggestion, "telling the story of Totum, if we could only decipher it."

"That's one project I hope to take up soon," Delight said. "I mean reading all about Alaska. I don't suppose there's a library in town?"

"I'm afraid not. And the general store's paperbacks don't run much to respectable history," Mason added with a smile.

"Then, unless the Bentleys or some of the town's first citizens have something more educational, I'm doomed to ignorance until I can send to the States," Delight conceded.

"No need to wait in complete igorance." Bill Mason smiled. "Get yourself a map of Alaska and start learning its history from the place names on it. A lot of Indian names came first, of course, and then those given by the Russian discoverers, like Chichagof or Golovin. Later the British explorers took a hand in the christenings with such echoes of home as Chatham and Salisbury, and Spanish sea rovers with their Chacon, Muzon and Valdez, up the coast a short way. And finally the miners and fishermen arrived, and got right down to earth with their Bear River, Moose Pass and dozens of Grouse and Porcupine creeks." He laughed a trifle self-consciously. "Pardon the lecture, which I should call 'What's in a Name?' "

"A great deal, apparently. At least up here," Delight admitted enthusiastically.

"Not necessarily in Alaska, either." Mason studied the girl from a corner of his eye while apparently absorbed in the building. "Whoever named you Delight certainly hit the bull's-eye!"

"A gallant speech, and thank you, even if I don't actually deserve it." At his indignant protest she laughed, then explained, "You see, that name was Jim's doing. He was quite grown-up when his father married for a second time, and for once that worked out well, because Jim adored his stepmother.

"Anyway, they say that when he got the news of my arrival in the world he played hooky from his boarding school to rush home and see us both. He gave me the name Delight, and Delight I've been ever since, although I was formally christened Geraldine."

"A decided improvement."

"I've never objected so long as it was Jim who named me. He has been my hero from earliest years, right through West Point and down to the present moment. And it turned out to be a constant help when Jim married another Geraldine. *Dee* and *Gerry* avoided a great deal of confusion."

"Not a happy marriage?" Mason asked. "I'm judging that from the shadow on your face when you spoke of it."

"Not happy," was her only comment as she turned away and hit on a more pleasant subject. "Heavens, look at the Totum market place! You know, if someone doesn't keep me firmly in hand I'm liable to spend my household allowance on souvenirs."

Between the trading post's doorway and the street squatted two lines of chattering Indian squaws. Every day they camped there to offer their wares to the camp personnel or any chance tourists, wares knowingly created to intrigue the folks at home.

The women were young and old, comely and ugly, some with shining white teeth, some with no teeth at all, clean and dirty, humble and disdainful, voluble and taciturn. Their costumes varied from a few modern garments to the ragged blankets of their ancestors. The one universal gesture to civilization was the rubber band which secured each and every braid of black hair.

"The original Fifty-seven Varieties," murmured Lieutenant Mason, and won a smothered laugh from Delight. "As a matter of fact," he advised, "you're fairly safe in buying from these people. We're so far off the beaten track here the tourist trade hasn't commercialized them yet, and everything they are selling is genuine—their own handiwork. But take your time before you decide."

Together they inspected the offerings set out on blankets: spoons carved from elkhorn, beaded and quill-embroidered moccasins, carved and marvelously painted miniature war canoes of fragrant cedar. One squaw displayed a few flint or bone spearheads and arrowheads from the past, but, as Mason had said, all the other articles were the work of the women who offered them. Always in the background lounged a few low-browed Tlingit men, keeping watch over their wives, growling guttural advice, touching their dilapidated felt hats respectfully to the officer.

At one blanket, on which were laid delicately wrought silver chains and bracelets set with polished bits of Alaskan jade, Delight gazed longest.

"I could really go for some of those!" she told Mason, speaking softly lest the squaw snatch at the words as a bona fide offer.

"A safe buy, you know." Mason copied her cautious whisper. "Uncle Sam stands behind every one of them."

"What do you mean?"

"The Indians get the metal for them by hammering out silver dollars."

In spite of this added endorsement Delight tore herself away from temptation. "I'm not going to rush into anything," she asserted firmly. "There'll be plenty of time to make up my mind." Resolutely she continued up the street.

Mason accompanied her. Such was his state of mind that he would not have left her then for a king's ransom. Later, when absence weakened her spell, he might regret this lapse from his customary reserve, but for the moment he had even forgotten that.

Totum itself offered little material for conversation, being a typical isolated village of fishermen and lumberjacks. One large building, the cold storage plant, represented the principal industry. One long building, a warehouse near the dock, served the Army. For the rest, a scattering of small houses clustered around the steep road up from the wharf and dotted the steeper hillside behind. Some of the houses near the shore were built on piles to stand clear of the winter tides, and the plank sidewalks, too, ran on piling in many places above the rutted, muddy road.

It was a quiet town, as far removed in the tempo of its life as in miles from the mechanical bustle of the cities Delight was accustomed to. Like the Indian merchants around the trading post, Totum's inhabitants seemed to drift peacefully through their days perfectly content with their town and their life.

The few people they met were roughly dressed fishermen who gave the girl admiring glances as they passed, or stolid Indians who did not lift their eyes from the sidewalk. The only sign of activity Delight saw was at the dock, where a battered white schooner lay moored. A towheaded man, barebacked above oilskin pants, was painting the wheelhouse with long, deliberate strokes as though he had all summer to complete the work.

Bill Mason halted beside Totum's single restaurant.

"How's for a cup of coffee, my treat?" he suggested. "That is, if you are a slave, like all of us, to the morning coffee break."

"A willing slave. I'd love it. I haven't sampled the Aurora Café's cooking yet; isn't coffee supposed to be a good gauge of any eating establishment?"

"I can tell that you are a seasoned gourmet," Mason chuckled. "Have no fear. If the Aurora doesn't sport a Duncan Hines endorsement, that's because Dunc hasn't visited Totum as yet in his travels."

He seated Delight at an oilcloth-covered table in one of the two booths and went to the counter. The imposing blond waitress, almost as tall as Mason and considerably heavier, was talking to the only other customer, who sat leisurely dunking a doughnut in his coffee, but she paused long enough to lift an inquiring eyebrow at the officer.

"Two coffees, please," he ordered.

While the woman went to the urn Mason lounged against the counter facing the other customer.

"Nice morning," he offered amiably.

The man looked up, holding the soggy doughnut suspended above his cup. He was slender, thin-faced, of no apparent distinction. His gray flannel suit, Delight considered, would have been vastly improved by pressing and cleaning.

"Hello." Noting the silver bar on Mason's cap he added, "Lieutenant" politely, before taking a bite of the doughnut. "Must be an Army camp around here, or are you just passing through?"

"If you call that dump a camp!" Mason growled. "Have you *seen* it?"

Delight, at her table, looked up in surprise at the scorn in his voice. Until now it had never occurred to her that Bill Mason's stony reserve might be covering a career man's bitterness at being sidetracked in this wilderness outpost. Somehow that did not seem a satisfactory explanation; certainly a disgruntled officer would not have carried out his duties so well that he would be considered a splendid officer by Jim.

The coffee dunker missed or ignored the slurring reference to the camp and only answered the question.

"I haven't seen anything of the town yet," he admitted, dipping the doughnut again. He pushed one foot toward the small suitcase on the floor beside his stool. "Came in last night on that jerk steamer, and the manager up there," he nodded toward the freezing plant, "put me up for the night."

"Oh?" Mason took the two cups which the waitress passed to him but delayed for more conversation. "You in the fishing business?"

"Nope," the stranger answered with a full mouth. "I'm

selling freezing machinery. And believe me, brother, that takes you into some real shanty towns along the coast. This one don't look so bad by comparison."

"You must have been in some pretty hopeless ones, then!"

"What's the odds? I don't stay long. I'm through here, and grabbing the boat when it comes back this afternoon."

"Lucky you!" said Mason, moving away. "Be seeing you."

"Not around Totum!" The salesman grinned. "Unless you're still here when I drop in next year."

"God forbid!" Mason joined Delight and over the coffee seemed to forget his displeasure with the camp in pleasure at furthering their acquaintance.

While they talked the salesman departed with his suitcase, leaving the waitress to improve her mind with—Delight could read in blood-red capital letters—MURDER BY MOONLIGHT.

Still troubled by the lieutenant's caustic remarks, she took advantage of a pause to ask hesitantly, "Do you really hate this assignment so much?"

"Hate it?" He stared in surprise.

"From the way you spoke to that man—"

"Oh—well—" He hesitated a moment and leaned forward to whisper something for her ears alone, but caught himself in time. He sat back and sipped his coffee.

"I was just striking up a conversation with him—seeing he's a stranger in town, you know. We're supposed to be friendly with everyone. Part of our job. A lot of times if you crab about the service," he explained smoothly, "they open up and talk to you. They sort of expect it from a soldier—the old Army habit of grumbling about everything."

"I suppose Totum *isn't* exactly a soldier's dream of the perfect assignment," she admitted smiling.

"Forget what I said to that fellow," he begged. "I told you it was just an act. This duty is practically a rest cure after some of the places I've been stationed."

"But didn't they have at least the fascination of being foreign—and romantic? I understand that you had all sorts of strange assignments overseas, and I'd love to hear about them some time. I have an insatiable thirst for adventure," she confessed. "All the more because so far it has consistently avoided me."

Mason's subdued snort was partly amusement and partly disgust. "You've come to the wrong shop for any tales of romantic adventure, child; no sinister Orientals or exotic female spies—*they* have consistently avoided *me*. So let's talk about you."

"I wonder if you are politely hinting that your work with

Army Intelligence—I've been led to believe that was one phase of your job—isn't to be discussed. Sorry, I should have remembered that myself, Jim has warned me often enough."

"I didn't mean that!" he protested, and then gave a sigh of resignation. "It's no use, I see; you've been conditioned by movies and novels to believe that every Intelligence operative goes around risking his life every hour on the hour. I assure you I regret the cold hard facts of truth because nothing would please me more than to intrigue you with yarns of hairbreadth escapes. Failing in that," he said with a grin, "what can I offer? More coffee?"

"No, thank you, I must stop dallying and go about my business."

Delight went to the door and waited while he carried their cups back to the counter and paid the waitress. It seemed as though that simple business deal took an unusually long time and entailed considerable discussion in tones too low for Delight to hear. She wondered how well Mason knew the burly blonde.

Actually the delay was not caused by either business or pleasure. Mason handed the waitress a dollar bill and while she made change asked quietly, "Ever see that salesman before today?"

The blonde slanted a look from him to the waiting girl and copied his lowered tone. "Saw him come in on the boat yesterday, like he told you."

"And he went up to the freezing plant?"

The woman slowly counted change into his hand.

"Don't know about that. But he came in here for coffee with Mr. Swenson before you did."

"Swenson's the manager up there, isn't he? Did you hear them talk business?"

"Some. And when Mr. Swenson left, just before you two showed up, the guy thanked him for the order and they shook hands. They knew each other, all right. Talked about a ball game they went to in Seattle last time Swenson was down there. You worried about him, Lieutenant?"

"Just checking. A stranger in town. Force of habit, I guess. Thanks, anyway."

Outside the Aurora Café, Mason asked, "What's next on your schedule? Shopping?"

"'I've got a little list, I've got a little list.'" Delight hummed the *Mikado* refrain. "But you are dismissed if you wish, Lieutenant. I'm sure you have more important duties than carrying my bundles."

"At the moment I can't think of any." He spoke truthfully,

having completely forgotten his intended visit to the warehouse by the dock, and walked happily beside her toward Totum's general store.

Before they reached it one of the detachment's jeeps brought their companionable hour to an end by drumming from the camp at the usual breakneck pace and screeching to a halt beside the lieutenant. The driver, after a knowing leer at their evident preoccupation with each other, saluted Mason and solemnly announced that Major Tremaine was "having a hemorrhage" because no one had been able to locate the lieutenant.

To Delight's disappointment that officer immediately resumed his habitual granite countenance, bade her a correctly formal farewell and departed, jeep-borne with the speed and fury of Jehu in his chariot, for the post.

"And at the very moment," she sighed, watching the jeep bound away up the street, "when I would have bet anything that Bill Mason's glacial front was thawed for good. Darn the luck!"

VI

DELIGHT would have regretted making any such wager if she could have seen her late companion, Lieutenant Mason of Baker Company, standing before Major Tremaine's desk in Headquarters. The pleasure of that hour with her had been sternly banished from his thoughts; his lips were drawn to an inflexible line, his gray eyes gloomed down on his commanding officer.

"But, sir!" he protested. "Why send me? I have already made a trip to the ice fields, seen the glacier, even taken a crack at the halibut fishing. Young Peck, or any of the officers who've never been out there, would jump at the chance."

"Very probably," the major acknowledged without enthusiasm. "However, I have selected you to accompany my sister."

"Besides, sir," Mason hurried on, "you know I have those new replacements to train, practically overnight, and from scratch as far as this special duty goes. My company should be at full strength to handle the guard duty at the airstrip; we can't afford to fill in with inexperienced men."

"Just a minute!" the major snapped, his brown eyes hard, the determined chin jutting more than ever, signs which the camp's personnel had learned meant impending fireworks. In further warning a flush of impatience spread from the square jaw to the top of his bald head. "Perhaps it wasn't clear, Lieutenant, that I was not making a request. I gave an order!"

The junior officer sprang to ramrod erectness.

"Yes, *sir!* I beg your pardon for misunderstanding. I shall report as directed, Major."

Tremaine grunted an acknowledgment, fiddled with some papers on his desk, glanced up at the rigid figure before him and concealed a smile.

"At ease, Mason, at ease. Now will you give me an explanation of why you confined Private Crane? I looked for you around camp last night after the Bentley party, but you weren't here."

"No, sir." Mason had obediently relaxed from his stiff attention and stood slackly with his hands clasped behind his back. "I rode out to the airfield with the guard."

Tremaine, still shuffling his papers, looked up quickly.

"Trouble there?"

"No, sir. But I like to go along with a detail once in a while, just to see how they're acting, and to check on the situation."

"Everything under control? No friction with the Air Force guards?" the major asked with a trace of worried frown.

"None at all, sir. But Baker Company's responsible for guarding a large area and I believe in knowing exactly what conditions my men face at all times."

"Quite right, Lieutenant," the other agreed and pushed his open cigarette case across the desk. "Have a smoke and let's have an informal discussion of the Crane situation."

He watched silently as the younger man lit up, leaned an elbow on the window sill, and studied the parade ground.

"Steele kicked to me about what you'd done to his orderly." Tremaine slid a probing look at Mason and pursed his lips. "Not very good feeling between you and the captain, is there?"

Mason wheeled from the window as though to bark a furious answer, then caught himself and stood with lips clamped shut while he gave his commander a long smoldering glare. When he did speak, it was to ignore the question in favor of supplying the requested information.

"I learned that Crane has been messing around with my mail, sir." Further explanation was interrupted by the sound of hurrying footsteps in the corridor and the entrance of Captain Warner Steele as though on a well-timed cue.

He saw Mason as he came in, and the blue eyes flamed. With a perfunctory salute to the major he snapped, "Good!

Glad to find Mason here. Perhaps he'll explain why he picked on my orderly yesterday!"

"My report is already going through channels, Captain," Mason countered sharply.

Tremaine's knuckles rapped the desk.

"Never mind that. Answer the captain!"

Mason's face was colorless, but he repressed his anger and met Steele's glare steadily.

"Sir, Crane has been stealing my mail."

Warner Steele laughed. "You have proof, of course," he demanded with heavy sarcasm.

Contempt hardened Mason's eyes, but instead of answering with words he drew a letter from his pocket and held it out to the major. The envelope showed unmistakable signs of having been steamed open—the flap was wrinkled but untorn.

Tremaine took the envelope, stared from it to Mason, then at Steele. His fingers drummed a tattoo on the desk.

"The supply sergeant brought that to me yesterday," explained Mason, watching the captain narrowly. "He said that he'd found it in a field jacket which Crane had turned in for exchange. It's postmarked Washington, but it is not an official communication, of course. If you look inside, Major, you'll find a check, made out to me. Evidently the captain's orderly was stumped to know how to cash it."

Steele swore under his breath and stepped forward as if he meant to examine the evidence, then stopped.

"I don't like this!" he growled.

"Neither do I," Mason pointed out coldly, his eyes still on the other man. "And I don't quite understand why the captain is in such a stew about it."

"Crane happens to be my orderly," Steele blustered. "No one is going to pick on him if I—"

"No one will," Tremaine broke in, "if he behaves himself."

Steele jerked his shoulders impatiently.

"I'm not so sure, Major. This looks like a frame-up, and I'll bet I know the answer. You claim the supply sergeant gave you this, Mason?"

"That's what I said, *Captain*."

"Hah, there you are, Major! That sergeant has been trying to make my man's Indian girl friend—and he's been getting nowhere. Any number of the men made a play for her, but she's so crazy about Crane that she won't give them the right time. The sergeant pulled this trick to get Crane out of the running."

Mason laughed scornfully. "Don't you think, Captain, that you're giving the sergeant credit for rather subtle scheming?"

"Oh, these men here will do anything to get a girl."

"They might fight over her, but I wouldn't expect them to cook up such comic-opera stuff as planting letters—"

Tremaine banged down his fist.

"All right, gentlemen, that's enough! This is too serious for a personal argument; we'll let a court-martial handle it. Then, at the proper time, Captain Steele, you can present any *evidence* you may have. Lieutenant, you have no objection to my holding this letter for the present?"

"No, sir."

The major placed a paperweight on it and swung on Steele.

"Now, Captain, regarding that disturbance in town yesterday which we discussed. The Navy has failed to locate any unidentified ship, but they will continue the search." He nodded to Mason. "You may go, Lieutenant."

Mason saluted and without a glance at Steele went out.

On the Headquarters steps he stood staring across the parade ground dotted with formations at close order drill. Beyond, the sea sparkled like an immense blue mirror, merging far out into a sky as clear and blue, where an invisible plane was tracing a long curving white line of condensed vapor. The stillness was broken by a ringing bugle call: *"All you hungry GI's, come and get your chow!"*

Oblivious to the call and to the beauty of his surroundings, Bill Mason stood, hands on hips, his mind working fruitlessly.

"What the devil could that Crane want with *my* mail?" he growled. "And how many other letters has he lifted? Some besides mine, I wonder? He's been soldiering five years and broken to private half a dozen times. An 'odd ball,' the men call him, but I never heard that he was a thief. But why pick on me? Unless—" he scowled at a thought—"unless someone put him up to it, someone who wants to know what's in my mail. Captain Steele's orderly! Hmm!"

His face paled and his hands balled into fists. Then he shook his head and advised himself crossly not to be a fool. Better get over this enduring distrust of Steele.

"But what infernal fate," he muttered, "landed me in this setup with my former pal ranking me!" A cynical smile creased his face as he repeated the major's, " 'Not very good feeling between you and the captain, is there?' Lord, if the major only knew the half of it!"

Shaking his head, he crossed the parade ground to the detachment's post office. Only the mail orderly was inside and Mason called him to the door.

"Duveen, don't put mail in my box after this," he ordered. "And don't have anyone deliver it, either. Hold it aside, I'll pick it up myself. Give it to nobody but me, understand?"

Duveen was startled by this deviation from routine.

"Well—yes, sir! O.K. But, Lieutenant—"

"And don't lose it, either," Mason advised curtly. "You keep it close or I'll have your hide!"

"Yes, *sir!*" The man's eyes bulged; his ears twitched nervously as he shuffled his feet. "Is—is something wrong, sir?"

"I'll say there is, but not with you, soldier." A friendly smile calmed Duveen's alarm. "Just do as I say and we won't have any more trouble."

In the afternoon Mason remembered the warehouse inspection from which Delight had so thoroughly sidetracked him. As he made his way along the winding road and across the bridge into town his mind reverted with a shock to the major's unwelcome assignment.

"Why'd he pick on *me* for his sister's escort?" he wondered aloud impatiently. "Every *single* officer here—and some of the married ones, too—has fallen for her, and I—I don't dare go near her again because I'm half in love with her now. And I've no right to become even interested in a girl."

Half in love? He laughed bitterly, visualizing Delight's startlingly beautiful face, her charm, her rather boyish friendliness. *Half* in love? After this morning the damage was complete, irremediable. Who ever claimed there was nothing to this love-at-first-sight idea? He might as well admit that he was head over heels—and *that*, worse luck, meant more struggle, more bitter regret.

His brain thrashing helplessly among conflicting thoughts, he passed the old Greek church which stood near the center of town.

"Plenty of troubles that place has seen," he admitted ruefully. "Probably worse than mine—but not for me!"

A bulky figure blocked his path so suddenly that he was forced to side-step to avoid a collision, and almost stumbled off the plank sidewalk. As he recovered his balance the sight of the mark left by chevrons on the worn olive-drab jacket gave him a quick stab of annoyance at the carelessness of a reduced corporal—until he looked up to meet the laughing eyes of Father Darley.

The priest, who divided his time and strength among six villages, was short and built like a wrestler; his chest strained the buttons on the tailor-made blouse which had been presented to him by a soldier of less girth. From the shelter of his impressive figure the anxious face of Tamara Rostov peered at the officer.

"Got a minute to spare, Lieutenant?" asked the priest.

"All the time in the world for you, sir."

"Not for me, on this occasion. Tamara, here, begged me to gain an audience for her with the handsome officer approaching." Darley's eyes twinkled. "That was you, boy! Her description, not mine."

Mason looked his surprise. "An *audience?* What's the idea, Tamara? Do you think I'm the governor of the Territory!" To the priest he confided with mock horror, "If that's the case, she must have been paralyzed at the honor when I actually spoke to her the other day on the dock."

While the girl grinned sheepishly, the priest explained, "As this is a military matter she has in mind, perhaps that makes the difference. Now, Tamara, here is Lieutenant Mason, ready, willing and able. Carry on!" With a jovial salute he went off along the sidewalk, leaving Mason still in puzzled study of the Indian girl.

Her dark face was streaked with tears but still lovely. Jet-black hair, parted in the middle and drawn with satin sleekness over her ears, set off her smooth olive skin, warmed by a flush at her temerity. She was slight and dainty, and her brilliant orange sweater, black and white checked skirt and worn saddle shoes made her appear more like a teen-age sorority sister than a backwoods mixture of Indian, Russian and Scandinavian.

As she stood mute before him, hands tightly clasping either elbow, Mason's eyes flicked to her massive silver bracelet set with small gold nuggets. That had been the subject of conversation at their first and only meeting—but this was "a military matter."

"What's on your mind, Tamara Ecklund Rostov?" he prompted with friendly sympathy. "Why tears on a beautiful day like this?"

The girl's eyes filled anew at his gentleness.

"Oh, Lieutenant, sir, why did you put my Jed in jail?"

"Sorry, but I had to. He was bad."

"He's not bad, he's a good man!"

"No, he isn't," Mason insisted quietly. "He's locked up because he's a thief."

"That's not true!" The savage broke through civilization's thin veneer; her large black eyes flamed in the flushed face. "Why do you and everybody say such terrible things about my man?" As her anger grew her English deteriorated. "Some day we marry! How can we, if he shut up in that place?"

Mason was silent for a moment, regarding her narrowly while an idea edged into his mind.

"Look here, Tamara, if you want to get him out of the jug, there might be something you could so."

"Me? I do *anything*," she gasped with tragic intensity.

"Take it easy, youngster. Here's what you can do. Crane stole a letter of mine." He stopped her indignant denial with

39

upraised finger. "I know he took one, he may have taken more. Maybe he didn't do it on his own, though; someone else might have put him up to it. Get him to tell you why he stole my mail. Then you tell me."

"Then you'll let Jed go?"

"If he tells the truth, I'll try to get him let off, maybe with just a fine or some extra duty. It's the first time he's really stepped out of bounds that I know of, so I'll do my best for him—and for you. But remember, you've got to get the *truth*," he added compellingly, "or he'll stay cooped up until he's an old man. You understand?"

The girl's face lighted with a confident smile. "Sure, I get you!" She drew slim fingers across her damp eyes, then reached for his hand and shook it violently. "You're O.K., Lieutenant, sir. I'll do what you say." A frown replaced her smile. "But how can I get to see Jed?" she demanded. "The soldiers will never let me inside the fence!"

"You promise to do what I ask if I get you in?" Mason insisted. At her nod he drew a pad from his pocket, wrote a note and handed the slip of paper to her. "Show that at the gate whenever you want to see Crane and someone will take you to him." Beaming with anticipation, Tamara slipped the pass under her belt.

"Now here's something else," he cautioned. "There will be a soldier watching you all the time, so you whisper to Crane and don't let anyone hear what you two say. This has to be a secret between us, and if anybody asks questions, you know nothing. Catch?"

Tamara nodded vehemently. "Catch! Everything okey-do-key now." With a giggle she announced, "I got a secret with the lieutenant! Imagine that!"

"This isn't anything to fool about!" he warned gravely. "Remember, your boy friend won't get out unless you do your part *right*."

"You bet! I'll do it *right* and right away. But first I got to get some things for Miss Delight at the store. And thank you, Lieutenant, sir. Maybe sometime Tamara can help when you're in love. Maybe, huh?"

Mason stared at her, his cheeks slowly flushing under her calculating gaze.

"Why, thanks, but I shan't need your help, Tamara." Involuntarily he blurted, "The girl I'm in love with will never fall for me," touched his cap and turned away toward he wharf.

What got into me, he wondered disgustedly, spilling a re-mark like that to her? She must have a sympathetic nature which encourages confidence. Sympathetic! He snorted in derision. About as sympathetic as a Kodiak bear, if she's
40

ever crossed. But she did have loyalty; ready to fight for her lover at the drop of a hat. Too bad the man happened to be Jed Crane, who doubtless had left a sweetheart at every post, if not a wife back home.

So she was going to battle for his release, but how honestly would she fight? If Crane did confess anything to her, Mason doubted that it would be the truth, or that Tamara would pass it on if she thought silence would better serve her turn. Father Darley, in discussing his work, had referred to her as the brightest Indian he had ever taught—not only in schoolwork but in adapting herself to civilized ways. But he had admitted one fault in her character: she had no ethics; tenaciously she clung to the creed of her Indian ancestors, and Father Darley's philosophy of turning the other cheek fell on completely barren ground.

If the truth about Crane was reached through Tamara, Mason admitted gloomily, it would be only because she decided that the truth would help her. And ignorant as she was of Army ways, that was not apt to be her view. Better forget the girl and try to work through other channels.

Returning from the dock and passing the trading post, Mason saw the squaws still assembled with their wares and was reminded of his morning meeting with Delight. That brought up the major's order and set his jaw in grim determination. Better tell her at once that he was to be her escort and get it over with!

"Boy, how I dread this sight-seeing junket!" he muttered bitterly. "All day on a boat with the loveliest girl in Alaska —and points south!—and nothing can come of it. Besides, I ought to be on hand here every minute, just in case Tamara fools me and does want to report. If she should decide to come through and not be able to find me, she might change her mind. Wouldn't that be a tough break!"

Passing the camp gate, he returned the sentry's salute automatically and tramped disconsolately up to Officers Row.

"No way out of it, I guess," he growled. "I'll tell her I'm elected and beat it fast!"

In his anxiety to get the unpleasant task behind him he ran up the steps of the major's quarters so rapidly that he tripped at the top and went stumbling across the narrow porch. For some reason the screen door was propped open and the front door ajar. As he fought to regain his balance his outthrust hand smacked against the door and slammed it against the wall. Quick as an echo, from inside the house came a crash, followed by a series of anguished wails.

VII

WHILE the lieutenant was inspecting the warehouse Delight had begun another project. Singing a soft accompaniment to the music from the radio in the kitchen, she assembled, with painstaking care, the ingredients for two apple pies. Her maiden effort in that direction a few days ago had not been quite what the cookbook promised, she admitted, although her brother bravely devoured them. This time she'd show him!

The kitchen was vastly improved, she felt, by the candy-striped gingham curtains which she had discovered in Totum's general store. Why not paint the cupboard handles in the same Chinese vermilion? There was a small can of this paint left by a former tenant among the odds and ends on the closet shelf. She wouldn't ask Jim to assign one of the men to the job; Do-It-Yourself had become her daily motto.

From the window, while she worked, she looked across the rolling green slopes of the mountains splashed with patches of blue lupine and blazing fireweed as though a careless painter had wiped his brush at random. Where the river made leisurely curves between the hills the airfield showed like a giant O.D. handkerchief spread out in the hot sun, its hangar and administration building making a monogram in one corner. Near them tiny figures of men labored around a jet plane shrunken to miniature by distance.

A knock from the back porch announced a caller, and immediately a large, white-haired woman elbowed open the screen door and leaned in. Her face wore a harried look, she clutched a shopping bag with both hands.

"Oh!" she exclaimed, her brown eyes enormous with surprise. "Excuse me, Miss Tremaine! I saw someone here and thought it was Tamara. I was going to ask her—But never mind."

"I'm trying—not too skillfully—to take over the cooking duties," Delight explained. "Can I help you?"

"Well—" The woman hesitated, then took the plunge in a breathless Southern accent. "I'm Mrs. Kent, next door—Captain Kent's mother, you met him at the Bentleys', didn't you?—and I have to run over to town for a few minutes." She lifted the shopping bag level with her ample bosom in explanation. "But Henry—that's Captain Kent—and Sue—that's my daughter-in-law—are away and I'm supposed to be minding Harry—" She halted momentarily to draw breath.

"Harry being your grandson?" Delight supplied, smiling.

"Yes." With renewed vigor Mrs. Kent took up the tale. "He's been playing in the yard, and I'm sure he'd be perfectly all right there, but Sue would worry if she thought I wasn't on the job every minute."

"Bring him in here, Mrs. Kent. He can help me make pies until you come back."

"Well, thanks. That's real nice of you, Miss Tremaine. I don't believe in bothering the neighbors, but—"

"It won't bother me in the least; I'd love company." Delight went to the door. "Call him over."

Instead, Mrs. Kent removed enough of her wide expanse to reveal a small red-haired boy with a replica of her large brown eyes and pink cheeks.

"Here he is. Harry, you stay with Miss Tremaine, and do mind your manners, you hear? Grandma'll be back directly." She was off with the last words, moving with the same scurrying rush in which she spoke.

"Come in, Harry," Delight invited politely.

The wide eyes inventoried her from somewhat ruffled hair to blue-striped apron.

"O.K.," he said and entered.

As Delight turned to resume operations, a rumbling growl spun her about in alarm to confront a ferocious black and white Husky whose bristling head bulged in the screen.

"Go away!" she gasped, feverishly anxious to close the inner door, but dreading to approach it.

Harry Kent trotted past her to bat the straining screen door.

"It's my Igloo," he announced carelessly. "Sit down, stupid!"

The man-eater sank on his haunches and protruded a dripping tongue to lap the wire separating him from his miniature master.

Somewhat reassured Delight said, "He'd better wait for you out there." She found a sliver of lamb in the refrigerator and offered it to the boy. "Would Igloo like this?"

"Sure." Harry opened the screen door and held out the meat. Delight shuddered at the formidable teeth which seemed to snap shut on the little fingers, and marveled at the unconcerned way Harry withdrew his hand.

Feeling that the situation had been well handled by all she went back to her work.

"I'm making apple pies," she explained, rolling out dough. "Do you like them?"

"Yuh."

"You can have a piece with your supper then, if they turn out as well as I hope."

Harry nodded gravely. "Thanks."

Well, Delight thought, smiling to herself, he may have inherited Grandma's eyes, but not her volubility. Still, that might develop with added years. "How old are you, Harry?"

"Seven."

Determined not to allow monosyllables to discourage her, she persisted. "Any brothers or sisters?"

"Nope." The boy climbed up on the stool and gazed dreamily out the window at the mountains, and then, as she groped for another question, surprised her by adding cheerfully. "I had an older brother. His name was Randolph, but he's in Heaven. Much older," he amplified. "He went to Heaven when I was very small."

Oh dear! Delight thought, he *can* talk, but why did I choose that subject? Hastily she chopped off a few inches of pie crust and handed it to him.

"See if you can make a little man out of that, Harry, and we'll bake him along with the pies. Flatten it out in that pan there."

"O.K." He began to mold the dough carefully, but his train of thought was not sidetracked. "He was pretty bad, I guess; he was sent to the chair!"

There was such satisfaction in his tone that Delight stared.

"What chair? You mean the electric chair? *Who* was sent to the chair?" she gasped.

Harry frowned. "Richard," he answered impatiently.

"And who?" she demanded, now thoroughly confused, "is *Richard?*"

The boy heaved a prolonged sigh, as one tried beyond endurance by such stupidity.

"My brother who's in Heaven, of course!"

"You said his name was Randolph!"

The brown eyes regarded her solemnly. "I did? Shucks!" Again he sighed, this time with real regret.

"You were making it all up, weren't you!" Delight accused, smiling in spite of her annoyance.

"Sure," Harry admitted cheerfully.

"But you mustn't tell such stories!" she protested. "Harry, you know you should always be truthful."

"Why?" he demanded, rounding a head from the dough and carefully poking his finger to make eyes and a mouth. "Is Jack and the Beanstalk true? And things on the radio? And that movie about a mouse?"

"But, Harry, those are—are entertainment. Everyone knows they aren't supposed to be really true."

The boy shrugged. "So I was trying to entertain you. Everyone knows I didn't have a brother—" He cocked an eyebrow at her. "What did I say his name was?"

"Never mind," Delight said firmly. "We'll forget him and fix up your pie man. We'll put in raisins for the eyes and sprinkle him with cinnamon and bake him brown as a berry."

"O.K." Harry patted the head of his pastry man until it began to flatten on top and bulge at the sides. "Hey, it's starting to look just like an Indian!" he announced happily. "They're brown as a berry, like you said he's going to be. You know, I shot an Indian once."

"You didn't!"

"Sure. He was trying to get in our house—"

"Harry!" She raised a warning finger.

He poked the dough impatiently.

"Gee, you don't believe anything I say, do you? Guess you're too smart." Seeing her smile he completely disarmed her by remarking, "You've got dimples, haven't you! Like me. See?" He proved his point with a grin.

After that they were boon companions, and Delight managed to keep him so occupied with the completion of his Indian for baking that he launched no more attempts at "entertainment." She felt genuine regret when Grandma returned and retrieved her lively charge and his canine guardian.

With the two pies and dough man finally in the oven and the timer set on the electric stove, Delight busied herself with further preparations for the evening meal. Some time later she happened to glance out the window. What she saw sent her hurrying to the door for a clearer view.

Evidently Harry Kent had evaded his grandmother's watchful eye, for he was down at the river's edge engaged in a wrestling match with Igloo. Because of their frantic activity and the flying mud Delight could not decide if the boy was hauling the dog away from the water or being himself dragged in.

Debating whether interference was called for she went out and crossed the field to where it dropped steeply toward the river. From there she was relieved to watch a victorious Harry emerge from the mudflat towing a subdued Igloo by his collar. The two raced toward the bridge, where a uniformed figure was crossing from town and waving violently. Probably, Delight guessed, that would be Daddy Kent coming home. Let him deal with the wanderer.

She spent a moment admiring the patchwork quilt of colors spreading away in the valley before she turned back to the house. She paused again; out here she could see the slope of the hillside which had been hidden from her kitchen window. As she looked along its blossom-sprinkled curve her heart gave a sudden leap of apprehension. Was that a—*a body*—stretched out in the gully halfway down the hill?

Through the tall grass and scattered bushes she could glimpse sections of what looked like tan and yellow clothing. And two red shoes with white soles, their toes buried in the grass. It *was* a body! Motionless, face down. Someone dead—or badly hurt. In an instant she was running at full speed across the slope.

On the brink of the gully she halted even more suddenly than she had begun her errand of mercy. Viewed at close range the alarming corpse became nothing more tragic than a bearded man lying at full length in the grass, chin propped on hands while he looked down into the valley. It made a picture of such solid comfort in contrast to the suffering Delight had envisioned that she laughed.

The man started, tilted his bullet head enough to locate the source of the merriment and then turned back to pick up a pair of sunglasses and slip them on. Rolling over he sat up, brushing twigs and grass from his rumpled yellow sports coat with one hand. The other held a pair of binoculars.

For a moment Delight's mind, conditioned by years of movies and TV, seethed with suspicion. The combination of a remote and extremely hush-hush airfield, a bearded stranger armed with "powerful field glasses" and a camera slung from one shoulder reeked of melodrama—for a moment only. Then, remembering her initial acceptance of Harry Kent's fiction and chagrined by the absurd outcome of her rescue dash, the girl reined in her imagination to take calm inventory of the suspicious character.

He was young, she decided. No hint of gray in the rumpled black hair or beard. The latter was evidently a first attempt and not an unqualified success. Although he was deeply tanned his snub nose and high cheekbones were red from sunburn, and the large dark glasses gave him an owlish expression. White teeth glistened through straggling whiskers when he smiled up at the girl.

"I uttered a curse at the interruption, but having met its author, I repent," he confessed with facetious eloquence. "It was annoying, though, after I spent an hour stalking a marmot, to have even such a charming laugh scare him into his burrow."

"You were only watching a marmot? Oh! I thought—" She barely repressed announcement of her suspicion. "Let this be a lesson in restraint for me," she sighed. "I thought you were hurt and dashed over to apply first aid—a holdover from Red Cross training, no doubt. I'm sorry I frightened away your quarry."

"Think nothing of it," the boy grinned as he climbed out of the gully. He was short and heavily built; standing, he appeared more mature. "Who wouldn't swap a wild animal for Miss America in person?"

"Well!" Delight was unprepared for such gallantry.

He gulped and rubbed his nose in awkward embarrassment.

"Sorry if that sounded fresh, ma'am," he mumbled. "It sort of slipped out. Haven't seen anything around town today except ninety-year-old Indian ladies, so you're kind of a shock." When Delight turned back toward the house he fell into step beside her.

"Have you just arrived in Totum?" she asked.

"This afternoon, ma'am. A freighter from Juneau dropped me off at Kuski—that's down the coast a ways—but that town's dead, so I hiked up here." He extended a canvas shoe. "Tough going, in these."

"A real tenderfoot, aren't you?" she joked.

" 'The most unkindest cut of all!' " he muttered sheepishly. "You wouldn't believe I grew up in Alaska, would you? But I've been away quite a while, so I'd sort of forgotten what it's like. This vacation I thought I'd bum around the old place. Hitchhiking, you know, on boats, planes—anything that moves."

"That must be fun." Delight paused to gather a handful of unfamiliar blossoms. "What a delicious shade of pink! I'm going to put a bowl of them on the mantel tonight."

"That's bird bill. Some people call them pink shooting stars." He found another small patch, picked them and held them out to her. "You won't find many now, they come early with the violets."

"Thank you." She smiled at the discord of the flowers against his flamboyant yellow jacket, which, with the light tan slacks and red shoes, suggested his possible status. "I'll bet you're a college student."

"Right! And that takes cash, you know; that's why I can't afford to travel de luxe." Chuckling, he held up the camera. "I was smart to get this in a Seattle drugstore for two dollars. Up in Juneau they want five bucks for the same junk."

Most probably, Delight thought, his binoculars had come from the same bargain counter.

"Are you going to stay in Totum?" she asked.

"No, ma'am! As I told you I grew up in this section, and it's even deader than I remember. I want to get further north where it's more exciting and really rugged. Get pictures of walruses, Kodiak bears, maybe." He glanced at his wrist watch. "I'll grab a meal in town and see if I can catch on with some boat or plane headed north tonight."

As they neared the house Delight yielded to impulsive friendliness.

"Why not have supper with us?" she suggested. "I dare to promise it will be as good as the Aurora Café."

"Well, gee, that's nice of you, ma'am!" He beamed at her. "But won't I be barging in, upsetting things?"

"Not at all. I'm housekeeping for my brother, Major Tremaine, who commands this post. We'd love company."

"Oh!" The young man ran his tongue over his lips, rubbed his nose, hitched the camera strap higher on his shoulder. "Well, gee, thanks, but, on second thought, I guess I ought to get right over to town. I might miss someone who's pulling out tonight, someone eating at the Café, you know. Or someone there might know of somebody who's going—" His involved explanation trailed off to a mumble. He turned away. "Nice to have seen you, ma'am," he called over his shoulder as he tramped toward the road.

VIII

DELIGHT stood gazing after him, wondering at the sudden change of heart. Next door she saw Harry Kent sitting on a boulder; he, too, was watching the departing stranger. Igloo slouched out to sniff the young man as he passed and received a friendly pat on the head in acknowledgment.

The bell on the stove rang warningly and she jumped. The pies! She hurried into the kitchen, opened the oven door, and with two potholders removed the bubbling pastries. They were evenly, toothsomely browned. She sniffed. They smelled divine! Success at last! She surveyed the kitchen for a secure, out-of-the-way place to set them aside until they cooled.

Came a thunderous crash from the front hall. The girl gave a convulsive start, both pies upended and crashed to the floor.

Horrified, she glared at the mass of crumpled pastry, clutched her head in agonized hands and perched on the stool with a piercing wail of frustration.

"Oh! O-o-h—" No expletive she knew was strong enough to fit her fury and she rocked back and forth in speechless impotence.

Without warning a firm hand gripped her shoulder and a man's voice demanded, "What's going on here? Pull yourself together or you'll have hysterics!"

Delight looked up to find Bill Mason's worried face bent to hers.

"I dropped my pies—my beautiful pies!" she moaned and pointed forlornly. "Right on the floor!"

Mason burst into a roar of relieved laughter.

"And I thought you'd severed an artery, at the very least!" He patted her shoulder with comforting gentleness. "Cheer up, no one can accuse you of crying over spilt milk."

"It's no joking matter!" she stormed.

"Pardon the ill-timed merriment," he grinned. "Let me help you clean up the mess."

Delight shook her head and gulped down the last of her moans.

"I couldn't bear to touch them after all the work I put into them. Tamara can do it when she comes."

"But what happened anyway?" he persisted.

"I don't know. I remember a terrific bang—probably one of the guns at the airfield—and they just seemed to fly out of my hands."

Mason looked stricken. "Oh! Well I—the door—"

"How do you happen to be here?" she interrupted, not noticing his agitation. "Looking for the major?"

He was suddenly conscious that his hand still rested on her shoulder with more than friendly sympathy. His alarm for her safety had driven his carefully planned formality from his mind. Flushing, he released her and took a backward step. With stilted politeness, he stated his errand.

"Major Tremaine has detailed me to act as your escort on the glacier trip. I haven't a doubt, though," he suggested hopefully, "that if you request it he will send someone else."

When the girl stared at him wordlessly he added with the same stiff dignity, "Mrs. Bentley sent word to Headquarters that the coaster will leave the town wharf at six A.M., and asked that you be there in plenty of time."

Delight continued her silent study. She was searching for a sign, the slightest twinkle in the gray eyes, anything to warn her that he was being purposely ridiculous. She could not believe that he was serious. His manner was too far removed from the friendliness of their morning encounter; it was like a slap in the face. When she could find no hint of humor she was forced to accept the truth, that he found no pleasure in the assignment.

"Thank you, Lieutenant," she said with equal formality. "As to asking for a substitute, I never interfere in military matters. I'll be there on time. I'm sorry that you find it so boring to go with me."

"Not at all—a pleasure."

"How very convincing," she whispered sarcastically. Then, because she was hurt but would not for the world have him guess it, she struck back. "I wonder why my brother inflicted *you* with the distasteful duty. Oh—" with an exasperating air of military wisdom—"is it punishment for disobeying orders or something?"

The flush of Mason's cheeks deepened at the suggestion; uncomfortably he remembered Tremaine's sharp, "I was not making a request. I gave an order." Then annoyance filled him, resentment that this girl could make him feel like a fool at will. *Make* him feel so? Sooner or later he acted like one at every meeting.

Coldly he suggested, "Perhaps the major selected me as the most unlikely of his command to fall into the heart-line."

"The heart-line?" Her eyes darkened to purple with indignation, but her smile was undiluted sweetness. "Oh, I see! But really, I have never thought of my *friends* standing in line like a lot of hungry down-and-outers hoping for a handout!" She slipped off the stool and walked to the doorway. "Now if you will excuse me—"

Her gesture was dismissal enough. Mason tramped glumly out.

Delight watched him go down the hill, then stood in the doorway staring thoughtfully at the front steps. Why had she sent him away so abruptly? For that matter, why should she resent his reference to a "heart-line" when anyone could see the officers making pretexts to talk to her, sauntering up to the house for unnecessary conferences with the major, trailing her when she shopped in town? He might have been attempting a compliment, and only inexperience made him seem brusque.

Inexperience? Hah! She doubted that—and discovered a slight twinge of jealousy at the thought. Pull yourself together, gal! she admonished silently. Hands off Jim's boys— by his orders.

She raised her head hopefully at the sound of rapid footsteps. But it was not Bill Mason returning. Captain Steele hurried into the yard and ran up the steps. Blue flames flickered in his eyes as he glared down at her.

"Is it true that Mason is going with you on the trip?" was his rasping greeting.

Delight was in no mood to humor his apparent displeasure. "Good afternoon, Captain," she said evenly.

Steele smothered his anger for a moment to plead, "You knew I planned to go with you, was working on Bertha Bentley to put in a word for me with the major. You could have stalled him off until I managed it."

"I could have? But why? Why are you so convinced that

50

I'll be utterly heartbroken if *you* aren't a member of the party?"

The taunting suggestion whipped red into his cheeks, but he answered with confidence. "I want you to myself, Delight. A whole day with you—on a boat where you can't walk out on me as you did this morning."

"Are you sure I couldn't? I'm an excellent swimmer."

His smile was maddeningly assured. "I'll gamble that you won't want to."

"You overwhelm me!" she scoffed and, anxious to end the unpleasant discussion, abruptly turned back into the hall. When he followed she stopped and faced him. "Won't you come in, Captain?" she invited icily.

Brushing aside the sarcasm he persisted, "I'm giving you fair warning, Delight, in the words of the old song, 'You're the girl for me!' I've known a lot of charmers, but—"

"I'm sure you have!"

"—but never one like you," he finished with an ardent look. "Give me a chance. Let me go with you."

Delight almost laughed in his face. "Dare I refuse? I dare! And anyway, Lieutenant Mason has already been selected for the duty."

"Major Tremaine should not allow it!" he stated harshly.

"Really?" Dislike coupled with annoyance in her voice. "On the contrary, Major Tremaine ordered it."

"He's crazy! If he knew what I know—" Steele choked with fury and pounded a fist in the palm of his hand.

The knife-in-the-back innuendo destroyed the last doubt as to Delight's feelings for the captain. She had turned for an idle look at herself in the hall mirror. Now she whirled to confront him, cheeks flying combative pink flags. Blazing eyes locked with his.

"If there is something the major ought to know, why don't you tell him?" she challenged hotly. "Why come crying to me!"

"If you put it that way, I *will* tell him!" Steele was fairly shouting by this time. He stamped to the door, where he nearly collided with Tamara. "Get out of my way, you trouble-making klootch!" he snarled and pushed past her.

Tamara watched his retreating figure with flashing eyes and angrily pouting lips before she followed Delight to the kitchen. Intent on depositing her bag of groceries on the counter she almost stepped on the scattered pies and drew back with a gasp.

"Did *he* do that?" she shrilled, jerking her head toward the front of the house.

Still shaking from anger Delight gave a nervous laugh.

"Captain Steele? No—it was—something startled me and

I just dropped them. The captain arrived after—after the accident. Will you clean it up, please?" She unpacked the girl's purchases to quiet her own jangled nerves. "Why were you gone so long?"

"I met Lieutenant Mason and asked him why he put my Jed in jail. He's so nice," Tamara sighed, "and so handsome when he smiles. Polite, too, not like that Captain Steele. He's a dirty pig!"

Delight smothered a fervent desire to agree with the last statement and asked, "Did the lieutenant tell you why your boy friend was in the guardhouse?"

"Sure, he did. But I promised not to talk with anyone about it. Not even you, Miss Delight." Two tears started down the girl's cheeks. "He's really in bad, I guess!"

Delight, amazed to see this independent, self-sufficient youngster cry, laid her hand gently on the girl's shoulder.

"I'm sorry to see you upset, Tam, but I'm afraid you always will be if you count on a man like Crane. Can't you fall in love with somebody more your type? Think of all the nice village boys who have tried to make you like them."

Tamara tossed her head defiantly.

"Those good-for-nothings! All they think of is hunting and fishing, and they'll live *here* always. I want to marry a soldier who'll take me places. An officer would be better, but anyway a soldier. I picked out Jed right off because he's the best soldier in the camp and has been a lot of places."

She nodded, grinning. "Yes, sir! Everybody thinks he's just a lazy, easygoing good fella. But I love him and he loves me, and with me back of him pushing, he'll go places, just see if he doesn't, Miss Delight." She carefully skirted the ruined pies and helped the other put away the groceries.

That done, Delight perched on the stool and studied the girl thoughtfully.

"Doesn't it make any difference to you what kind of man he is?" she asked curiously. "I understand he drinks and gambles and has been broken to private I don't know how many times. That proves how irresponsible he is."

"No sirree, ma'am! It makes no difference to me as long as I love him and he loves me. Once I get him hooked tight, I'll show him. Then he'll really get somewhere, you bet! I'd do anything for him. Father Darley at the mission says it's very wrong to hate or lie or steal, but I'd do any of those things—I'd shoot to kill—for Jed. Wouldn't you, Miss Delight, for your man?"

Her mistress shook her head decidedly.

"No, Tamara, I wouldn't, and when it comes to the test you wouldn't either. You'd remember what the Bible says and what Father Darley has taught you about being a Christian. Then you'd begin to wonder if the savage ways of your ancestors were good enough for you now. You'd compare his ideas of right and wrong with theirs and his would win.

"After all, you'll have to admit that civilized Christian ways have done a lot more for you than ancient Indian customs. You can't just accept a few and discard the rest and be honest."

There was a short silence, while Tamara thoughtfully followed a design on the linoleum with her toe, then Delight continued:

"Remember that you are an exceedingly charming and capable girl, with a good life ahead of you, because you accepted and followed some of our Christian beliefs and customs and pulled yourself out of the rut of these people here. Remember that every time you do wrong it makes it easier for the Devil to win you to his side."

Delight paused and stared at the other uncertainly. The fervor of her own words shocked her. Was she preaching? That was no way to influence Tamara; it might only antagonize her. She switched from the subject hastily and forced her voice to lightness as she scoffed, "You talk about shooting! Heaven protect the person who depended on me for that sort of help in an emergency. Let me tell you about my enlightening experience with guns, while you get those sorry-looking pies into the garbage pail. Throw away that burned doughman which I forgot, too."

"You bet, pies coming right up!" Tamara agreed, adding with a smile, "Go ahead and tell me. I love to hear about what you did outside." Seizing a large spoon she attacked the litter on the floor.

Delight reached for a pack of cigarettes on the counter and lighted one.

"When I drove for the Red Cross in San Francisco we sometimes had to go into pretty rough sections of the city, often late at night. I was ordered to carry a little automatic pistol, and I hated every inch of it. Cold and treacherous and deadly. I couldn't get over the creepy feeling that I had a venomous snake in my pocket."

"Did you bring it with you?" Tamara asked eagerly.

"I certainly did not! I never wanted to see it again. So, imagine how I felt, shortly after my arrival here, when Major Jim insisted that I go out to the pistol range with him, when no one was there, to practice. He knows I detest it, but his excuse is that in this kind of country there could be an emergency when I would need to shoot—and shoot straight."

"That's so. The major knows what he's talking about."

"But he didn't know *me*," Delight sighed. "He does now— knows the worst. Unfortunately I am perfectly hopeless when it comes to hitting anything. I get the cold shivers every time I hold one of those things in my hand. My poor brother wanted to disown me, I'm sure. Most of the time I automatically shut my eyes when I pull the trigger. When I do manage to look I jerk in fright the instant before it goes off and miss the target by a mile."

She laughed self-consciously. "There are just two things in the world that petrify me, Tam, and both of them are guns!"

The girl squatting on her heels gave Delight a serious and prolonged study. Then she shook her head.

"Just the same, Miss Delight Tremaine, you don't fool me. In spite of all your talk I think you'd shoot for your man— and shoot *good!*"

"Just the same, Miss Tamara Ecklund Rostov"—smilingly she imitated the girl's positive tone—"in spite of all *your* talk I think you *won't* shoot or steal or do anything wrong for your man."

"Maybe." Tamara went to the sink, rolled up her sleeves, wet a rubber sponge, and then stood looking thoughtfully at the floor. "Miss Delight," she sighed, "sometimes I think love makes everybody unhappy. Lieutenant Mason said he loved somebody very much, but he had a hopeless look on his face when he said it."

"Did Lieutenant Mason tell *you* that he was in love?" Delight demanded incredulously.

"Sure. But I knew before, anyway. One time he tried to buy my good-luck charm." She raised her arm and watched the massive silver bracelet slide to her elbow. "It's very old. Great-grandmother Tatima Kadyana made it. It's—what you call an heirloom?—and very lucky, maybe."

She knelt to scrub the last traces of pie from the floor.

"The lieutenant offered me twenty dollars for it; said a girl back home would like it very much."

At the sink she rinsed the sponge and then stood eying the bracelet.

"I wouldn't sell it to anybody—not even the lieutenant, who is just *dreamy!* No, not even to Jed! Me, I think the lieutenant is wrong, that his girl must love him very much. But—" her black eyes flashed to Delight's face, then away —"she's way down there while he's up here. You think *he's* a good man, maybe?"

"Tamara, let's stop gossiping and get to work," Delight suggested crisply as she slid off the stool. "You carry on with the floor here, I have a dress to mend."

"I got an errand right away!" Tamara remembered breathlessly. "When I come back I'll finish. Okay?" She slipped out the back door and ran.

54

IX

IN THE post guardhouse Tamara's black eyes hungrily searched the pale face of Jed Crane. The mop of blond hair which usually covered his massive head like a shining cap now stood erect in crisp, disturbed points; his hazel eyes with deep crowfeet at the corners were clouded with worry. Ordinarily the big man was carefree and easygoing as a boy, but now his thick fingers picked nervously at the seams in his blue fatigues.

Getting into the place had proved surprisingly easy for Tamara. Mason's note achieved that, and effectively silenced the guard before he could more than suggest a date. Now he lounged at a distance, well out of earshot. Everything had worked out as the lieutenant promised. But gaining the confidence of Crane was proving more difficult.

"How do I know you're shootin' square, Tam?" he muttered. "Too many guys have been trying to make you; maybe one of 'em sent you to pull a fast one on me. I ain't goin' to spill anything to get me in worse, so's they can take over!"

The girl's eyes widened in reproach.

"I never fooled with any of them after I saw you, Jed. You know that. Lieutenant Mason thinks you didn't steal his mail on your own—that somebody made you do it. And you'll be in the lockup instead of the other fellow!" She brushed away sudden tears. "He promised that if you tell me the truth he'll try to get them to let you off easy. But it's a secret," she warned tensely. "Nobody knows what we're trying to do, only him and me."

Crane hitched uneasily in his chair, stood up and paced slowly to the grated window. He stared out at freedom, represented by a hillside of sunlit green against a mountain of green and brown forest, slashed with purple shadows. When he came back he leaned close to whisper to her, "For the love of Mike, don't cry, Tam! I'll tell you the truth, so help me. I've got to trust you, I guess, but my story won't keep me out of the jug, whatever the lieutenant promised you—fat chance of that in this man's Army!

"But I don't give a damn about that. I'm coming clean because I've felt like a heel ever since—since I took on the job of snitching his mail. Honest, Tam, I never done anythin' that low before and I ain't going to try it again, no matter who pressures me."

"Who got you to do it, Jed?"

He hesitated, stalling while he reached out a foot to hook his chair nearer and sit beside her.

"Never mind his name!" he ordered roughly. "I ain't squealing on him—I didn't *have* to do it, remember," he muttered with sudden honesty. "A guy in the camp, that's all you need to know. He's kind of interested to know what goes on in Mason's letters, he says, and never mind why. He's one smooth operator, Tam; soaped me up with a great line of talk, offered good money for the job, and kept high-pressuring me until I bit."

Crane mopped sweat from his forehead with a grimy sleeve and lowered his voice still more.

"I agreed to get hold of Mason's mail, see—letters posted from Washington, that is—and steam 'em open. If any of 'em mentioned—uh—a certain thing, I was to light a match to 'em, see, and then tell the—this guy—what they said. He wasn't touching a single letter, the smart cookie! Not with a ten-foot pole, for fear *he* might get into trouble. And any letters that wasn't about this matter, see, I was to slip back into Mason's box, so's he wouldn't suspect anything."

Jed Crane sat back, scrubbed his blond hair roughly with both hands and sighed.

"Well," he whispered, "I got nothing he was after until yesterday; when I read the letter I damn near dropped. 'Hey, Crane! *Hold it!* No dice!' I says. Honest, I had no idea what I was gettin' into, Tam!"

The girl gasped, "What was it, Jed?"

"You keep out of this, kid; no need for you to know. And I figured *I'd* better get out of it quick; I wouldn't be such a heel for anybody, no matter how much I was paid, and I'd slip the letter back in Mason's mailbox P.D.Q. and say nothin' to nobody." He squirmed on the chair. "I thought I'd be so damn smart!"

"What happened, Jed?"

"Before I got a chance to return it I'm picked up and jugged —for another letter! One that didn't have anything to do with this matter I was working on, either. I hadn't put it back —that's how smart I am—figuring I had plenty of time. But that Lieutenant Mason's the sharp John, not me, and he's a fast worker."

He glanced sharply at the guard, who now stood back to them in the doorway, talking to someone outside. Cautiously he drew from his pocket a small Indian flute carved from walrus tusk, and handed it to Tamara.

"Put that away quick. Don't let anyone see it!" he commanded. "Especially not an officer. You take it straight to

56

Mason, see, nobody else. Tell him to pull off the mouthpiece, his letter's inside."

"The bad letter, Jed? What's it say?"

"I keep telling you, Tam, *never mind!* Don't you dare look at it, I'm trusting you. I wouldn't mix you in this at all, only I'm scared they'll find it on me, and it ought to get back to the lieutenant before anyone else reads it. The dopes didn't search me when they threw me in here." He grunted a bitter laugh. "If Mason finds out they didn't, he'll have *them* on the carpet so fast they'll be dizzy!"

Overwhelming relief at being rid of his guilty burden flushed Crane's pale cheeks.

"Don't you fool with that flute, Tam. Take it direct to Mason. Put it right in his hand, understand?" His own big hand jerked her glossy hair gently for emphasis. "I'm trusting you, sugar, but you cook up any funny business and I'll beat the tar out of your hide, so help me. Now get going. Scram!"

Tamara went slowly down the guardhouse steps, the flute tucked out of sight in the sleeve of her sweater. Behind her sounded a rough laugh and then the guard's voice as he drawled, "That babe is something to look at, Crane boy, but watch yourself! Sure as shooting she'll stick a shiv in you sometime. They say the only safe Indian's a dead one and brother, what I mean, *she ain't dead!*"

With a guttural grunt of contempt Tamara walked away. That, from a man who had more than once tried to cut out Jed with her! So that was how they talked about her. Smoldering with fury she shook her head.

The soldier was right about one thing, though. Even though Jed trusted her to deliver the letter, she wouldn't do it. Never! Jed wanted to get rid of it, so they wouldn't find it on him. All right, he'd done that. And Lieutenant Mason had said the truth might save him. Tamara laughed with bitter knowledge. Mason had tricked her with his sympathy, his friendly persuasive way.

Now she saw her own version of the truth; this letter could be just the confession of guilt the Army was looking for to convict Jed. And that would come about through her innocent action. She laughed again, this time scornfully. She could still fool them all.

Thoughtfully she walked to the main gate, followed by the guard who had brought her in, unconscious of a passing truck whose driver whistled admiringly, and then came back to reality with a jolt. The officer she hated, the man who had insulted her not an hour ago, was approaching. She saw his frosty blue eyes sweep from her toward the guardhouse and jerk back to her in a fixed stare. When he grasped her arm she flung his hand off with contempt plain in her face.

"Don't get excited, baby," Captain Steele advised with a sneer. "I only want to talk to you. Have you been to see Crane?"

A suspicion born of hate and encouraged by Jed's story now crystallized into startled conviction. This must be the man who was interested in the lieutenant's mail, the man responsible for Jed's trouble! Hiding her flaming anger behind an expressionless mask inherited from her savage ancestors, she proceeded to lie elaborately and convincingly.

"I saw Jed, but the guard wouldn't let me talk to him. I had some candy I bought in town, and I asked the soldier to give it to him. He said he would, but I'll bet he won't. He'll eat it himself, won't he, huh?"

Steele, somewhat baffled by the ready flow of invention, studied her through narrowed eyes. "You're a smooth little talker, aren't you!" When Tamara only stared woodenly he growled, "Don't know whether to believe you or not, but I can check with the guard, you know. If you're lying to me I'll make it tough for you."

Tamara shrugged. She had expected that, and countered without hesitation, "Why should I lie to *you?* Go ahead, ask the guard," she urged scornfully. "Of course he'll say I talked to Jed, because he'll want to cover up that he kept the candy." With a rapid shift to wide-eyed innocence she demanded, "And if I do go and talk to Jed, with someone's permission, of course, what's wrong with that? Has he a secret I shouldn't know about, maybe?"

The captain grunted something and stalked in through the gate. Tamara watched him out of sight, but had no consciousness that she did so. Her mind whirled with conflicting ideas. Two officers, Steele and Mason, so different in their manner, in their treatment of her. Which one truly represented the Army, that vague but powerful force which held her man? How could she know whom to trust? Could she trust anyone but Tamara Rostov?

Instead of returning to the major's house she walked on into town. Passing the old Russian church, she looked up at the panel above the doorway, the patron saint now dimmed and stained by many generations of exposure. Something about the calmness of the painted face stirred her, brought back an echo of Delight Tremaine's earnest words, scarcely heard at the time.

". . . I think you *won't* do anything wrong for your man."

The girl sighed. "Miss Delight doesn't know what love is," she whispered. "For Jed—I think I'd do anything! But—" Her eyes fell to the great bronze doors of the church. They stood flung wide, invitingly, revealing the peaceful white and gold interior. Against her will, one hand clutching the hidden flute, she moved slowly up the steps and into the church.

It was empty at this hour. She passed the main altar with its relics of Russian days, the massive silver candlesticks, the tapers, the smoke-dulled painting of the Last Supper, and entered the chapel. How many times she had been there, always inwardly scornful of the kneeling Indians who had abandoned the teachings of their fathers to accept this new Christian idea of turning the other cheek, forgiving their enemies.

She stared up at the Madonna and Child in the ornate and heavy gilded frame. That she had seen many times, too. But now it made her think of Miss Delight again. Miss Delight! A lovely person, so often she had longed to be more like her. Could she have been right in what she said? And Jed. A wonderful man, in spite of the bad talk about him. Could *he* be right about what he wanted her to do? Then there was Lieutenant Mason. Her eyes glowed. He seemed that knight in shining armor about whom Father Darley read wonderful stories. He had told her what to do. But even he could be wrong. How could she know?

As she looked at the picture, the face of the Mother seemed to gaze back with tender pity, the mystic eyes to glow with sympathetic understanding. With a sob of passionate entreaty Tamara dropped to her knees and flung out her arms. "What shall I do?" she whispered. "What *shall* I do?"

Half an hour later Delight was alarmed to find Tamara crouching in a corner of the kitchen, her attitude that of a trapped and desperate wild animal. Her mental state was dangerously close to hysteria, Delight thought, when gently sympathetic questioning drew floods of tears alternating with unintelligible muttering and bitter denunciation of "the white men." The nerve-racking session ended only when Delight gave up attempts to understand and sent the girl home to rest. Tamara departed with tears of gratitude for her mistress, but stubborn imprecations against the rest of her race.

Delight, too recently arrived in the wilderness to have confidence in her own ability to handle this crisis, yearned for counsel, but not from Jim, who had more than enough on his mind already. Nor was she willing to call on Mrs. Bentley; that lady's curiosity was nothing to turn loose on poor Tamara's personal troubles. Seemingly she had nowhere to turn, since she doubted that any of the other wives in camp knew more about the savage temperament than she herself.

Then chance came to her aid. She felt a flood of relief and a strong inclination to believe in miracles when she saw Father Darley striding past the house. If anyone in Totum knew the Indian mind surely here was the man. She hurried down the road to overtake him.

The priest heard her and turned to wait. Breathless with haste, she begged, "Father Darley! Can you tell me about Indians?"

He chuckled at the question and looked at her with twinkling eyes.

"Miss Tremaine, I presume," he greeted. "I can't promise to tell you *all* about Indians," he hedged while the keen eyes studied her. "And if you happen to have a problem with one Tamara Rostov," he hazarded with another twinkle, "I make no guarantee at all. But let's hear about it." He clasped his hands behind his back and teetered back and forth comfortably.

"You *expect* problems with Tamara, it seems." Delight attempted, but found it difficult, to give him a clear description of the girl's actions.

Father Darley sighed. "They have so many troubles, these poor people. She wouldn't say anything definite?"

"She was practically incoherent most of the time, mixing Indian with her English. Jed Crane is concerned in some way, I don't know how. She kept wailing that something was *yek*—at least it sounded like that."

"She would say that! *Yek* is so handy to blame any misfortune on. It's the Tlingit name for a supernatural power which they believe often interferes in their lives. An interesting creation, really, an aimless, mysterious something which meddles with human affairs.

"Then perhaps Tamara was blaming *yek* for her troubles —and for Crane's." Delight made an impatient gesture. "She is a savage still, in spite of your teaching."

"But never forget," the priest said quietly, "these *savages* have many qualities which civilized people could adopt with advantage. Contrast their life with the brawling, quarreling and cheating whites here, who live in similar poverty. The Indians live together in amity, honest and considerate of one another, sharing good fortune or bad. They have some beliefs which seem foolish to us enlightened ones, beliefs which I don't attempt to change except when they might endanger the salvation of their souls. *Yek* I consider harmless. Even though Tamara blames it for her troubles, I bank on her to work through them to happiness."

"Even with Jed Crane?"

"Perhaps. She visited him at the guardhouse this afternoon."

"Are you sure of that?"

The other nodded. "Quite sure."

"She didn't mention it to me."

"I imagine the interview was not pleasant. Later on she may talk to me about it. Tamara is a good girl, Miss Tremaine. I have great hopes for her. And for Crane. Not promising material, but there's no telling what a good woman could make of him."

"How odd that you should say that, when Tamara used almost those words earlier today. I'm sorry, but I can't imagine him as anything but a no-good—"

"Perhaps," the priest interrupted mildly, "Tamara is wiser than either of us. Who knows?"

X

AT SUPPER that evening Major Tremaine sat preoccupied, and there was a grimness in his expression which warned his sister not to trespass lightly in the realm of military affairs. But she was tinglingly anxious to learn whether Steele had carried out his threat to tell what he knew about Lieutenant Mason. Her circuitous approach to the matter would have done credit to the most oily diplomat.

Opportunity offered when the roar of a jet plane swept in from the sea, rolled over the roof like thunder and died away. Jim heaved a sigh of relief.

"Another flight completed! They may get some results if this weather holds."

"And we," she added, "should have a glorious day for the ice fields."

Jim took the bait. He had been engrossed in the food without the slightest consciousness of what he was eating. Now he looked up and two deep creases appeared between his eyebrows.

"Did Mason deliver my message?" he asked sharply. "Did he tell you when Mrs. Bentley expects you?"

"He did. Is—is he still going with me?" Delight allowed a shade of anxiety to cloud her eyes and tinge her voice.

Tremaine glared across the table. "He is, but don't cry about it. Good Lord, you haven't changed your mind about wanting him, have you?" he exploded.

"Of course I want him, silly. It was only that you yourself haven't confirmed that he was going, and when he was here—"

"Didn't he make it clearly understood that I had *ordered* him to go?" His fingers drummed irritably on the table.

"*Ordered* him!" the girl exclaimed aghast. "Good grief! Is that your idea of the finesse I asked you to use? Jeepers, the iron fist in the concrete glove! As a matter of fact he did tell me that he was going, but one never knows what may happen in this man's Army. It moves in a mysterious way, its wonders to perform," she added flippantly.

Her brother lighted a cigar, leaned back with folded arms, and stared at her absently. She smiled back at him affectionately. How very good to look at he was, she thought. His skin was bronzed, his brown eyes clear with health. Even the bald expanse rimmed with short, red-tinged hair, seemed to suit him. She couldn't imagine Jim with a bristling crewcut, although that might fit his quick temper. She brought her thoughts back from his irascible personality when he spoke.

"There's something going on between Steele and Mason, Dee," he mused. "Some kind of a rotten deal somewhere, or I miss my guess. They're like a couple of bulldogs, ready to fly at each other's throats whenever they're in the same room," he explained worriedly.

"Well, I'll pick Steele for the underhanded individual, every time. The *treacherous dog* would be more like it," she corrected herself. "You don't really believe that Bill Mason would do anything wrong, do you?" she accused, eyes stormy with protest. "Why, just to look at him you'd know that he's as fine as they come."

Jim shrugged his shoulders and blew smoke ceilingward, but his eyes never left his sister's face.

"I'd hate like the devil to think that he'd step out of line," he admitted. "So far he's the best officer I've ever had under my command, bar none. He's got everything! Of course I've never seen him in action, but I'll bet my bottom dollar he can take anything in stride."

Tremaine laid his cigar aside and rubbed his face vigorously with both hands, then rested his elbows on the table.

"I'm absolutely sold on him, but, take it from me," he added seriously, "you never know what a person will do. You may think you know them from inside out, but comes temptation or a crisis and they are liable to fool you."

Delight's thoughts flew back to Tamara's revelation.

"Do you suppose that that—that their trouble has anything to do with a girl?" she asked hesitantly.

Tremaine pushed back his chair and stood up. His glance lingered for a moment on his sister's downcast face, while a curious expression flashed in his eyes and was gone. His voice was gruff as he answered impatiently, "A girl! Good Heavens, it's something a darned sight more important than *that!*"

Delight blew a kiss from the tips of her fingers as she rose in her place to make him a sweeping bow. With exaggerated humility she simpered, "We, the women of America, thank you, Major. You are so subtle in your compliments."

Sometime during the night Delight started awake and lay wondering what had roused her, why her heart pounded so. The house was silent except for the electric clock beside her bed which hummed softly to itself. The greenish glow of the hands marked half-past one and she felt a fresh stirring of alarm.

Already she had become accustomed to Alaska's summer sun which, even at this hour, should be filling the room with pale twilight. But it was dark. Beyond the windows she could barely make out the dividing line between the Stygian blackness of the mountains and the lowering clouds that blanketed the sky.

Nothing more ominous than a cloudy night! She sat up and peered about the room. Still bemused with sleep she eyed the long hangings at the windows. Nothing, not even a breath of wind, disturbed their apple-green folds. Dreamily she reminded herself that it was impossible to tell their color now, although she had thrilled to it when Bertha Bentley trotted in to offer them.

"My contribution to Major Jim's Love Nest," Babbling Bertha had giggled. Because Jim flatly refused to "clutter up my quarters with such frippery," Delight had appropriated them as a first step in brightening her own room.

She settled down once more, planning further decorative improvements. . . .

The creak of her brother's door and soft footsteps on the bare boards of the hall shot her out of bed. Flinging a blanket around her brief pajamas, she crossed the room and gently opened her own door.

Major Tremaine halted in midstep. Still struggling into his Windbreaker he waved her back.

"Go to bed, Delight; it's only me."

"Where are you going?" she demanded breathlessly.

"Got a phone call. Some trouble at the airstrip, that's all. Nothing to worry about."

Delight saw the automatic holstered under his coat, and subconscious memory swam to the surface of her confused mind.

"Something woke me. Was it shooting?"

"Maybe—a little," Tremaine admitted. "Probably one of Mason's trigger-happy guards massacring a shadow. Don't worry, Dee, go to sleep. I expect to be right back." He waved again. "Orders, soldier! Hit the sack."

Dubiously she watched him hurry down the stairs, heard

the front door close. A machine churned away up the river road, the sound of its motor trailing off to a faint whine like a gentle breeze through pine trees.

This is the Army, Delight told herself firmly. Alarms and excursions at any hour of the day or night. Usually meaningless, but one day it might be—war. Until then, become accustomed to it, inured to it, or live in endless anxiety. Reluctantly she went back to bed and resolutely fell asleep.

In the morning, so obscure was her recollection of the incident that she would have set it down as a nightmare had not Jim been still absent at breakfast. That brought back her anxiety redoubled.

With difficulty she conquered an impulse to telephone or rush over to Headquarters for news, knowing how he would dislike such an exhibition of feminine weakness. Instead she filled the long morning with a thorough house-cleaning program, stopping more and more often to look out the window toward the camp. Maddeningly it preserved its normal appearance.

It was almost noon when Jim at last tramped in and found her desperately dusting the kitchen. She faced him expectantly.

Ignoring the wordless appeal he perched on the stool and wearily massaged cheeks and forehead.

"Make coffee, will you, Dee?" was all he said.

"Coming right up, Major. I just made some fresh—in case." She turned up the heat under the coffeepot.

"Swell!" He raised his head and called, "Come out here! Coffee's hot!"

"Company!" gasped Delight, forgetting her curiosity in the night alarm at his typically masculine disregard for a proper warning. She whipped off her apron and darted a glance in the mirror beside the sink. Darn! A smudge of dust gave her half a mustache! A lightning stroke of the apron erased it and she turned to see Lieutenant Mason loom through the doorway.

He took off his cap. "Hello, Tam—Oh, excuse me! I thought—Good morning, Miss Tremaine."

"Everybody thinks I'm Tamara!" Delight sighed. "Because she was always in the kitchen before I came—evidently. And now I'm here all the time—evidently. But really, Lieutenant, must we be so formal in the kitchen? *Delight,* please. *Dee* to my friends—in case you care."

A responsive smile lighted his grave face. "Then the name is *William*—not Lieutenant—*Bill,* to my friends."

"Much better all around, Bill," she laughed. "Sit here in the breakfast nook, both of you." She placed cups of coffee for him and her brother and went to the refrigerator. "Cream?"

"Black, no sugar!" the men voiced together and laughed at the emphatic chorus.

"Me, too." She brought her cup to sit opposite them. "We are all watching our figures, I see."

"And well worth watching—" Mason began and then snapped his mouth shut. He scalded his tongue with a hasty gulp and gasped.

Delight felt her cheeks glow, not only at the compliment implied, but as much as its unexpectedness. Would she ever fathom this man, she wondered, one moment friendly, as at the trading post and in the café; then appearing at her door as icily formal as an official courier. And now—! She saw her brother's narrowed eyes shift from the lieutenant to her with a curious glint in them, and made a quick diversion.

"How about doughnuts or coffee cake, Jim?" she asked.

"Fine, Dee! Make it both. Strange as it may seem, we haven't had breakfast. Too busy."

"You poor men!" She was on her feet and heading for the refrigerator again. "Bacon and eggs, then. They won't take a minute."

"Haven't time. The other stuff will have to do."

Delight brought a plate of doughnuts to the table, and as she passed him Jim gave an approving pat to the sleeve of her cherry linen dress.

"You must have been *expecting* company, Dee—or do you doll up like this for housework? Pretty, isn't it, Lieutenant?"

"It certainly does something for her."

"Why, thank you, sir!" She dimpled. "And now that the subject has come up—" She fixed an imploring eye on her brother. "Actually I put on a bright dress to lift my spirits while waiting for the Lord of the Manor to come home—or be brought home on a stretcher. Just what did happen last night, anyway?"

Mason choked on his doughnut.

"You mean nobody let you know he was all right?" He glared at the major. "Didn't you call her when we got back to camp this morning?" Belatedly discipline penetrated his indignation and he added a lame, "I mean, *sir?*"

"I am sorry, Dee." Jim's propitiating smile faded as he muttered, "I'm not used to having someone at home worrying about me, you know."

The loneliness in the quiet words tugged at her heart, but she managed a shaky laugh.

"You've got someone now, Major, and how! So give— before I perish of curiosity."

"I guess you do rate an explanation." He grinned at Mason. "There you are, son, the horrible plight of an Army man with a demanding wife—or reasonable facsimile—at home. No peace!"

The jesting remark drove the color from Mason's face and he set down his cup with a clatter.

"I'd better—I'll run over to camp now and—and see how things are with my company, sir," he muttered. He stood up, groping for his cap. "I'll be at your office as soon as I've checked."

"You needn't rush off," Delight protested. "I'm sure I'm not going to hear anything you shouldn't. Have some more coffee."

"Thank you, no." Mason worked his way out from behind the table, put on his cap and saluted Tremaine. "Thank you for the breakfast, sir. I'll be waiting for you." He strode out of the kitchen. The front door opened and closed decisively.

"Well!" Delight exclaimed indignantly. "Exit Lieutenant Mason—and I thought I was being supremely entertaining!" She eyed her brother with suspicion. "If that sudden departure was meant to divert my attention, it didn't work. I still want to know what went on last night."

"I doubt if that was his intention," Jim said with a shrug. "But here's the story, Dee. Sorry I made you wait and worry for it. I guess you know that there is a highly secret project under way at the airfield."

"I've heard rumors," she admitted dryly.

"No doubt you have, worse luck. Science has made great strides but they haven't yet come up with an invention to stop people from blabbing. However, it's an Air Force project, so *they* handle all matters of security around their laboratories and buildings. But due to the isolated position here, and other considerations, the Army assigned this task force to assist in guarding the entire area. That is why I, Baker Company and various auxiliary units are in Totum."

"A sort of outer cordon of defense?" Delight suggested.

"Exactly. As to the project, I don't mind telling *you* that it's in the field of electronics. You know about the equipment we have to spot enemy planes—radar and so on?"

"I've read about them."

"Obviously other nations have them as well. This station is working on something with which a plane might defeat those spotting devices—blind them. A kind of cloak of invisibility."

"That sounds fantastic, Jim."

"It is—or will be, if it's successful. But it must be kept secret, of course. That is one reason why they work in this isolated district, and we guard them. Now, as I said, this is the baby of the Air Force—of SAC, to be more exact."

"Strategic Air Command," Delight translated.

Jim nodded. "When they have anything like this in the works they make occasional tests of the security measures surrounding it. Sometimes they send in a crew of their men, especially trained for the work, to try and penetrate the guard lines. That happened last night."

"And that's what woke me? A fight?"

"Yes. Four of their operatives attempted a sneak infiltration at one-thirty. Their primary objective was to test the Air Force guards, but the Army is happy to state that they never got a chance. Bill Mason has trained his men well and kept them on their toes, so we nailed all four synthetic spies before they reached the inner cordon of defense."

"Good for us—I mean, for Bill!" Delight applauded. "But the shooting, Jim! Surely you don't kill these raiders!"

Tremaine shook his head. "The shooting you heard took place at the same time, but at the far end of the field. Corporal Fanning, on guard there, found a man behind the hangar, challenged him—and was shot before he could fire his rifle. He did fire then, but missed, and the man shot again."

Delight's heart jumped painfully. "Killed?" she whispered.

"No, no. Chest wound from a small-caliber pistol. The second shot only hit Fanning's hand and made him drop his gun. He tackled the stranger, just the same, but couldn't hold him—he got away."

"But—but"—her stare was incredulous—"you mean one of *our* Air Force men shot one of *our* men for practice? I don't—"

"The Air Force sent in four men. We caught four. Nobody knows who the fifth man was, but believe me we're going to find out."

"Oh! Maybe a *real* spy?"

"Maybe." Jim spread his hands, smiling. "Now you have the whole story, Dee, and you see that you needn't have worried about me."

"Of course not!" she scoffed. "After this if you race out in the middle of the night I'll just say, 'Another spy—with a small-caliber pistol! Phooey!' and go back to sleep."

"You might as well, my dear." Jim stood up and stretched. "That coffee hit the spot. Now back to work. I expect to be home in plenty of time for supper," he threw over his shoulder as he left, "so have a good one to make up for my lost breakfast!"

XI

DELIGHT had no appetite for a lonely lunch; she made a sandwich from leftovers and drank another cup of coffee.

"This Army life will make a caffeine case out of me," she sighed. "If I sleep a wink tonight it will be a miracle. Coffee —and spies!"

Her uneasiness was not allayed when, an hour later, a jeep-driving corporal delivered a peremptory summons to her to come to Major Tremaine's office. With renewed foreboding Delight made the trip beside the strangely silent driver.

Entering Jim's room she felt as though she were stepping into a full-dress court-martial. Her brother was pacing the floor, again rubbing his face nervously. Warner Steele, Bill Mason and another officer in Air Force blue rose from their chairs. To her dismay there wasn't a welcoming smile visible in the room.

"Hello again, B—Lieutenant Mason." Delight covered the too familiar address hastily. "And the same to you, Captain Steele."

"This is Captain Whitaker, Dee." Jim indicated the fourth man. "Of Air Force Security."

"How do you do, Captain." Delight took in the short, slim flier, his sober brown eyes and rust-colored crewcut. "I haven't seen you around before, have I?" she asked with assumed cheerfulness, sitting down beside the major's desk.

"Flew in this morning—too late." Captain Whitaker dispensed with a formal greeting and merely nodded. "Due yesterday but we were grounded by fog. Too da—darn bad!"

"I don't know what more *you* could have done than we did!" Steele growled.

The airman waved a placating hand.

"No criticism intended, Captain. No one here was at fault. Major Tremaine should have been notified that we were setting up a test raid. But something went haywire this time, Major, and you weren't informed. Possibly there was a mix-up because the date couldn't be fixed until the last moment, since they had to wait for a cloudy night. Difficult to work unseen," he smiled, "when your twilight lasts all night."

Mason sat forward.

"Were your men in Totum ahead of time, waiting for the weather?" When the captain nodded, Bill snapped his fingers in disgust. "One of them was selling freezers to the plant here? At least, that was his cover?"

"You spotted him?" demanded the airman sharply.

Mason shook his head. "I let him slip. Didn't like his looks, and pumped him—gently." He threw Delight a look that was almost a wink. "The usual Disgruntled Soldier approach; must have done it well, I think it upset Miss Tremaine. But you fellows are too thorough. When I checked with the waitress in the café she gave him a clean bill." He shook his head regretfully.

Delight remembered his prolonged conference with the statuesque blonde and could not repress an indignant, "Why didn't you let me in on it?"

"And show myself up as a sucker?" Mason sighed. "That waitress saw him get off the steamer, and said the plant manager himself brought him in there for coffee. Seemed I was barking up the wrong tree, so"—he spread his hands—"like a sap I let it ride."

"We try to set up an ironclad story," Whitaker said complacently. "Now, to business. Miss Tremaine, the major has filled you in on what took place last night, I understand. The net result was all four of our operatives rounded up in jig time—very satisfactory, Lieutenant Mason—and one apparent enemy agent at large. Not satisfactory! Miss Tremaine, we have got to find him, and we hope you can help."

"*I?*" Incredulity rounded her eyes. "What can I do?"

The captain hesitated, darting a questioning look at the major, who shook his head and walked away to the window. Whitaker shrugged.

"He leaves the dirty work to me, Miss Tremaine. All right, I admit it's my job. We have heard from—well, I'll put it this way—one of your neighbors saw you with a suspicious-looking stranger yesterday."

In spite of her perfectly clear conscience Delight felt a stab of alarm at the portentous tone. Then reason took charge and instilled a wild desire to laugh at the quartet of grim faces.

"What busybody neighbors we must have, Major Jim," she observed lightly—and in the next instant memory nudged her to even more amusement. One of her neighbors! Suppressing an anticipatory chuckle she demanded, "*Who* saw me?"

Tremaine answered from the window. "Captain Kent reported that his boy watched you—"

"Harry Kent!" Her explosive laugh mingled merriment and relief. "I knew it! Now I suppose my best defense will be to cast doubt on the credibility of your witness. Isn't that the proper legal maneuver?" she queried airily. "And can I do it!"

With counterfeit drama she described her experience with

the boy and his tragic history of the nonexistent brother, Randolph.

"Or it might have been Richard," she finished brightly. "Harry couldn't quite make up his mind." She snapped her fingers. "So much for your witness!"

The four officers exchanged rueful frowns and Steele slapped the arm of his chair in disgust.

"And I thought we had something hot!" he snapped, flushed with chagrin. "That kid ought to be paddled every day for a week! He can cause trouble if he goes around making up those yarns out of whole cloth. The infernal little liar!"

"That's not fair!" Delight defended her small friend. "Harry doesn't mean to lie, he claims he's only trying to be entertaining."

"I'd *entertain* him, if he was my brat!" Steele growled.

Mason intervened. "Luckily he isn't, so cut out the crabbing." When the captain whirled on him angrily he growled, "Lay off, will you? You're just burned up because you fell for a cock-and-bull fairy tale—from a seven-year-old boy."

"I don't know why *you* horn in on this business, anyway, Mason!" Steele blustered. "Just who do you think—"

"You forget, Captain Steele," Mason interrupted levelly, "that Corporal Fanning, one of *my* men, was shot. I make that my business. Let's not waste any more time."

"I'm not going to, you can bet on that!" Steele left his chair and addressed the major with more force than courtesy. "I wasn't at the field last night, so I can't be of any help, and Captain Whitaker has taken over for the Air Force. He should handle this from now on. With your permission, sir, I will leave the inquiry in his hands." He flung a salute toward the general vicinity of his commanding officer and stalked toward the door.

Delight could not refrain from sending a parting shot after him.

"It just happens, Captain Steele, that Harry Kent *didn't* make up his story about me out of whole cloth, as you said." When he ignored her and disappeared, she smiled at Mason. "I remember now, that I did talk to a stranger yesterday afternoon."

"Where?" demanded Whitaker sharply.

"Behind our house. But he was hardly a spy, Captain, even if I did think so for a minute." She smiled reminiscently. "Too many exciting movies, I suppose. I thought he was surveying the airfield—through binoculars, in the approved cinema fashion for secret agents—but he was watching a marmot, until I frightened it away."

The Air Force man scraped his chair around to face her directly.

"If you'd be so kind, Miss Tremaine, I'd like a complete description of this meeting—and of the person you met."

His determined gravity amused her. Evidently this captain was the bulldog type, loath to let go of an idea, no matter how farfetched it might be. To humor him, she recounted, step by step, her supposed errand of mercy and its embarrassing denouement.

"Did *you* see the animal he was watching?" asked Whitaker.

"No. I told you it went into its den—burrow or whatever you call it—when I laughed."

"*He* said that," the captain pointed out. "Perhaps you think I'm making a lot out of nothing, Miss Tremaine, but your man is the first *stranger* we've learned of who was in town yesterday."

"But, Captain, it's foolish! He was a college boy on vacation, very pleasant and friendly. He told me he grew up around here, and came back to see Alaska again. Not much money, so he landed from a freighter at Kuski yesterday and walked up to Totum."

Mason stood up. "We can check that, Major Tremaine?" When Jim nodded he went out hurriedly. They could hear his staccato directions to a clerk in the next room. In a moment he was back in his seat.

"Let's have a description of your college boy, Miss Tremaine," Whitaker resumed.

Resignedly she complied. "Short but well built; he looked husky. Black hair, and a typical collegiate attempt to be bizarre by growing a beard." She laughed. "It looked rather like a moth-eaten fur piece. He was tanned, and with his black whiskers, his teeth seemed startlingly white. But then perhaps they are, anyway," she added lightly.

Whitaker shifted irritably in his chair, but before he could speak, Major Tremaine said quietly, "Try to treat this as a serious matter, Dee. An attempt has been made to spy on us. And a man has been shot."

Delight flushed. "I beg your pardon, Captain Whitaker. Of course it isn't a joke. But this boy was so completely innocent. If you had seen him—"

"I wish to God I had! But go on. His clothes?"

"Very collegiate, I suppose. Anyway, they were very loud. A painfully yellow sports coat and tan slacks, very light in color—almost *café au lait*. Hardly the costume for a spy who hoped to remain unnoticed, I should think."

"Or a good cover for a spy," Mason disagreed. "Who'd think of suspecting a man in such blatant clothes?"

"And he wore the most fiery red shoes—those canvas things with crepe rubber soles—"

"Now you're starting to roll!" Mason broke in. "Fanning reported that the man who shot him made no sound when he ran away."

"Any more details?" Whitaker prompted.

Delight concentrated, her head bowed, fingers pressing her temples as she recreated a picture of that afternoon. She was walking across the slope beside the young man, talking of nothing important. Flowers.

"I think he did come from around here, as he claimed," she murmured. "He knew the name of some blossoms I picked. Bird bill."

The sunlit meadow was clear in her mind now, Jim's house with the screen door giving a darkened glimpse of the kitchen, Harry Kent staring from his yard—no, that was afterward —after the stranger had declined her invitation to supper, pulling up his sleeve to consult his watch—

"He wore a wrist watch!" she announced, and then quickly, "I noticed it because it was unusual. Large—larger than yours, Jim—and quite thin and flat."

Captain Whitaker reached into his pocket and laid something on her lap.

"Like this, Miss Tremaine?"

While she stared with pounding heart at the silver watch and its broken leather strap, she experienced the dizzying sensation of whirling helplessly downstream through churning rapids.

"Yes," she gasped. "It looks exactly the same."

"That," the Captain informed her with the patient calm of a teacher instructing the very young, "is an imported watch, highly accurate—and extremely expensive. A split-second stop watch, too. Doesn't seem like the sort of thing a struggling college student would want or could afford, does it?"

Delight shook her head, whispered, "Where—"

"Corporal Fanning, the wounded guard, grappled with his assailant but couldn't hang on. When the man broke away he left this in the guard's fist."

XII

SILENCE hung over the room, a silence so electric that Delight's nerves tingled. Wordlessly she prayed that no one would suggest that it would be well if she left them to continue their council of war in private. She would perish of curiosity.

She jumped when knuckles rapped on the closed door and a corporal stepped in and stood at attention. At the major's nod he reported, "I just had Kuski on the line, sir. No boats have touched there this week, from anywhere. And no strangers have been seen there, either." After waiting a moment for further instructions, and getting none, he retired—reluctantly, Delight thought, and sympathized with his evident thirst for enlightening details.

Tremaine moved to sit at his desk. Chin on clenched hands he mused, "Captain Steele investigated some trouble in the town over an unidentified ship offshore the other day." At Whitaker's questioning look he explained, "The fishermen claimed it was a floating cannery, Jap or Russian—a foreigner at any rate. But that was only suspicion, they're always on the lookout for such boats. It could have been there for another purpose."

"Putting a man ashore in some out-of-the-way place near here, for instance. You checked on it, Major?"

Jim shrugged. "We alerted the Navy and they sent a destroyer down from Cordova and a reconnaissance plane from Anchorage. No dice. There are a thousand straits and inlets among the islands in this section; it would take a long time to search them all. Besides, fog rolled in from the ocean before they had covered much of the area."

He cracked his fist on the desk.

"Wouldn't you know that would happen, just when we most need to see! But fog does that up here, Captain, without warning, and even on the clearest day."

"Certainly, I've been caught in it." Whitaker eyed Delight thoughtfully. "Before we go any further, perhaps Miss Tremaine can add to her description of this man. Anything may help, you know. He came from this part of the country, you said. Was he white?"

"He must be. Indians don't have whiskers," Tremaine asserted.

"Oh, definitely white," Delight said. "A broad face with high cheekbones, and a sort of a button nose. The Slavic type, isn't it? Of Finnish descent, perhaps?"

"Perhaps," was the captain's cautious agreement. "Notice the color of his eyes??"

"Why, no. He wore dark glasses." Mention of them jogged her memory once more. "It was queer; he had them off to look through his binoculars, but put them on before he turned to speak to me."

Mason's short laugh and an exchange of looks between the three men expressed satisfaction.

"A careful young man," said Bill approvingly. "So he had a pair of binoculars?"

Delight nodded. "And a camera, but it was the cheapest kind of box camera. He boasted about what a bargain it was, which made him seem quite young and unsophisticated, if you know what I mean. I assumed the binoculars were of the same bargain type. They were quite small."

"Not always a sign of inefficiency," Whitaker sighed.

The major tilted back in his chair and put his hands behind his head.

"It looks as though we've identified our spy, Captain."

"No question about it. Now we find him—if we can. For the moment, let's assume that he did land from that strange ship you mentioned. He made his try at the hangar last night. What's his next move?"

Tremaine arched an eyebrow at Mason. "You've had considerable experience with Red espionage overseas, Lieutenant. What's your opinion?"

"They are thorough planners, I can tell you that!" Mason said slowly. "Every possibility is considered—and covered —before they start anything. Captain, I'd like to ask a question, which you may not care to answer."

"Shoot!"

"Did the spy succeed?"

Whitaker spread his hands. "I'd be glad to answer that, if I knew. He was coming out of the hangar when the guard met him—or so your man thought. We don't know how long he'd been in there, if he was, or how much he found out."

"If he got in," Mason admitted gloomily, "he succeeded. Probably a trained engineer with a photographic memory. Our *friends* overseas don't send dopes on espionage missions!"

Jim smiled at Delight. "Your description didn't indicate a mastermind."

"An excellent description of just that," Mason corrected. " 'What bright eyes you have, my dear'—er—Miss Tremaine!" he amended the quote quickly, but his eyes remained fixed on her.

Nervously she wondered if his stare expressed admiration or speculation as to the propriety of a girl—even the commander's sister—sitting in on this kind of a conference.

"An excellent description of a 'mastermind,' as you referred to it, Major," Mason continued soberly. "And every word of it worries me. They really picked a star for this show. Look at him! Who's going to pay attention to a crazy kid in zoot clothes? But he grew up around here, knows the people, the country. Perhaps not as young as De—Miss Tremaine thought. Collegiate? I'll bet—probably majored in electronics.

"Somehow the Reds got a strangle hold on him, trained him and put him to work." He banged his hand on his knee to emphasize his words. "He *must* be tops, gentlemen, or they wouldn't send him up here. *They* know how vital this experiment is as well as we do!"

"That's true, I suppose," the captain nodded agreement. "Then we assume he secured the information. What next?"

"A prearranged meeting place, where they pick him up," Mason answered decidedly. "Probably a small boat would sneak in from the ship."

"Likely. And the place would have to be some distance from here; contact made during the night, such as it is. Not last night, certainly, that wouldn't give him time to accomplish anything at the field. So he has to hide out today at least."

Mason nodded assent. "He must have got away down the road." Half-closed eyes seemed to be reviewing the scene. "The only possible way. The airfield switched on their floodlights and had men all along the river and on the hillside within minutes of the shots. But he could have sneaked down the road, dropping into the ditch whenever a truck came along. Captain Kent and I moved two platoons up there on trucks as quickly as we could assemble them, but everyone was looking for trouble at the field, not on the way. They could easily have missed seeing him."

"Then he goes to ground out in the hills to wait for tonight?" the captain suggested.

"Possibly. But I have a hunch that he expects us to figure it just that way. So he hides in town." Mason leaned forward. "O.K. if we comb the place, Major, including the Indian village?"

Tremaine hesitated. "I suppose you'll have to, but handle the Indians with kid gloves. Don't stir them up; we're supposed to be their friends."

"The townies are more apt to give us trouble than the Indians, who are A-1 Americans, every one of them. If I tell them we're hunting a spy they'll turn the village inside out for me."

"Go ahead, then." The major sighed tiredly. "Let's break this meeting up now, Captain, and get on with our witch hunt."

"Right!" Whitaker jumped to his feet. "Think I'll post a man on the observation tower, with glasses. He just might get sight of the guy if he did take to the hills." He started for the door and stopped.

"You'll be sure and not broadcast any of this, won't you, Miss Tremaine?" he demanded.

Before she could speak Bill Mason snapped, "That was unnecessary, Captain, and insulting!"

Whitaker took in the lieutenant's slowly reddening face, and the girl's surprised smile at such stanch defense. With a knowing twinkle he bowed to Delight.

"It was indeed," he admitted gravely. "I humbly apologize," and went out grinning.

The noisy clearing of the major's throat drew Delight's eyes from the embarrassed lieutenant. Her brother assumed his most rigid poker face.

"If you want to go back to the house, Dee," he suggested, "ask my driver to run you up there. I have a few details to clear up with Lieutenant Mason."

Delight laughed. "As obvious a brush-off as I've enjoyed for some time. But—very well, sir, I depart."

Tremaine waited until the door closed before he said, "That spy's timing was lucky, wasn't it? To be sure, he had to pick a dark night, just as Whitaker's men did. But was it *accidental* that he moved in just when everyone was engrossed in a test raid by Air Force Security?"

Mason stared. "You think there was a leak, sir? That someone tipped him off the test was coming up?"

"I wondered," the other mused. "There's this trouble over Captain Steele's orderly intercepting the mail."

As always that name brought a look of cold enmity to Mason's face and he ground a fist into his palm. Then he shook his head.

"No, Major, even I can't see Warner Steele mixed up in anything so—"

"Damn it, man, I didn't mean Steele! Never thought of connecting *him* with it! But Jed Crane? His record isn't too good."

"Just ordinary hell-raising, sir," Mason said with conviction. "He'll make a good man yet; all he needs is a jolt hard enough to knock some sense into him. This may be it, unless he loosens up and spills the truth."

The lieutenant saw no reason to mention his attempt to get the facts through Tamara; she needn't be involved at all if she was unsuccessful.

"As for Crane looking for secret information to pass along —it doesn't add up, sir," he continued. "He took a personal letter and who would expect that sort of thing to be sent to an infantry lieutenant."

"That's true," the other admitted resignedly. "Scratch my brainstorm."

"If our spy had that information he got it from someone

with a pipeline into Air Force Headquarters. And that," Mason admitted gloomily, "wouldn't surprise me. They're clever people on his side."

Delight, after her sugar-coated dismissal from Headquarters, had resigned herself to the prospect of no further information on the progress of the spy hunt. Jim, she knew, was not one to "bring his office home with him"; in fact he never discussed military matters with her unless backed into a corner. And she was determined not to take advantage of her involvement in this affair by pressing him for news. So, unless the information came to her from some other source, this business, she foresaw sadly, was going to be as disappointing as a mystery novel with the last chapter torn from the book.

But fate took pity on her. At six o'clock Captain Kent knocked on her door. The jovial and slightly rotund Virginian, whom she had met at the Bentleys', could not have looked less like a fairy godmother, but such he proved himself. He presented the major's regrets; her brother would not be able to get home for supper as he had promised. In the same breath the smiling captain suggested that Delight should honor the Kents by joining them for the evening meal.

Her spirits, which had sunk to subterranean depths at his announcement, rebounded at the invitation.

"I'll accept so fast it'll make your head spin!" she exclaimed gratefully. "Keeping house all day for Nobody is a wearing experience; I couldn't stand another solitary meal. What time?" Laughing, she apologized, "I don't wish to appear too eager, but I am!"

"Come along with me now."

"If this dress is all right—"

"What's the matter with it?" was his practical answer. "We're not dining with Babbling Bertha, and if we were, what that aqua blouse does for you—it is aqua, isn't it?— would turn her an unbecoming green with envy. Come on! I haven't given Sue much notice, so there's no telling what she'll whip up to grace the festive board, but if it's lack of solitude you crave I can guarantee plenty of that."

While they crossed to his house the captain satisfied her curiosity about the spy hunt without waiting to be questioned.

"Quite a day we've had," he announced. "Spent most of it making a thorough search of Totum for the Disappearing Man, from fishermen's shacks to Indian shanties. Unfortunately, no dice. Bill Mason is disgusted—with himself—because he fell for what he terms 'A moss-grown double-cross.'"

"What in the world is that?" Delight asked.

"Moss-grown refers to its hoary age; otherwise it means the unknown agent outguessed us." Kent stopped to stare across the river at town and shadowed hills and shook his head. "He knew that we would figure the woods to be his likeliest choice for a hideout. Anyone would. But he counted on our being smart enough to figure, also, that *he* would be smart and cross us up by sticking to town."

"That's what Lieutenant Mason thought," Delight remembered.

"Yes, and that's the way we played it. So he double-crossed us by taking to the hills after all."

"So he may be miles away by now?"

"We don't think so; we believe he'd make contact with the ship that brought him as near here as safely possible, because he'd be in a hurry to get his information aboard. We think his contact is that unidentified ship which was reported a couple of days ago, because there hasn't been any ship or plane into Totum that wasn't checked in and out. So, in order to rejoin that ship he has to stay fairly near this town."

As he started homeward again he continued, "Probably you noticed a good deal of extra activity in the air today, planes watching to try and spot either him or his ship. And Mason has a couple of hundred men beating the bush, so somebody may flush him out. In the meantime, Miss Tremaine, let's forget shop, and enjoy our supper, whatever it is."

The captain's guarantee of "no solitude" proved well-founded. Delight was welcomed cordially by the two Mrs. Kents, who emerged from the kitchen pink of face and breathless, and rapturously by red-haired Harry. Even his attendant shadow Igloo threatened to lay her low by the vigor of his welcome, until dragged outside by his young master. The Husky then took up his favorite station on the porch, leaning heavily against the screen door to watch what went on inside with panting attention.

Delight waited with some misgivings for the boy to refer to her meeting with the spy—misgivings because she was not sure how much should be said about it. But her apprehension was wasted; Harry was too full of today's exciting adventure of living to waste a thought on yesterday.

He plunged at once into a step-by-step history of his trip to Totum wharf, where he made a new friend in Swede, a fisherman who impressed him as particularly genial and talkative.

"His schooner didn't go out today," Harry explained, "so he took me off in a little boat. A—a dopey, or something—"

"Dory?" suggested Delight.

"Yuh—dory. We rowed along the shore and he sang most of the time. Funny songs, I couldn't understand the words 'cause he didn't say 'em plain. He had a cold, he said, and kept taking cough medicine."

Delight and Captain Kent exchanged a glance of comprehension; evidently Swede's geniality had been induced or enhanced by alcohol.

"Thank goodness," murmured Kent, "he didn't tip you both out into the drink."

"Aw, I can swim!"

"*What!*" The explosive reproof showed that father was aware of son's flair for "entertaining" fiction.

"Well, pretty near—honest, Miss Tremaine!" Harry retreated to safer ground. "Then we rowed up the river—"

Again Kent snapped, "You didn't go near the airfield?"

"No, sir! You told me not to, remember?" Virtue personified. "We just went up past the Indian village. We were going to try fishing there, because Swede said the tide wasn't right in the bay. But when we were rowing under the bridge a guy hollered at us. He works at the wharf in town and asked us to take a message to Kasan Charley. He's an Indian," Harry threw in for Delight's benefit, "and lives in a shack quite a ways beyond the village. This guy didn't want to walk way out there."

Here Captain Kent essayed to stem the conversational flood by offering Delight a cocktail. When she declined but urged him not to deny himself, he retreated toward the kitchen.

"Chuck that boy out in the yard if he gets on your nerves before either Sue or I get back," was his parting advice.

Delight banished the worried look from Harry's face with a broad wink and received a heart-warming dimpled smile in return. No wonder the captain glowed with loving pride in his son, gruffly as he might attempt to conceal the emotion. Delight could have hugged the boy for his inexhaustible enthusiasm for life.

"I think the Indians are fascinating," she said. "Did you give the message to—to Kasan?"

"Sure. Swede didn't want to bother with any"—a wary glance toward the kitchen,— "'*lousy* native,' but I told the man we would. It was just a call from Captain Pepper—he runs the ship that's going to the glacier—Hey, Pop!" he shouted so abruptly that Delight gasped.

"Now what?" Kent wandered in, glass in hand.

"Mom says I can go on that trip with her if you say so. Can I, Pop?"

"If she's rugged enough to stand being cooped up all day on a boat with you, Young Dynamite, go to it."

"*Yay!*" Without a lost breath Harry resumed his saga of

adventure. "Captain Pepper wanted Kasan Charley on the trip—Swede says that's all the work Charley ever does, and even then he only sits around looking wise—and for Charley to surely be at the wharf in the morning at four o'clock."

"Four?" Delight wondered. "I was told we'd leave at six."

"Sure, but the steamer's coming down from Valdez and gets in here at four. So Swede rowed us up there, grumbling a lot. The shack's on the bank of the river, and Swede had finished his cough medicine by then, so he slung the empty bottle at the door. He hit it, all right, but Charley didn't run out swearing, the way Swede says he usually does."

"Did you go up to the shack then?"

"Didn't have to. Some man looked out the door and Swede said it wasn't Charley, so I asked, 'Where's Kasan Charley?' and the man said something I couldn't hear, but he pointed inside so I guessed Charley was busy or something. So I told him to tell Charley the message from Captain Pepper and he nodded and went back in.

"It was kind of funny," Harry mused. "He had a fur coat on, like the Indians wear, with the hood over his head. I should think he'd have roasted, but Indians are crazy that way, Swede says."

"And then did you catch some fish?" Delight braced herself for a fantastic catalogue of finny monsters.

"Well—" For a moment he wavered between soaring romance and pedestrian truth, but the parental eye was on him. "Well, no," he admitted with reluctance. "I would have all right, only when Swede was getting out the line for me he stumbled and dropped it overboard. The sinkers took it right to the bottom. We laughed like anything."

Further revelations were curtailed by the call to supper and the dispatch of Harry to his bed. With his departure Delight noticed a distinct drop in the conversational tempo, rather like the lull after a hurricane.

XIII

DELIGHT'S eagerness for the trip to the glacier was somewhat dashed when she arrived at the Totum wharf in the early morning hours and found Bill Mason standing apart from the laughing group of guests. His tanned face betrayed no sign of anticipation, unless an anticipation of boredom to be stoically endured.

It was unfortunate that she could not know the cause of his depression, another futile argument with Major Tremaine over his assignment to the expedition. This time Mason could with honesty plead the necessity of remaining in camp to continue the search for the spy, a duty which he considered a personal obligation as the wounded guard's commanding officer.

Tremaine had curtly informed him that any further search by *his* men was to be abandoned, in accordance with Captain Whitaker's advice, in hopes that if the spy had not already left, with the heat off, he might show himself; that the four men the captain had sent in, being specialists in this kind of work, would continue the hunt on the quiet. Unwilling to state his real objection to escorting the girl, Mason was forced to give up the argument.

Because she knew nothing of this Delight assumed that his dour appearance was a throwback to that frigid formality of the other afternoon when he informed her of his appointment. Had she been less strongly attracted to the tall lieutenant she would have sympathized with his reluctance; unhappily she discovered that it irritated her to the point of reprisal.

Mason did summon up a vestige of a smile as he greeted her. "Wonderful day for the trip, Delight. I've been off a couple of times and always drawn a heavy mist to start out in. You've brought us luck."

She chose to ignore the peace offering. "I never expected to see *you* here, Lieutenant! You seemed quite anxious to secure a substitute the other day."

For a moment he looked steadily at her, then accepted her scorn with a wry smile.

"You know how it is in the Army," he countered with a shrug. "Orders are orders." He moved away to speak to Sergeant Hogan, who was crossing the dock.

It was too late for Delight to retract her angry gibe, much as she would have liked to. She tried to forget it by chatting with the Bentleys' friends, several of whom she had already met at Bertha's or on shopping trips to town. Since most of them were too sleepy and chilled to be entertaining she turned to watch the spectators who had gathered to see the steamer depart.

In spite of the hour there were a number of Indians, concealing any interest they might have behind expressionless coppery features, and a dozen townspeople and fishermen whose business brought them out early in the day. Delight noticed Tamara, who had been given the day off, leaning against a pile near the little steamer, her head down and eyes intent on slowly twisting fingers.

Bill Mason dismissed the sergeant and walked across the pier to the Indian girl. From under scowling brows she watched his approach. She straightened and took a step as though to leave the wharf, then halted at a word from him.

Delight was too far away to hear, but it was obvious that he asked some question which Tamara answered with a shake of the head. Another question elicited a similar negative, this time with an expressive shrug.

Apparently impatient, Mason raised his voice.

"If you intend to see him, Tamara, don't wait too long."

"Why?" demanded the girl with equal vehemence. "You going to shoot him, maybe?"

The lieutenant laughed. "No fear of that. But he may be sent away for trial, and it will be too late then."

"Too late?" She lifted a sullen glare to his face and then looked away. "For me—or *you?*" Switching away from him she plodded up the pier toward town.

Mason came over to stand beside Delight near the ship's gangplank. She wondered if the dull redness under the tan on his cheeks showed embarrassment at the girl's jeering question. He must have asked her if she had visited Jed Crane, and the girl denied it. Yet Father Darley seemed quite positive that Tam had been to the guardhouse on that errand. "Too late for me—or you?" What could that mean; how was Bill Mason concerned in their meeting?

Without turning, Delight angled a probing glance at him —and immediately blushed at her action. In exactly that furtive way Tamara had looked at Mason when he approached her. Were white girl and Indian more sisters under the skin than she had realized?

She shivered and drew an orange scarf more closely about her throat. Although the sun had been up for hours there was still a nip in the air, that penetrating chill which comes from the proximity of snow and ice. In silence she accompanied Mason onto the steamer.

The others who were to make the trip had already gone aboard with the Bentleys. Delight saw Sue Kent, but not Harry. Before she could express disappointment at the absence of Young Dynamite he put in an appearance, although far too busy exploring the ship from bow to stern to give her more than a whoop of welcome in passing.

From the wharf Jim Tremaine was questioning the steamer's commander about the weather. Captain Pepper admired the major, in part because Jim never attempted to boss him when the Army made use of his ship. Some of the junior officers had been less careful about that delicate matter, which compelled the testy captain to put them in their place with seagoing bluntness. But not Tremaine. The major, in Pepper's opinion, would have made an excellent ship's captain; no higher praise was possible.

Now he waved careless reassurance from the window of the pilothouse.

"This day's made to order for a look at the glacier," he bawled. "Warming up, too, there'll be plenty of melting." Leaning out the window he tugged at his bristling mustache while he cast a professional eye at the sun.

"We ought to be back by ten tonight, Major, but don't worry if we're late. I've spent most of my life in these waters and I know this—you never know what will come up to delay you. You'll see us when you see us—that's all I guarantee." With a parting wave to those on the wharf he jerked the handle of the engine-room telegraph.

As the boat swung clear a jeep came bouncing down the steep road to the pier. Automatically Captain Pepper rang for full astern to check the forward motion of the ship, prepared to return if Tremaine should signal that someone on board was wanted. He watched the jeep's driver scramble out, run to the major, and after a few hurried words follow him to the machine, which then roared off. Pepper shrugged and resumed the interrupted voyage.

"What do you suppose that was all about?" Delight asked.

"Might be anything," Mason answered. "A post commander, like a doctor, is always on call. In a task force of four or five hundred men such as this, with equipment, quarters, kitchens, guardhouse, medical unit and what have you to be maintained at top efficiency, the major is kept busy."

Major Tremaine was indeed busy. The jeep whirled him through town to the river and turned off on the muddy road between the tar-paper huts, log cabins and unpainted frame houses which made up the Indian village. A few women stared at him from doorways, but there were no men in sight. They would be at the scene of whatever excitement offered, Jim knew, while the squaws remained patiently at home in obedience to their lord-and-masters' commands.

At the end of the road, which was now no more than a cart path, and well beyond the other houses, he saw the decrepit shanty of Kasan Charley. One of the post's ambulances stood at its door, surrounded by a crowd of Indians. Before Tremaine reached it the ambulance driver yelled a warning, gunned his motor thunderously to part the spectators and started up the road.

"Pull out!" Jim commanded, and the jeep promptly jumped

the ruts and nosed into some low bushes to clear the way. He leaned from the car and waved the ambulance forward when it slowed, catching a glimpse of a medic bent over a blanketed stretcher in the back as it lumbered past. Halting them for explanations might be a dangerous waste of time and the details could be soon learned from Father Darley, whom he saw standing in the cabin doorway.

As Tremaine jumped from the jeep before the shack he recognized one Indian in the crowd, saluted him and held out his hand.

"Chief Peter, they say that Kasan Charley is hurt. I'm sorry."

The mahogany face, wrinkled like a dried raisin, preserved its stolid blankness as the old man gripped Jim's hand to give it the Indian's customary limp single shake.

"We'll do everything we can for Charley," Tremaine assured him. "May I go in his house?"

Still silent, Chief Peter nodded and began pushing the staring Indians aside to clear a path, as Tremaine walked to where Father Darley waited for him.

"Am I glad to see you, Major!" the priest sighed with no trace of his usual geniality. "This is serious. Attempted murder, I think. I took it upon myself to commandeer the ambulance when I couldn't contact you at once. Captain Kent assures me that I was justified."

"Certainly, Father."

Kent appeared in the doorway behind the priest.

"I've told him it was no time to wait on regulations. You coming in now, sir, to look around?"

"Is the Indian badly hurt?" asked Jim as he entered.

"I'll have to leave that to your surgeon," Darley said. "Someone evidently gave him a murderous blow from behind. I don't know whether his skull is fractured or not; it looked too serious for my limited first-aid knowledge, and I couldn't get hold of Dr. Bentley."

"When did this happen?"

"Sometime last night, Major, or early this morning. Chief Peter tells me that Charley spent yesterday in town. Several people heard him come home very late."

"Heard him?"

"Er—yes—he was singing." At the pointed query in Jim's eyes the priest nodded. "Yes, he had been drinking."

"Couldn't he have been so drunk that he fell down and struck his head?" Tremaine suggested.

The other was emphatic. "Kason Charley never got *that* intoxicated. I don't think he could have walked after he received the blow, and what could he hit his head on in

84

here?" He gestured around at the sparse furnishings of the shack. "Even that sheet-iron stove would collapse, not make a wound such as he had."

"Wait a minute," Captain Kent said with a thoughtful frown. "Didn't you say he was away yesterday?"

"According to the chief, yes. All day."

"Harry was up here in the afternoon and thought Charley was at home then." Kent retold the boy's saga of delivering Captain Pepper's message through a third party.

"Another Indian in *here?*" Father Darley shook his head in doubt. "It's not likely, you know. Chief Peter!" he called out the door. "Was one of your people in Charley's house yesterday afternoon?"

The old man edged inside. "No, Father. No one here any time, sure. Charley no like visitors."

"That's what I thought."

"But he had one yesterday," Kent insisted.

"Unless Harry was making up one of his stories," Tremaine suggested.

"That's possible, I know. But he gave such a lot of details —I think he saw somebody," the captain persisted.

Chief Peter moved further into the room, his beaked nose twitching suspiciously. "Bad smell here," he muttered. "Burn smell!" He opened the top of the stove and bent over it sniffing loudly. "In here." He thrust in a hand and poked among the ashes, grunted and withdrew a charred button with bits of burned cloth still attached.

Peter examined it, scowling as he brought his old eyes close to see better.

"From white man's coat—white man here," he growled and held the button out to Tremaine. "Not from Indian coat."

"I wouldn't know, Chief. Are you sure?"

"Sure." Peter turned slowly, still frowning, to scan the tumbled dingy blankets on the broken-down bunk, the corners of the room, then raised his eyes to the walls. "Where Charley's coat? Not here. Not on him when he go?"

"No," agreed Darley. "He only had his plaid shirt on."

The chief nodded. "I see now, maybe. White man here when Charley come home. Hit him on head. Much blood, maybe? Man burn own coat in stove, take Charley's coat."

"Had to get rid of his bloodstained coat?" Captain Kent amplified the chief's deductions. "Could be, at that."

"But," the priest objected, "there wasn't that much blood —on Kasan Charley, anyway. Peter, you're sure it wasn't an Indian who was here?"

"White man," the Chief repeated stolidly, taking the button from Tremaine. His gnarled fingers worked at the twisted scrap of cloth still sticking to it until the blackened folds uncovered the inner surface which had not been touched by the flames. He held it out for Tremaine's inspection.

"Yellow cloth, Major. Yesterday you look for stranger in yellow coat. This it, maybe?"

Tremaine came within a breath of swearing, but smothered it out of deference to the priest.

"That must be it, Chief," he growled. "The man was just too darned clever for us! He evidently hid out in the bush until we finished searching the village and then calmly moved in behind us."

"It wasn't blood he was concealing, then," Kent argued. "He wanted to duck the clothes he thought we'd tie up with him." He bent over the stove and sniffed. "No smell of burnt rubber. Wonder what he did with the red shoes. Charley probably came back, caught him hiding here, and he fought to get away."

"No Indian would attack a man in his house," Father Darley protested. "Even if he came uninvited he would be considered a guest and treated generously."

"Perhaps Charley said something to make our spy suspect that he knew who he was and was going to turn him in," the major pointed out. "So he had to be silenced. Isn't that likely, Chief?"

Old Peter, who had been poking around the room, showed no interest in suppositions.

"Moccasins gone," he growled. "Man took Charley's coat and moccasins. A thief!"

"He's worse than that." Tremaine started for the door. "Perhaps he didn't hook up with his friends last night after all and is still around for us to pick up." He turned to salute the Indian. "We'll do our best to help Charley, Chief," he encouraged. "If the doctor gives the word we'll fly him to the hospital at Anchorage, or even Seattle. Trust me for that. And if any of your men want to help us hunt for this spy that hit him, send them down to camp. We can use them."

To the priest he said, "Father, I'm on my way to the post now. If you're interested in the medical verdict I'd be pleased to have you ride in with me."

XIV

ABOARD the steamer Dr. Bentley joined Delight and Mason where they stood at the rail to watch the receding shore.

"I've settled Bertha in a double order of pillows and rugs in a chair below the wheelhouse, fed her the second dose of her favorite seasick remedy, and now I can enjoy myself," he announced with an unconscious sigh of relaxation.

"Isn't she a good sailor?" asked Delight, amused.

"Fair, as long as she doesn't talk. When she does her stomach is apt to go on strike. Aboard ship is one place where she has deep respect for silence."

"But if she's afraid of being sick why did she arrange a trip like this?"

The doctor winked. "Between you and me, I think it was self-defense. Her sister Grace is coming to spend a month with us, and she's just back from a winter in Paris. I suspect B.B. wanted to have a glacier to counter Grace's tales of the fashion salons and Montmartre."

He glanced at the lieutenant, whose silence was distinctly noticeable, and then at the girl. With a knowing grin he remarked conversationally, "This ought to be quite a voyage. You've got a mighty pretty girl to squire, Bill. Perhaps she'll be able to make a dent in that walrus-hide heart of yours." Before either could answer, if either could have thought of a suitable retort, he patted the girl's arm. "Sure you've brought wraps enough? Our usual summer heat will turn to arctic chill when we reach the ice fields, you know."

Welcoming the diversion she assured him, "Jim made me bring his lined trench coat as well as my leather jacket, and in spite of its size it fits me if I wear it over my own. I had to promise to take it with me if I left the ship for any reason." She laughed in derision. "Do you suppose he pictured me doing a Little-Eva-Crossing-the-Ice stunt with a couple of polar bears after me?"

"In that event," Dr. Bentley said smiling, "you won't need either coat, believe me. Even if you only catch sight of a bear or a whale the excitement will warm you up. I know the first ones *I* saw gave me a real tingle. How about you, Bill?"

The sudden question jerked Mason from the depths of absorption. He had not needed the genial doctor's earlier comment to call his attention to the girl, whom he had been studying covertly since their departure. Her face was alive with anticipation, her eyes sparkling with eagerness. He was admiring her suit of golden flecked tweed and the dash of orange scarf when Bentley's abrupt words penetrated, and with no idea of what the two were discussing he said hastily, "Right, Doctor! Tweeds are just the thing for an ice trip, and her high boots are a good idea, too." Then he wondered why Bentley exploded with laughter and Delight blushed most becomingly at this betrayal of his preoccupation.

"Good!" The doctor was still chuckling. "The lieutenant approves of your costume as Little Eva, so now all we need is the bear to chase you."

"No thanks," Delight shook her head with decision. "I'm not interested. I'd rather comb a beach for fossils or arrowheads. I understand the ice sometimes leaves them there."

"Deliver me!" groaned Bentley. "Bill, we've got a rabid collector on our hands. Sure as shooting she'll pester us until we unearth the backbone of a mastodon for her. Since I've had my fill of modern bones for years I guess you're elected to stir up the past." Something like a shadow of pain darkened the officer's face and disturbed him, so he quickly digressed, "What's this, Bill?" pointing at the pistol belted to the other's waist. "You're under arms? Oho! Guard duty, eh?"

"Yes, Doctor," said Delight before Mason could speak. The lieutenant is on duty. Orders are orders, you know."

Dr. Bentley looked from the girl's flushed cheeks to the officer's stony glare and needed no gift of clairvoyance to guess that some sort of clash was in the offing. With careful nonchalance he shrugged his coat higher and turned up the collar. "Think I'll see how B.B. is getting along," he said, and strolled away.

Delight kept her eyes on the receding shoreline and counted the gulls as, with white and lavender wings outspread, they circled and dove above the blue waves rolling in. The drab buildings of Totum glistened pink and cream-colored in the morning sunlight, bright against the deep green forest which rolled up in successively higher folds to towering snow-capped mountains. The white Greek church with its faded green roof, steeple and bulbous dome, shone like a jewel. Beside it the pale crosses in the old Russian cemetery gleamed and disappeared in ghostly fashion as the breeze stirred the gigantic fern fronds surrounding them.

Mason cleared his throat, hesitated, and then spoke with determined lightness.

"Dr. Bentley seems to have taken over the 'Babbling' for his sea-conscious wife, did you notice?"

"Perhaps he felt that the conversation needed a little stimulus," she retorted. Before she could say more the faint silvery notes of a bugle call drifted across the water. Reveille. From the camp near the river the Stars and Stripes slid smoothly aloft and floated, a speck of fluttering color in the sun.

Emotion swept away the last of Delight's anger. With pleading eyes she looked up at Mason.

"Lieutenant—Bill! I apologize for every nasty crack I've made. I know you hate being here with me, and I'm not particularly set up over being thrown into your unwilling arms—figuratively speaking," she amended with a rush. "But this day is too perfect to be spoiled. Suppose—suppose you forget that I'm just one more troublesome female in your life and pretend that I'm a very good pal, and I'll pretend that you are—you are—"

"Himself? Nothing doing!" Mason interrupted with emphasis. "I'll be *your* very good pal and *myself,* thank you." At her expression of surprise he smiled. "Of course I heard of your toast at the Bentleys', Delight. Did you expect a thing like that to pass without comment here, where *anything* that happens out of the ordinary is broadcast to the four winds? Every poor hermit consigned to this howling wilderness has to have something to talk about—when there's anyone around to talk to. I'll bet that tasty bit of excitement has reached Anchorage by now, and even points north."

"I had no idea—"

"What's more," he went on, ignoring the interruption, "that ring of yours, pal Delight, fairly shouts a warning to even the most hardy adventurer. It states in no uncertain terms, 'This gal is spoken for, no trespassing!' But do we heed the admonition? Not a chance. We all tumble over each other to get our wings singed at the candle."

"All?" Delight twisted the diamonds on her finger till they shot out sparks of fire. "It seems to me that this beacon has kept away one cautious soul."

"For this day—all," he insisted. "Don't you realize," he asked blandly, "that we crave excitement up here? And for myself I can't imagine anything more thrilling than a day's sail with—with an attractive girl. So count me in on the heartbreak line for today."

At a loss for suitable reply and desperately searching for a less explosive subject Delight recalled the doctor's question about guard duty.

"Is a gun generally considered part of the costume for the

well-dressed man on a sailing party?" she asked pertly.

"I warned you that I'm weak on social graces," he reminded easily. "And I'm beginning to feel embarrassed by my forty-five. Force of habit is my only excuse. It has been my unfortunate experience to discover that under certain conditions a gun, like a dog, is man's best friend. Since I'm unable to foresee future 'certain conditions' my *friend* goes with me, day and night." He leaned his elbows on the rail and turned his attention to the passing scene.

The volcano, seen from Totum as a distant cone far up the bay, was now looming nearer, its snowy peak pure gold in the sunlight.

"Has anyone told you the legend of that extinct volcano?" he asked, and at a shake of her head bowed grandly. "Then brace yourself. Here goes Professor Mason astride his hobby of Alaskan history and mythology.

"The Indians believed that a gigantic spirit—a genie of incredible power and uncertain temper—inhabited the inside of that mountain. This, by the way, was years and years ago, before any white men came to Alaska—even before there were any white men, according to the legend. The genie of the mountain was deeply in love with the lady-village across the bay, and the occasional bursts of fire, smoke and steam were his attempts to dazzle her with his power and magnificence."

"Could he be induced to indulge in some of his pyrotechnic courtship today?" Delight asked hopefully. "I would love to view an eruption."

"A little too close for comfort. Luckily he hasn't been heard from for years."

The hours slipped away unnoticed as the steamer forged on, every moment bringing some scene of interest to be discussed. It was near noon when a white-bloused deck hand shuffled toward them.

"Captain sent message for you, miss," announced the sailor, his English thick with Indian gutturals. "Captain say go over there." He motioned toward the other side of the ship. "Over there whales blowing now."

"How exciting! Thank you!" Delight smiled, but no answering friendliness stirred in the broad brown face. If there was any emotion evident in his small black eyes it was dislike. He made an awkward attempt to salute Lieutenant Mason, touching half-closed fingers to the oily black hair plastered low on his forehead, before he shambled away forward.

"Why did he look daggers at me?" Delight wondered, unable to avoid a little shiver of revulsion.

"Don't worry about him," Mason encouraged. "Seems part

Indian, part Eskimo, with a touch of white man somewhere along the line. There are a lot of them around here, but civilization and the Army have simmered them down from the wild men who used to ramp around the settlements raising Cain. Some of them are bitten by the Yankee urge for money and take jobs on ships instead of following their old habit of hunting, fishing and lying around the cabin waiting for the squaw to feed them. Or they hire out to the Army until they've made a few dollars and then quit.

"Retire to their cabins to rest," he chuckled, "that's their excuse, but it's only a stall. They don't need rest! Strong? We have a gang of them unloading at the warehouse, and they throw crates around like balloons, smash practically everything if they're not watched. Sergeant Hogan is at the nervous-breakdown stage with them most of the time."

"That one who was just here didn't look much like a sailor."

"They're not actually sailors; the ship captains take them on because they know the currents among the islands and where the ledges are, and because they're wizards when it comes to navigating in floating ice."

He pointed down the deck at two Finns in leather Windbreakers and blue jeans who were coiling some rope.

"Those men are some of the regular crew in their working clothes. Quite a contrast to the man who was just here. The captains know how Indians love a uniform of any kind, so they keep a stock of white sailor blouses on hand for them to pretty up with."

He took Delight's arm.

"Let's try the other view as Captain Pepper suggested. If there's a killer whale on the loose over there it will be something to see." They crossed the deck and Mason pointed forward. "Look there, the ice is beginning to show up."

Delight's eyes widened. At first glance she thought that the water ahead was sprinkled with giant snowflakes, but in a moment she saw that they were varied blocks and pans of ice heavily frosted with snow. The air above them was swarming with gulls. Sparkling jets of vapor shot up continually from a school of black whales, and on the distant horizon a cloud of smoky haze drifted up from a volcanic peak.

While she tried to see everything at once Delight was staggered by an interruption—the reappearance of Harry Kent. The boy embraced her as though they had been parted for years, tossed a happy, "Hi, Bill!" at her companion and loudly beseeched her to "Come and watch the engines!"

"Can I see them without actually going down in the engine room?" she demanded cautiously.

"Sure. Through the skylight or somep'n. It's open. Mom

won't let me go down even if Captain Pepper said I could. I wish Pop was here, he'd take us right down there."

"Thank goodness he isn't," Delight murmured to the highly amused Mason. With a covert grimace for his benefit she permitted Harry to drag her forward to the fascinating spectacle of huge diesel motors thumping at their endless labor.

When at length she was able to detach herself from the absorbed boy, she made a desultory tour of the steamer without finding anything as interesting as the company she had quitted at Harry's urging. She therefore returned to her former position, found Mason still at his station and contentedly resumed her place at his side.

"More wonders to behold?" she asked.

"A new one every minute," Bill promised. "But let's go up to the bow, where we can see both sides and not miss anything."

They had just reached their new position when he exclaimed, "Here's a sight coming up now that should give you something to remember!"

The steamer had rounded a point of land and disclosed the shoreline of a deep bay. On a small plateau, bare of trees and backed by saw-toothed rocky hills, lay the ruins of an Indian village. So dilapidated were the buildings that it might have gone unnoticed but for the totem poles still standing over the desolation. They rose from a tangle of bushes and rank grass like dead trees left by a forest fire. The boat passed so close to shore that Delight could make out some of the carvings on the poles, a grotesque face, huge teeth, widespread wings.

She drew a long, unsteady breath of appreciation and impulsively put her hand on Mason's where it gripped the rail.

"Isn't it marvelous!" she whispered. "I'm hugging myself with satisfaction because I'm actually seeing all this instead of merely reading about it!" When he was silent, his jaw set and a frown creasing his forehead, she pounded his hand with her clenched fist.

"Please enthuse with me, Bill! You're the only one I can enjoy this with. Mrs. Bentley has abandoned her comfortable chair behind us, reduced to a jellyfish state by fear of seasickness, and the doctor has discovered that one of the sailors has a reconstructed leg, and nothing in the world could get him away from that. Sue Kent, at long last, is riding herd on Harry, and—and none of the others really interest me. So won't you *please* give up your denatured attitude, be a nice friendly guy?"

The other met her look squarely, his face pale.

"Do I seem indifferent, pal? Don't you believe it, because I'm having the time of my life."

"Don't perjure yourself on my account," she retorted and turned away.

He caught the hurt look in her eyes and found it unbearable. His hand on her shoulder swung her to face him.

"You've got me all wrong, Delight!" he pleaded. "Honestly, I'm enjoying every minute of this. Being with you is—" He hesitated, searching for words, then slowly released her, and shook his head as though to clear it. "All I can say is this," he muttered bitterly, "I just can't tell you what this day means to me," he laughed without merriment. "And don't ask me to explain that!"

The repression that strained his voice, the blaze in his eyes startled her. She leaned against the rail, schooling her voice to casual friendliness.

"I won't ask you anything but to enjoy today with me."

"That I can't help doing," he admitted quietly, and was relieved to see Captain Pepper coming toward them, forcing an end to the discussion.

XV

THE SEA was so calm that except for the steamer's wake, not a ripple disturbed its surface. The floating cakes of ice were increasing in size, those disturbed by the ship bumping and grinding noisily against each other. The numerous islands were less heavily wooded and showed a marblelike smoothness at the shore line. Suddenly the morning quiet was broken by a distant roar.

"What was that?" demanded Delight breathlessly as the captain joined them at the rail.

"That noise? A brand new berg being born, miss," he answered facetiously. "But that's nothing, just wait till we get real near to the glacier. Then you'll hear and see something to write home about."

Mrs. Bentley, apparently rallied from her state of coma by the smoothness of the sea, joined the group in time to catch the captain's words.

"I hope there's no danger in going in close, Captain Pepper. I'm not only nervous for myself, but—but I do feel responsible to the dear major for his sister's safety," she fluttered.

"This trip was made at my suggestion, but I didn't realize there might be danger."

The captain contemplatively wriggled the moth-eaten mustache below his vein-netted nose. He looked from under bushy white brows at the girl, then at the officer beside her.

"Don't think you need to worry yourself, ma'am. Being responsible for Miss Tremaine looks to me like a man-sized job, and I hear the lieutenant's the one who's hooked for that."

There were whole colonies of gulls now perched on the floating masses of ice, drifting serenely toward the open sea. The ship lost headway. From time to time the bow struck a glancing blow against a seemingly small piece with a force which sent a shiver through the hull. The air grew noticeably colder when a towering island of gleaming ice slid past.

Mason grasped the girl's shoulder.

"Look! Quick! See that bear?"

The girl stood motionless as she stared at the huge brown animal which had emerged from an ice cave only a few hundred feet across the water.

"Oh-oh-oh!" she exclaimed. "Isn't he lovely. What a beautiful fur coat! And he has such a winning smile on his face. Are they really very dangerous?"

Mason nodded soberly. "I understand that when they are cornered, or even think they are, they're about the last word in destruction. There's nothing bigger up here than these brown bears, except a Kodiak. I've seen a number of them, but never one so large or so near. Handsome, with a pleasant smile, as you say, but hardly the kind of playmate I'd recommend."

Delight broke in with another breathless long-drawn "Oh!" of admiration. Speechless, she tugged at Bill's arm and pointed ahead. On all sides floated peaks, spires and ridges of ice, and beyond them a glacier reared its two-hundred-foot-high face in a sheer palisade of glistening white, seamed and veined with a hundred crevasses and fissures.

The tumbled body of it sloped back for miles between raw brown and rusty-orange granite cliffs, a frozen cataract transformed to dazzling brilliance by the sunshine. Here and there on the face the sun flung purple shadows of spur or pinnacle, or sparkled in the green torrent of a stream cutting its way through the ice to join the blue water of the bay.

Awed by the magnitude of the scene, spellbound by its beauty, Delight stared wordlessly. Here was the very workshop of the elements, here Mother Nature was using this enormous mass of ice as a tool in her labors of creation. For centuries this same melting, grinding, smashing process had continued and would go on for countless centuries to come. Fashioning hills, boring out riverbeds, gouging hollows for lakes and ponds, and eternally grinding cliffs into boulders, boulders into gravel, gravel into sand.

Delight was not alone in her absorption. By now the entire party was clustered along the rail silently admiring the panorama of arctic splendor.

"As soon as we get closer," Captain Pepper announced, "I'll pull off to the side and anchor in the lee of that island up ahead, where we'll be protected from most of this floating ice. The view will be just as good as from here. We'll serve lunch then; there is so much to watch, so many changes taking place, that you'll need the whole afternoon to take it all in. If any of you want to fish, this is the place for halibut. Two of the crew will be at the stern with tackle and bait. They'll look after you."

Delight had an inspiration and stopped the officer as he started to walk away.

"Captain! Since we are to be anchored for some time may I go ashore on your island? I'd love to do a little beachcombing, and perhaps find some souvenirs to take home."

Dr. Bentley hooted. "I knew it! You're a 'now-why-did-I-bring-this-junk-home' addict, young lady. A messer-upper of the living room with useless impedimenta, b'gad!" He chuckled. "What were those lines from Carryl's poem? Hmm:

> "Then we gather as we travel
> Bits of moss and dirty gravel,
> And we chip off little specimens of stone;
> And we carry home as prizes
> Funny bugs of handy sizes,
> Just to give the day a scientific tone."

Delight laughed with the others, but returned to the attack.

"Please, Captain, be a sport!" Lips, eyes and voice pleaded.

"My dear young lady!" Pepper lifted an admonishing hand, but his intended refusal was interrupted.

"It's out of the question, Delight!" snapped Mason, stepping between them.

The old seaman's face darkened, his blue eyes protruded and heavy eyebrows bunched in a scowl.

"Hold on, Lieutenant!" he rumbled. "*I* make the decisions on this ship!"

"But you must admit that sending her ashore would be taking a foolish—"

"Are *you* taking command here?" Pepper's voice rose, as past irritations surged up in his memory and clouded his judgment. "Maybe I should be used to the Army running everything in sight, but I ain't! I've been working this region for fifty years, and I don't need any advice from a tenderfoot doughboy!" Puffing wrathfully he turned to Delight. "Sure, you can go ashore, miss. I'll have a boat and crew over the side after lunch, and you and your party can really comb the beach."

Mason, his face inscrutable, walked away. Inwardly he cursed the carelessness which had antagonized the captain.

"Even if you are my bodyguard, Mr. Mason," Delight called after him, "you needn't come if you're afraid. I'll interest some of the others."

Ignoring the taunt he propped his elbows on the rail some distance away and stared at the floe-dotted water.

With the ship riding quietly at anchor the passengers gathered for the buffet lunch in the stern, where a long table was heaped with a variety of food. Long loaves of neatly sliced bread were stacked in the center surrounded by mountainous plates of canned ham, corned beef and chicken. Quart jars of mayonnaise, pickles, olives and mustard filled any empty spaces. One end of the table supported a Gargantuan yellow cheese, the other a five-gallon coffeepot steaming on its alcohol stove. A smaller table nearby displayed an array of plated silverware, piles of plates and cups, pies and an enormous layer cake.

Delight suppressed a gasp of awe as she took in the layout. So this is roughing it in the wilderness, she thought, but à la Bertha. However, both she and the guests, after the early breakfast and hours of sea air, fell on the spread like a swarm of locusts.

It was near the end of the meal, when satisfied hunger allowed some conversation to mingle with the serious business of eating, that Bill Mason unknowingly clinched Delight's already high opinion of him. Harry Kent, who had made astonishing inroads on everything within reach, finished a second slice of cake and heaved a sigh of repletion.

"Gee, what a day!" he exclaimed. "Everything absolutely *super*, all the way." He thought a minute and then added wistfully, "Except that Mom wouldn't let me go down in the engine room."

There was such a world of disappointment in his tone that everyone but Mason laughed. Bill laid aside plate and cup and stood up.

"Then let's make *everything* super, bud. If the captain is agreeable, Mrs. Kent, you won't mind if I take Harry down there, will you?"

"I'll be eternally grateful," she promised.

"I'm agreeable, all right," Captain Pepper chuckled, "but

I can't answer for my engineer. If you want to try, go ahead."

"Yay!" Harry was up with a whoop of triumph. Then his face fell. "But the engines aren't running now."

"So what?" Bill countered. "We can see twice as much because we won't have to keep clear of them."

"Gee, that's right! Let's go!"

"Hold it, bud!" Mason lowered his voice to a conspiratorial whisper. "Remember the engineer. Let me give you a tip, soldier. When you're heading into strange country where the natives may be hostile, it's a sound idea to take along something to butter them up. Makes them more friendly. Like a piece of that lemon pie, for instance."

"Sure!" The boy watched breathlessly as Mason placed the suggested bribe on a paper plate, and thus armed, Harry trotted happily forward beside his tall protector.

"That," Delight murmured, as she watched them go, "is the kindest deed I've seen since I arrived, and I'd hardly expect it of the lieutenant."

"You don't know him very well, then," Dr. Bentley said quietly. "He shows a frozen face to the world, for some reason, but the ice is only skin deep."

When Mason returned a pop-eyed and thoroughly satisfied boy to his mother he found Delight standing expectantly beside the captain. Pepper was watching the crew make ready a diesel-powered whaleboat while he listened with half an ear to a tirade from Mrs. Bentley. Babbling Bertha was outdoing herself on the subject of the proposed expedition and only succeeded in exhausting the captain's patience.

"Do you think I'd let anyone go if there was the least danger, ma'am?" he inquired caustically. "I come up here three-four times a summer and most always let some of the crew ashore. Nothing's ever happened. Now, there's no ice, hardly, between us and shore, the sea is easy and the beach is in plain sight."

"Captain Pepper," Delight admitted, "none of the others seem to want to go. I guess I'm the only hardy soul among your passengers."

"Count me in," Bill Mason growled.

Delight feigned surprise. "Goodness, are you coming? I thought you didn't approve of this jaunt, Lieutenant," she teased.

"Where you go, I go, lady, approving or not." Mason smiled wryly. "My orders were to look after you, and if I don't the major will have my hide. I would brave any danger," he added with mock gravity, "rather than risk his displeasure."

Captain Pepper studied the two with a quizzical grin and

then called to the mate, "Belay the boat, mister! Only two going, we'll use the outboard."

The mate looked at the sky, where a faint haze dulled the blue, looked at the shore, at the captain. He opened his mouth as though to protest, thought better of it and shrugged.

"Nils, you and Stig check the outboard and get it ready to drop!" he barked. "The rest of you men get this tarp back on!"

One of the crew in a white blouse dropped the rope he was coiling and moved aft toward Pepper.

"I take them ashore, Cap'n," he offered solemnly. "I know all this place. That King Crab Beach; lady find plenty nice things there, maybe."

Delight saw that it was the sour Indian who had brought her the captain's message and wondered at his sudden amiability.

Captain Pepper nodded. "That's so, Thomas, you come from around here, don't you. You savvy outboard motor?"

"Sure. Long time."

"All right, Thomas. You run the lady and this officer in there, and wait for them." Pepper addressed the two. "I'll give you an hour. Don't go anywhere but on that beach, and stay in sight of the ship. Understand?"

"Yes, Captain," said Mason politely.

The Indian, who had scuttled below, now returned at a dogtrot. He had exchanged his sailor blouse for a shaggy jacket with a collar of long white fur, from which his brown face and shining oiled hair protruded like a turtle's head from its shell. Silently he took his place in the boat with Delight and Mason and, when it had been swung out and lowered, cast off the falls and crouched over the motor. One pull at the starter cord and they were off.

Mrs. Bentley fastened a grip on the captain's arm.

"Is that little boat safe?" she demanded breathlessly. "Shouldn't you—"

Pepper gently but firmly freed himself.

"That boat's a lot handier than the whaler for beaching, ma'am, and sound as a dollar."

"I thought that Indian looked positively villainous!"

"I don't pick my crew for a beauty contest," he assured her wearily. "Thomas is some kind of a relative of old Kasan Charley, who's been going with me for years. The boy came aboard this morning to tell me Charley's laid up with a hangover and wanted the young feller to take his place this trip. Looks like Charley's coat he's wearing, as a matter of fact. And if Kasan Charley recommends 'em, ma'am, they're really good."

As the boat left the ship's side Delight looked up and waved at the peering faces hung over the rail.

"Stick-in-the-muds!" she called gaily. "I wouldn't miss this for anything!"

She drew Jim's trench coat more closely about her and folded her hands in her lap as she studied the man facing her from the bow.

"Please don't look so cross, Bill. Smile for the lady. You don't know how thrilling it will be to tell my friends at home how I collected the stuff I hope we'll find. You make me feel as though I were a very trying, very spoiled, very naughty child."

Mason remained silent and glowered at the fast receding ship. A long silver fish broke the surface with a burst of spray nearby and the girl jumped up on the seat and craned her neck to watch. Bill seized her arm and dragged her down with a swiftness that made her head swim.

"Sit *down!*" he ordered sharply. "Don't you know any better than to stand up like that in a boat? The slightest tip might throw you off balance and dump you in, and this beautiful blue water is extremely cold. I'm in command of this expedition now. One fool stunt per trip is plenty, so watch yourself!"

Silence, except for the whine of the motor, descended like a funeral pall upon the boat. It was impossible for Delight to object to Mason's criticism, even though his strenuous enforcement of his "sit *down!*" annoyed her. Of course her sudden action had been dangerous; pleading excitement as an excuse would only be adding stupidity to carelessness. Equally in vain did Bill Mason search for words to confess that his rough treatment had been a lightning reaction to agonized fear for her safety.

Avoiding his still smoldering glare, Delight turned with elaborate caution to look past the Indian toward the now distant steamer. It floated back against a pearly curtain of cloud on the far horizon. The fishing party was gathered at its stern, where two crewmen in a dory waited to gaff any trophy too large to be landed without help.

"Wouldn't it be wonderful if Harry Kent should haul in a halibut, a really big one?" Delight hoped the question might restart the stalled conversation.

Mason accepted the overture. "Wonderful, if the fish didn't haul him overboard instead," he chuckled.

"Goodness, you *are* obsessed with the falling-overboard idea today!" Instantly she regretted the gibe, but too late.

Mason flushed and swung around on the bow seat to look ahead. The boat had rounded a rocky point strewn with shattered ice and driftwood, and was entering a narrow passage between King Crab Island and its neighbor. Mason whirled.

"Hey, Thomas! What's the idea? You've run past the beach. Turn back!"

The Indian bobbed his head. "We go around here, boss. Much better beach for lady. Much more—more souvenir, maybe."

"Never mind that!" the other ordered impatiently. "You heard Captain Pepper. We land on King Crab Beach and stay in sight!"

Thomas sat immobile as a totem pole, his fur collar snapping white hairs against his brown cheeks, as the boat sped straight on.

"Don' worry, boss. I know all-a this place. Much better beach round in here—"

"Turn this boat!" Mason did not raise his voice, but the words cracked like a whip. He leaned forward, eyes steel hard, hands white-knuckled where they gripped the gunwales.

Involuntarily Delight shrank aside to be out of the line of that coldly furious stare. The look, she thought, of a man trained in a life where disobedience could mean death.

The Indian wilted. "Okay, boss," he muttered. Glumly he throttled down the motor, preparing to turn.

A sinister ripping crackle like a gigantic electric spark startled the girl and spun her head toward the glacier. An enormous jagged crack gaped across its face of weathered white ice, the black chasm widening while she stared. A section of the glacier, huge and rough surfaced as a mountain crag, split slowly away, wavered, hung suspended for what seemed hours, and then plunged into the bay, exposing a gaping cavern of brilliant blue ice. Seconds later a thunderous roar beat against Delight's ears and seemed to shake the boat.

Where the mass of ice plunged in, the water rose in a towering wall which spread outward with the speed of a tidal wave. Ice floes bobbed on its racing slope, spinning, grinding together, shattering, tossing at its crest as they hurtled onward with it toward the boat.

With a terrified yell Thomas swung the tiller and brought the boat around in a sweeping arc, then jammed open the throttle. The engine bucked, backfired, sputtered and stopped.

Sweat poured down the Indian's face as he whipped the starting cord again and again, but the engine remained dead.

From the glacier another roar like a salvo of a battleship's heaviest guns told that more ice had broken away and warned of a second wave to follow. Thomas darted a panicky look over his shoulder at the onrushing water. It was streaming into the narrow space between the islands in a churning smother of emerald green, milky froth and splintering ice. He dropped flat in the bottom of the boat.

"Get down!" he screamed. "Get under the seats! Hang on!"

XVI

MASON needed no warning to understand their danger. Even on the open bay they might have been swamped or dashed onto the rocky shore. But here, hemmed in by the islands, as a sluice confines a millstream, the mass of water rose higher and sped faster, its face a ragged slope of foam and ice. The first swelling of the wave reached the boat, lifted it like a giant's hand and hurled it forward.

Swiftly Bill dragged the girl from her seat, clamped his knees tightly about her and bent low as he gripped the thwart.

"Rest your head on your arms!" he ordered sharply. "This will be rough!"

Prone on the hard planking, Delight buried her cheek in a crooked elbow and shut her eyes. The tossing and plunging of the boat sickened her. A whistling wind tugged at her hair, whipping her eyelashes as though it would yank them out by the roots. Ice scraped raspingly along the planking, pounded the sides. She shivered at each impact which seemed to threaten utter and final annihilation. Water poured in over one gunwale, surged up her legs. The paralyzing chill shocked a gasp from between clenched teeth.

At the sound Mason's hand groped for her shoulder with a reassuring pressure. The boat heeled far over and he was forced to snatch the thwart again to keep his balance.

Delight opened her eyes, saw a ragged slab of gravel-streaked ice looming over her—and shut them quickly. The ice ground horribly along the gunwale, the vibration shaking her from head to foot. She heard a terrifying crash and felt the planks under her writhe and shudder.

As the crest of the wave passed and the boat staggered down the back slope, she knew the dizzying sensation of being trapped in a falling elevator. The second wave caught them then, and once more they whirled forward, spinning and careening violently through stinging spray and clashing ice.

Dazedly she wondered how soon they would be smashed by the ice. It seemed inevitable with so many pieces hurtling around them. She shivered. There was more water surging around her now and she propped her head higher to escape it. Were they sinking? She shivered again and felt Mason's hand on her shoulder. She slid hers up to cling to it.

Her bodyguard—the one she had selected. At first sight of him, she remembered, her thought had been that here was a man to have around if danger threatened. And here he was! How silly of her to be frightened.

Sometime later the boat stopped pitching, and when Mason released her she opened her eyes and sat up, still giddy from the wild voyage. What a changed world! The crystal, sapphire and emerald of the sunlit ice floes had disappeared behind a curtain of gray mist. White-capped water stretched ahead into the fog, with ice and driftwood bobbing aimlessly on every side. She realized that the boat was scarcely moving, that the Indian was standing erect, peering forward.

"That was some berg we saw born, as the captain would express it, Bill!" she exclaimed with a short hysterical laugh. Her voice caught in her throat. "What—what do we do next?"

"I haven't the slightest idea." Mason's face was pale, but he grinned encouragement. "We're on the knees of the gods —and of Thomas. I'm sure he'll know what to do. The steamer is somewhere back there, I judge." He gestured with his thumb over his shoulder. "Out of sight in the fog bank. And we are here—wherever this is—without a motor."

Delight looked quickly toward the stern. The outboard had vanished, the wood splintered and gashed where it had been attached.

"I don't want to scare you," he continued quietly, "and I don't think you scare easily. But you should know what we're up against. You'd better get out of that water you're sitting in, though." He leaned forward and steadied her as she struggled up onto the seat. "You're looking better every minute," he encouraged, as he dropped back on his own seat. "For a while your face was so white I thought you might pass out on us."

"I never fainted in my life!" she asserted indignantly, rubbing her arm, still numb from contact with the hard planks. "It's starting to rain, isn't it?"

Mason looked up, scowling. "Just to add to the gaiety of the occasion!" he growled. He stared around the narrowing circle of water at the impenetrable curtain of mist, then fixed his eyes on the Indian, who was peering down over the battered stern.

"If you're looking for the engine, Thomas, you're wasting time," he suggested dryly, and earned a sour grin from the native. "Where do *you* figure that darned ship is?"

A vague flap of the hand accompanied the Indian's guess.

"Back there, mile—two miles, maybe? Other side of the island. We come through—through—" he gestured while searching for the right words "—through narrow gut between islands. Water not deep, so we go pretty fast, eh?"

Mason winked at Delight, hoping to cheer her.

"His hydraulic theory seems sound enough. We certainly came fast!" He turned up the collar of his Windbreaker. "I thought this was a drizzle, but it's working up to a downpour, isn't it." Seeing that she was too emotionally exhausted to heed the rain, he gently buttoned her coat snugly around her throat and was relieved to have her smile tremulously.

The Indian had produced a pair of oarlocks from under the stern seat and was unshipping the two oars which were slung below the thwarts.

"How long do you think it will take us to row back?" Mason asked.

"We not go back, Lieutenant, sir. Too much ice over there. Too much fog. No good to fool with fog; ship move somewhere, maybe." He pointed ahead. "We go to shore there, make camp, wait for clearing."

"But we must get back to the steamer!" Delight protested. "Think how worried they'll be."

Mason shook his head. "Can we make shore all right, Thomas? You know where we are?"

The Indian nodded. "Sure Mike, make it easy." He moved forward and crouched to one side. "Lady go back seat so I use oars? Not to be afraid, lady. Thomas been here plenty times before."

"Hear that, Delight?" Mason encouraged. "Don't worry. I'll trust Thomas's judgment. Too bad that our friends are going to have some anxious hours, but we'll just have to make the best of it."

"Of course," Delight agreed bravely. "And considering that it's entirely my fault we're here, I should be the last to complain." She moved to the stern seat, watched the Indian ship the oars, and gave him a friendly smile. "I guess that the evil spirit you call *yek* broke that ice off the glacier to sweep us away, didn't it?"

Thomas favored her with a vacant stare, shrugged and began to row. Either he agreed, she decided, or he felt that this was not the moment for abstract discussion. There was a lot to be said for that practical view. Penitently she murmured, "I'm sorry to have dragged you both into this mess."

"Don't let it get you down," Mason advised cheerfully. "Captain Pepper isn't going to go home without us. When the weather clears he'll start hunting, believe me. Meanwhile, we're not too badly off. I noticed them putting blankets and equipment in these lockers when they were getting ready, which is probably standard procedure when any boat leaves Pepper's ship. Fortunately we didn't ship enough water to do any damage, and if you can wait, I'd like to keep them under cover so we'll have something dry when we land."

"Now that the danger is over I'm more comfortable than I deserve to be. But I can't see fifty feet in any direction, so how can anyone know where the land is, or anything else for that matter?" Bravely she added, "But if you say we're going ashore, Bill, that's good enough for me."

As the heavy boat limped ahead under the Indian's labored rowing, she gave up trying to penetrate the gray wall around them and fell to studying the stanch craft which had carried them so safely. In her excitement at the prospect of getting on the beach she'd not noticed it particularly, except that it had seemed small in comparison with the whaleboat they were readying and especially tiny when it floated beside the ship.

Now she realized that it was all of fifteen feet long, wide of beam and heavily built. Under the small decks at bow and stern were the lockers Mason had spoken of. If she hadn't known what it had just gone through, she still would have thought it looked very competent.

It seemed hours to the girl's excited fancy before the Indian, head over shoulder, pulled cautiously through a narrow rocky inlet into a shallow bay. Here the fog was less dense and visibility better. The boat pitched sluggishly on the swell of the incoming waves as the man rested on his oars.

"*Klosh!* Good!" he grunted, studying the heavily wooded shore. He shipped his oars and let the boat glide until it grated on the pebbly bottom. Leaping out into half a foot of water he struggled manfully to push the bow further up on the beach.

Sitting motionless in the stern, with a disquieting chill in her heart, Delight stared at the gray bearded trees which stood like spectral sentinels on guard. Weathered, irregular branches held great beds of moss in which grew ferns, grasses and seedlings, giving the effect of mammoth hanging gardens. The ground, where it was not choked with bushes, showed a maze of fallen branches and rotting tree trunks, some of them covered with a brilliant green fungus. The most wild and desolate place in the world, she thought with a shudder.

"Come on, this is the end of the boat ride!"

In her absorption in the wild surroundings Delight had not noticed what the others were doing. She turned her head with a start when Mason spoke. The two men stood in the water holding either side of the bow.

"Come on, come on!" Bill repeated impatiently. "It's cold, standing here while you daydream. We'll hold the boat steady —jump to the beach."

She stood up, stepped stiffly over the middle seats and up

on the forward deck, then paused, nervously gauging the distance to the sand. Mason leaned forward, lifted her in his arms and deposited her on the shore.

"You'll have to obey orders more promptly, ma'am," he warned, steadying her with an arm about her waist.

Color burned to her angry eyes as she shrugged out of the encircling arm and staggered aside. She opened her lips to retort, then clamped them shut with the unnerving conviction that if she spoke she would burst into tears—tears of helpless frustration. Mason and the Indian ignored her, rapidly unpacking the boat's lockers. She felt humiliatingly young and defenseless as she stood forlornly in the downpour.

Thomas drew a small anchor and coil of rope from under the bow seat and carried it aft. There he whipped the length of rope he had uncoiled around a cleat and flung the anchor astern. With the rest of the coil on his arm he took a turn around a bow cleat, jumped ashore and made the end fast to a boulder.

Mason was equally busy. With his lighter he had managed to start a pile of twigs burning, gradually adding larger branches as the flames grew. Now he rolled rocks around the blaze to form a fireplace.

With so much labor being expended in her behalf Delight felt ashamed to stand moping. No wonder Bill had grabbed her out of the boat when she fluttered there like a swooning Victorian female!

"Can I do anything to help?" she asked hopefully.

"Relax," said Bill, without looking up from his work on the fireplace. "Just talk to me." He began rolling a heavy stone into position and spoke between heaves at it. "Any bright chatter. *Come up there!*" This to the resistant rock. "Anything to amuse the peons—*ugh!* Tell me about your childhood. Sing a song. *Get in* there, you!" The stone ground into its appointed place among the others and he straightened to mop his face.

Delight laughed. "You sound exactly like Mr. Jingle in *Pickwick Papers!*"

"I do at that!" he grinned. " 'Revolution of July—epic poem composed on the spot—Mars by day, Apollo by night—bang the field-piece, twang the lyre!' " He stooped to another rock.

"You must have done all this many times before, from the way you go at it."

"Can't remember how young I was when I started camping out. Grew up on a ranch, you know." He wrestled with the stone, then waited a moment to get his breath. "If I hadn't learned then, I would have in the Army. Some places I've been in, you'd starve if you waited for the waiter to bring on the soup. Or waited for the waiter," he added, rolling another boulder into place.

"I'm still hoping to hear some of your adventures in Army Intelligence," she reminded wistfully.

"I can't convince you that it was humdrum routine all the way, can I! Oh, well, maybe around the campfire tonight I'll spin a few hair-raising yarns to entertain you—if I can invent some, that is. We should have Harry Kent along for that, though."

He walked to another rock and rolled it over. Noticing that the Indian stood staring at him instead of working, he jerked his head toward the ax.

"Better start cutting some poles for a shack, Thomas."

"Okay, boss." The man shouldered the ax and tramped into the forest.

"There's a lad we're lucky to have with us." Mason nodded toward the retreating figure. "A native can save you from a lot of mistakes when you're in strange country."

Two men she was lucky to have along, Delight thought. If she had to endure this predicament she couldn't imagine more efficient companions. She brushed a trickle of water from her nose, cuddled clammy hands together in the oversized sleeves of the trench coat, and in growing admiration observed the practiced speed with which the man accomplished every task.

In an unbelievably short time, and in spite of the rain, a sizable fire crackled inside the ring of stones, while a kettle hung over it gave forth the welcome aroma of brewing tea. Like magic, it seemed, a crude lean-to, thatched with pine boughs, rose at one side. Another fire, twice the size of the first, blazed and sputtered beside Delight. Let the cold wind blow and the rain fall—she felt wonderful warmth creeping up her numbed legs.

Obviously the boat had been prepared by experts with just such an emergency in mind. From its store Thomas had unearthed cooking utensils, canned foods, the ax and a small hatchet. The blankets Bill had mentioned appeared and were piled in the lean-to.

Sheltered under the fragrant pine thatch, a blanket over her shoulders, Delight found her spirits rebounding from the depths into which they had plunged. The heat from the fire surged over her in comforting waves; the tea she sipped from a tin cup was warming nectar. From a distance came the soft rippling rush of a little brook; dampness increased the pleasant odor of the pine and spruce forest and the curving ferns, the earthy smell of rich black soil.

She filled her lungs with the scents, her eyes with the unfamiliar sights, forgot her former depression and felt only a sense of high adventure. She looked at her wrist watch. Just five o'clock! It seemed days since they'd left the steamer.

"Do you suppose they're looking for us yet?" she asked Mason when he dropped down beside her with his own cup of tea.

"Not likely, Dee. Pepper isn't going to bat around that bay full of ice in this fog. I asked Thomas about it and he waxed positively garrulous, for him. 'No good out there now—danger—very danger,' " he quoted in a guttural monotone. " 'Too much ice—too much fog!' From his emphasis I judged that *he* wouldn't put out in it for a million dollars. We'll camp here until the weather clears—maybe tonight, tomorrow anyway, I'm sure."

"Where is Thomas now?"

"Fishing." Mason shook his head as water seeped down his forehead. He took off his sodden cap, leaned out the doorway, banged some of the water out of it on a stone and put it on.

"Exit one dress uniform after this unscheduled maneuver, I guess. And it won't be the first I've ruined unexpectedly," he added, as he leaned back again. "Just the same, we're in luck, you know. Thomas, bless his heart, says he's hunted this section a number of times and knows the lay of the land, and the water, too. That's why he could find this island so easily. This *is* an island we're on, by the way. It's a pretty small one, and he's never seen any large animals on it, which is very O.K. with me. He's gone up the brook a ways to try for some trout for our supper."

"Oh? Could I—?" Delight repressed her eager question in time. After all the trouble she had caused by her insistence on the souvenir beach hunt she would not chance adding to their woes by any further mishaps.

"Could you go fishing?" Bill finished the request for her, reading it in her eager eyes. He took in her muddy boots, wet skirt and bedraggled hat. "Sure you can. It's almost stopped raining now, and you couldn't get any wetter anyway. Exercise will warm you up. Come on."

He gained his feet and held out his hand to help her up, and she continued to cling to it as they went inland, tripping and stumbling over the ground, which was not only rough but crisscrossed with unseen vines.

"We're getting even more luck," Bill admitted. "No mosquitoes. Must be the fog or rain that's driven them to cover. Usually in the woods, or even near the woods, they tear you limb from limb."

"With all our other troubles, mosquitoes would be just run of the mill."

"Don't you believe it, pal! Alaskan mosquitoes are *murder!* There's the Indian."

They'd come on the brook where it tumbled its way beneath

heavy overhanging branches. Giant ferns with wide spreading lacy fronds lined the rocky banks. The broad tropical leaves of the devil's club and bushes heavy with golden berries thrust up from a tangled web of vines were reflected in the glassy black of a deep pool and the shining amber of the shallows.

Mason tugged at her hand for attention and pointed silently. Downstream in the shelter of an old beaver dam two marten were fishing, their wet brown bodies flitting soundlessly among the logs and boulders. Again Bill pressed her hand and this time nodded upstream. There a cataract only a few feet high plunged chuckling softly into a dark, brush-rimmed pool speckled with miniature islands of bubbly foam. Beside it crouched the Indian, fishing as industriously as the marten and as oblivious of them as they were of him.

Whatever their success, Thomas was doing well with the pole he had made from a slender alder and a line from the boat's supplies. Two good-sized trout already lay beside him on the bank. Somewhat reluctantly, Delight thought, he surrendered the tackle at Mason's request.

Her eyes sparkling, cheeks flushed with excitement, she cast the line baited with a fat white grub. Then, with an exclamation of impatience, she tucked the pole under one elbow while she twisted the heavy diamond ring from her finger. She held it out to Mason.

"Please keep this for me, Bill, it's terribly in the way. I can't imagine why I brought the darned thing on this trip!"

He wrapped the ring in his handkerchief and buttoned it in a pocket of his jacket.

"We'll handle the rest of the fishing, Thomas," he advised. "You'd better get a start on the other hut."

"O.K. You no get lost, Lieutenant, sir?" When they laughed he shrugged, picked up his trout and tramped away through the underbrush.

Delight watched him go. "I thought Indians walked with noiseless, catlike tread," she remarked. "Thomas trudges through the bushes like a weary old horse."

"Probably because he *is* tired. He did the rowing and most of the camp work—*watch it!*" he hissed sharply.

She faced about with a gasp of surprise as the pole quivered and bent. With a convulsive jerk she lifted an indignantly protesting fish out of the pool and held it aloft while she stared in awe at her catch.

"Look at *that!*" she exulted.

"Land him! For Heaven's sake, swing him over here!" Mason protested. "We can't eat him hanging on that line! Throw him on the bank."

Before she could follow this sound advice the thrashing
108

fish flipped himself free, splashed into the water and disappeared like a darting shadow.

Delight glared at the water, her line, and then at Mason.

"I lost him!" she announced with such innocent surprise that Bill roared with laughter. She smiled in sympathy, at the same time thinking that this was the first time she had ever seen him completely relaxed from his habitual sternness. It was a decided improvement.

"If you could have seen your face!" Bill gasped, and laughed again. "Did you expect him to hang on in that highly uncomfortable position all night? Try again, I see he didn't get your bait. But for the love of Pete, look alive! If you hook a fish, heave on the rod and throw him to dry land quick. Understand?"

"'Heave on the rod'!" she mimicked indignantly. "The Anglers' Club at home would blackball you for life for suggesting such a thing. However," she admitted, "as we must eat I'll throw all the rules of sportsmanship to the winds —and heave." She cast again and they waited hopefully.

XVII

FAR OVERHEAD a plane's motor droned, the sound dull and eerie coming down through the fog. It passed, flying to the south, and faded away. Then it returned, circled, and drifted northward into silence.

"An observation plane," Mason guessed. He shook his head. "Pepper must have radioed the post, he's probably frantic. But they haven't a prayer of spotting us, they're just making sure of that before dark."

"A bite!" shrilled Delight, and this time landed the trout successfully. Aglow with excitement, she confided, "I don't care if they can't find us, Bill! I'm having the time of my life."

The look of worry deepened on his face. "Cut out that kind of talk," he directed sharply. "This is no picnic, and you may not feel so perky before we get clear. I've been on plenty of these impromptu bivouacs, and sometimes they can turn out rugged."

"Are you sorry to be landed here with me? Is that what's bothering you?"

"And cut out that kind of question, too!" he snapped. Then he forced his tone to unemotional calm. "Play fair, Delight. Try to be serious, because this is a serious situation, in case you haven't caught on to that yet. Don't make it any harder for me than necessary. I never should have let you leave the steamer, whatever nonsense Captain Pepper talked. Just wait," he muttered unhappily, "until the major starts chewing me out for this escapade!"

"And *my* big mistake, I suppose," she retorted flippantly, "is to allow myself to enjoy it! You and Jim are alike—a couple of Grade A martinets, throwing cold water on everything I want to do. I wonder if Army life affects everyone that way." With a flash of scorn she added, "Officers first—human beings afterward!"

"That's what you think?" The sudden flame in his eyes gave her a momentary feeling of uneasiness, but he sensed her reaction and turned away to lean against a tree. "Thanks for your vote of confidence, anyway," he said lightly. "Being placed in the same category with Major Tremaine is highly flattering. He's my idea of what a soldier and commanding officer should be."

At her quick, grateful smile for the praise the tension of the moment evaporated.

"Poor Jimmy," she sighed. "Life has been no bed of roses for him." Always ready to embark on her favorite subject, she absently handed Mason the fishing pole and sat on the ledge at his feet.

"Jim made such a wonderful start in his career, but then came his marriage. A tragic mistake. Gerry—her name was Geraldine, I told you that, didn't I?—turned into a nagging wife who was bitterly unhappy because she couldn't have a settled home, expensive clothes, a lot of money to throw around.

"I can't imagine why she expected this from an Army captain, but she was peculiar in other ways, too. I know," she sighed, "how I know! A few years ago I lived with her while we waited for Jim to come home from Formosa and take a Washington assignment. And living with Gerry was no bed of roses for me, either!"

"Then why didn't you pull out?" He cast the line to another corner of the pool. "You didn't *have* to live with her, did you?"

"No, but I thought I could help Jim by standing by her, trying to keep her out of trouble. But she nearly drove me mad with her wildness—and her selfishness. Sometimes I could have——" She choked back the rest. "Why should I bore you with my troubles?"

"You're not. Go ahead, get it off your chest, pal." He was busy for a few moments with another trout, which he landed expertly. Then he propped the pole against a tree and sat beside her.

"If you've had something like this bottled up in you, it's time you let it out." The dreary tale of an unappreciative wife was far from new to him, but when it involved this girl for whom he cared so deeply, it depressed him as never before.

His sympathetic tone brought tears to her eyes and she brushed them away with a wet sleeve.

"It went on forever, it seemed. Jim was delayed, and delayed again, and Gerry grew more and more restless and—and hard to live with. But I stuck to her, hoping I could keep her more or less in line until he could take over." She pounded her little fist on her knee. "I hung on—and then, just when I might have helped the most, I passed out of the picture with a nervous breakdown. That's what the doctors called it, anyway.

"I remember the evening Jim was due, the telegram saying he couldn't make it and a frightful scene with Gerry—then nothing more until I came to, weeks later, without a single memory of the intervening time. A nervous breakdown!" she scoffed impatiently. "Me—of all people!"

"I don't wonder—with the load you were carrying."

The girl nodded. "The doctors said that I must have been building up to it for months. Worry—not over Gerry," she explained bitterly, "but what it might do to Jim if he found his wife running wild—proved too much for my feeble mind."

She was silent while she pulled a leaf from a bush and rolled it in nervous fingers.

"I failed at the crucial moment. From questions Jim has asked me—he never told me the whole story—and from gossip, I gather that Gerry got hold of some money somehow and went on a tear that ended"—she swallowed hard —"well, she died. A hit-and-run accident, they said. And if I'd been there, I might have saved her. But I don't know— I *don't* know! I can't remember anything! Oh, if I could see behind the cloud that obscures those last tragic days!"

The aching regret in every word overcame Mason's resolute pose of aloofness. Impulsively he slipped an arm about her shoulders and held her close.

"Don't think of it, my dear, don't brood on it. You fell ill because you tried so hard to help, too hard. But let it ride now—it's in the past. And those forgotten days may not prove as tragic as you imagine."

He laughed softly and patted her shoulder.

"Don't think I'm Old Doc Bentley, the Demon Quoter, but I do remember a poem I had to recite years ago in school.

111

One of Milton's, I think. I've never forgotten one couplet:

Was I deceived, or did a sable cloud
Turn forth her silver lining on the night?"

"I like that," she murmured.

"Your cloud may have happiness instead of sorrow behind its sable front," he said with conviction. Her tremulous smile of thanks was almost too much for his self-control, but he kept it firmly in hand and stood up. Picking up the trout and pole, he waved toward camp.

"Let's forget the past, think of the present, and rush these fish to the griddle," was his practical proposal. "I don't know about you, but I'm close to starving."

When all her proffers of assistance were politely rejected Delight sat and watched the men prepare supper. The Indian, who had already started to broil his trout, rapidly cleaned the other two. Finding the frying pan too small, he strung them all on a green branch, which he propped over a bed of glowing coals raked from the fire. There they curled and browned, sizzling and filling the air with an inviting scent which made her mouth water. Served later, with a cup of steaming tea and a half-dozen crackers, hers proved to be even better than she had anticipated.

In fact, now, everything about the camp belied her first gloomy impression and intrigued her. The smoke of the two fires rose only to the treetops in the heavy air, and hung there in a wavering gray-blue canopy. The lichened trunks of the trees and their long swaying beards of moss glistened with drops of water like tiny jewels. From the woods came the ring of Thomas's hatchet, as he cut branches to roof a second lean-to whose frame stood ready.

Mason, pipe gripped in his teeth, sat cross-legged by the smaller fire, methodically cutting holes in a ragged blanket, the most worn of those stored in the boat.

"Will the lieutenant deign to explain to an ignorant hanger-on in his expedition why he is further mutilating that already ruined blanket?" Delight inquired brightly.

Mason held the article at arm's length while he squinted critically from it to the girl.

"I'm designing a new dress for you." At her indignant protest he grinned. "Don't fly off the handle, pal. You certainly can't spend the night in those soaked clothes. I fully realize that you've worn a waterproof trench coat through all these proceedings, but even that is not proof against lying in three—four inches of water in the bottom of a boat, as you did.

"Of course you *could* spend the night in those clothes, but you'd wake up in the morning as stiff as a board. And I don't intend that you shall."

"If you think for one minute, Bill Mason, that I'm—"

"Hold it, dear lady, hold everything. No indecent exposure will be required, I assure you. Thomas is off cutting boughs for the shack for us menfolks, and shortly I'm going to help him haul them in here. While we're off *you* will be slipping into this latest Paris creation."

"Put on that dirty old thing? Never!" Delight gasped. "It makes me itch to even think of it! I'm perfectly comfortable as I am," she told him decidedly. Although this was flirting with the truth she felt that she put enough frost in her voice to end the discussion.

The frost failed to impress Mason, however. He knocked the ashes from his pipe and put it deliberately in his pocket. Then he stood up and tossed the blanket onto her lap.

"Get this, Dee, and get it fast! You're not going to sleep in those wet clothes. Either you take them off and climb into this, or I'll be forced to do it for you. Period!"

"You *wouldn't!*" Furious, she sprang to her feet, forgetting the cramped quarters. Her head struck a roof pole with stunning force and she sank to her knees. The pain drove every other thought away and she could only moan and rub the bruise. She shut her eyes tightly, but two tears trickled slowly down her white cheeks.

Instantly Mason was beside her, his hands steadying her as she swayed dizzily, and his voice was tender as he whispered, "Oh, Dee, I'm so sorry! Did it hurt a lot?" When the blue eyes flew open to flash speechless indignation, he stepped back with a sheepish smile. "Sorry, that was a foolish question, wasn't it?" Warily he returned to the subject under discussion, this time with placating reasonableness instead of stern command.

"Look, pal," he pleaded, "let's be sensible about this. You don't know this country and climate as well as I do. If the fog should hold we may have to stay here a day or two, so why court trouble by lying around in damp clothes? Believe me, it could be dangerous; that's why I can't allow it. There's nothing wrong with that blanket—"

"It's filthy!"

"It is not! Do you think I'd pick a dirty one for *you* to wear? It's just old and faded. Come on, be a sport." His rare smile lighted his face. "Do what the doctor orders and everybody will be happy."

When she neither replied nor looked up he grunted and strode away toward the sound of the chopping, but he turned when he was a few yards away to deliver an ultimatum.

"All right, you heard me! If your clothes aren't changed

when I come back, you know the consequences." Unconsciously his voice took on the driving staccato of an officer in the field. "I am in command of this expedition. My orders are to be obeyed to the letter!"

"Gr-rh! Cave-man stuff!" Delight flamed indignantly. Head cocked at a defiant angle, she watched him stalk into the woods. What tyrants military men became! Did he imagine for one minute that he could *make* her put on that ridiculous blanket? She lifted one end with disdainful fingers to throw it aside, and against her will admitted that it felt surprisingly soft and warm.

The lieutenant had been ingenious. She could see, as she held it up and turned it about, that with her arms through the holes he had cut, the blanket would form a sort of cape. There would be a rather fetching collar at the back formed by a loose fold. He had even strung a doubled length of fishline through slits to form a belt.

She wriggled her shoulders inside the trench coat. Even with its protection the top of her sweater was wet, the leather jacket sodden, and the thin blouse clung coldly to her skin. Besides the water in the bottom of the boat, which had soaked her tweed skirt and boots, the rain must have drenched her before Bill fastened her coat collar tight.

Bill Mason was right, it would be silly for her to go to bed in such a state when she could be much more comfortable in this contraption. And besides—although she side-stepped the thought, it would persist—she didn't quite dare test the strength of the determination she had seen in his eyes and heard in his voice. She felt a shivery conviction that he meant what he said.

Capitulation. She dragged some pine branches in front of the hut and crouched behind them while she struggled out of her clothes.

"As uncomfortable as undressing in an upper berth!" she muttered, but she was careful not to rise from her knees. Her head still ached after that one ambitious attempt to stand erect.

The blanket enveloped her in warmth to which she responded by tying the fishline belt in a festive bow knot. Then, since the rain had stopped completely, she hung coats, sweater, blouse and skirt on the branches of a dead tree embedded in the sand near the fire, pulled off her boots and propped them open toward the heat and added her stockings to the array.

"Surrender!" she muttered crossly as she studied her new outfit. "Shameful, unconditional surrender, that's what it is!" She hugged the blanket close. "But I guess it's worth it." Retreating to the hut, she rolled herself in another blanket and lay down. "It *is* worth it!" she sighed contentedly. "If I were a kitten I'd purr."

Comfortable, but lonely. The thumping of the hatchet sounded very far away. There were constant stealthy rustlings and flutterings from the woods, and whisperings from the misty treetops. The crackling fire was some company, but she was glad when she heard the voices of the two men approaching.

What a dictator that Bill Mason is! If he speaks to me, Delight thought pugnaciously, I'll pretend I'm asleep. She waited for the expected hail, but none came. They were back, though, she could tell by the dancing reflected glow in her shelter when more wood was put on the fire and a faint whiff of tobacco smoke drifted her way.

What a day this had been! It stretched back interminably, so that everything which had happened before today seemed long passed into history. Bill having coffee in her kitchen—and that other meeting at the trading post—and Captain Steele badgering her about Bill! She frowned, remembering his angry threat. What could he tell Jim that would discredit Bill Mason? *Nothing,* she was fiercely certain. The gods be praised that her escort had not been changed, that she was not here in this soaked wilderness with Warner Steele!

She closed her eyes and stifled a yawn. Disjointed thoughts raced through her mind, flickering like a badly geared movie. She was overpoweringly sleepy. Not much rest last night. As though the spy episode were not enough to banish slumber, she had been childishly excited over the coming trip. Because Bill was to be her companion? Perhaps. Even if he didn't respond as she hoped—

Who was the girl at home Bill loved, but who didn't love him? How could she fail to if she had a grain of sense? Oh, there were girls like that, women—If Gerry had been more of a wife to Jim—

Who's that crying? No, someone is *calling*—calling—

Delight sat up and rubbed her eyes. No sound now. Had she been asleep, dreaming? How still the forest lay, how black against the scarcely lighter clouds. The fire had sunk to red coals with an occasional leap of flame to flick shadows on the roof of her hut. On the shore the boat lay careened, abandoned by the receding tide, a black bulk among dimly luminous pools. The night seemed to press in from all sides, weirdly quiet, heavy with menace.

A distant wail from the woods made Delight shiver. She wasn't actually afraid, she assured herself without much conviction. Only it would be nice to have someone to talk to, to sit comfortably close beside. To be perfectly honest, what she would like most at the moment was to take tight hold of Bill's hand.

The eerie cry shattered the silence again, much nearer, and her heart went into a nose dive and then flew to her throat and stayed there, beating its wings. The wail lifted, note by quivering note, lingered and died away. In sudden ungovernable panic the girl struggled to her knees. She felt penned in, trapped in the little shack. Suddenly she couldn't breathe. Clutching the blankets close, she scrambled out of the lean-to and knelt rigid, listening.

XVIII

"WHAT'S up?" asked a calm voice.

Delight gave a convulsive start and swiveled her eyes to the right. Bill Mason sat muffled to the chin in a blanket, his back against a boulder. With a sigh of relief the girl relaxed. How silly of her to be frightened, she thought. Nothing could hurt her while he was on the scene.

"What time is it, Bill?"

"Nearly two. The blackest hours are over."

"Why are you sitting there?" she demanded. "Have you been awake all night? You need a guardian! Get in your hut and be comfortable. That's an order," she mimicked with a laugh. "Your C.O.'s sister commanding."

"I'm okay here. You go back to sleep."

"*Sleep?* With that wolf howling at my very door!"

"Thomas says there are no wolves on this island," he stated matter-of-factly, "because there are no deer. And anyway, what you heard was some kind of a bird. An owl, probably."

"A bird!" she jeered indignantly. "Don't be foolish! Any bird would split its windpipe producing that frightful sound. I know it was at least a wolf!"

She stood up, brushing back her hair, and saw his eyes fixed on her in frowning disapproval.

"What's the matter?" she asked. "Don't you approve of my costume? I put it on, by the way, because I wanted to, *not* because I was ordered to. If *you're* not satisfied with your designing," she taunted, "how do you suppose *I* feel? Answer —like one of those dummies the men use for bayonet practice!" She hugged her blankets more closely about her, padded in bare feet to his side and sank down on the spruce boughs he had arranged for a seat.

Mason's eyes lingered on her face for a moment before he shifted away from her.

"Got room enough?" he asked, staring at the fire.

"Plenty, thanks. I——" She was interrupted by a gurgling snore from the men's lean-to. "Heavens, did Thomas drive you in the open with that?"

"No, that's his first offense, and I haven't been in there yet."

She stared at him incredulously. "You mean you *chose* to sit out here—to keep watch—all night?"

"I'm used to it," he answered shortly. And after a pause, "I'm not much of a sleeper."

"Guilty conscience, yes?"

She was startled at the effect of her idle words. His face paled and froze in the tight-lipped mask she had seen so often, angry eyes drilled into hers.

"Has Steele been talking? Did he tell you?" he demanded in a hoarse voice.

"Captain Steele? No." Remembering how that officer's insinuations had disturbed her, she hurried to reinforce the denial. "He has told me nothing, and if he did try any character assassination," she added hotly, "I'd—well, I wouldn't believe him!" That was far less decisive than what she had started to say, but safer; her feeling for Bill was getting out of hand.

"My 'guilty conscience' crack was only a joke, and not a very funny one at that," she apologized. "Cheer up and snap out of it. You've been having a nightmare on your guard duty, and you're still living in it."

He rested his chin on clasped hands, eyes still fixed on the smoldering fire.

"A nightmare is right, but there is solid, crushing fact behind it. I might as well tell you, Dee." His voice shook with tension. "Some years ago I made a mistake. I wrecked my life by a stupid act of drunken foolishness."

The despair in the words tortured her. Her heart went out to him with a rush of tenderness and her hand would have followed, but she snatched it back in time. With only words she offered comfort. "Aren't you the one who told me about the sable cloud which turns its brighter side at last?"

"In this case there can be no brighter side, ever!" He shook his head decidedly.

"How can you know?" she argued. "None of us can see into the future, thank Heaven! And *you* advised me to forget the past."

"This," he muttered doggedly, "is something I can't forget as long as it hangs over me."

"Then why not face it and somehow put it right," she urged. "There's always a way of doing anything if you have the courage to try it."

"I haven't faced it because there is no way," he argued doggedly.

"How can you be sure? Perhaps it would turn out to be one of Grandma Tremaine's Disappearing Hills." At his puzzled frown she explained, "That's a family saying. Once when we were driving through the country the car started down a long, long slope. Ahead the road dipped into the valley and then climbed again in another hill. For some reason, perspective or something like that, the hill ahead looked so frightfully steep that I wondered aloud if we could climb it.

"Grandma gave one of her little snorting laughs that meant, What fools the young folks are! Then she said, 'Watch it disappear.' And sure enough, the nearer we came to its foot the more it flattened out, until it was just a gradual climb. 'Like a lot of our troubles in life,' Grandma remarked placidly. 'They look dreadfully difficult until we face up to them, and then they so often fade away.' A lesson," Delight concluded earnestly, "that I've never forgotten."

Mason turned to her and the warmth in his eyes made her pulses race. For a moment she thought he was going to put his arm around her.

"A lesson I'll remember, too," he said quietly. "My thanks to Grandma Tremaine, through her gallant granddaughter," and he resumed his study of the glowing coals.

After a short silence he continued, "I *have* let my trouble slide and not faced it squarely, dodging all the time like a coward. But no more! I doubt if it can be cured, but now I'm at least going to try to do something about it."

"Is it—whatever it is—the reason you can't marry the girl you love?" Delight asked with pounding heart.

"Yes." Quick on the involuntary admission came a harsh question. "Who told you I was in love?"

"Tamara," the girl admitted, pink with embarrassment under his angry glare. "You confided in her, didn't you? She said you wanted to buy her bracelet for a girl back home."

"Oh! Oh." His low laugh shook with relief. "Tamara has a taste for the melodramatic, hasn't she? I only wanted it for a cousin who's slightly cracked about curios and antiques, not for a best girl. At the time I didn't have one." He snapped his mouth shut on the words and sat grim-faced. *"At the time!"* he repeated with bitter irony. "Not at that time—or ever!"

"Don't say that! Remember the Disappearing Hills." Impulsively Delight laid her hand on his clenched fist.

Mason stared down at it for a tense second before he spoke. Then, "Put your hands under your blanket," he advised coldly. "They—they'll be safer there."

In hurt and angry silence she obeyed and sat outwardly calm, inwardly seething, while he scowled at the fire. There didn't seem much point in staying there. She stretched and looked up. Faint yellow light was staining the sky above the treetops, and the sight banished her resentment.

"There's the sunshine!" she announced happily. "It's going to be a good day!"

"Thank God!" Mason stood up and looked down at her soberly. "You'd better get your clothes on while I build up the fire for breakfast."

Obediently she retired behind her own hut to exchange the blanket for more tailored garments. She could hear the men moving about the fire, the clatter of utensils. When someone went to the brook for water she could tell it was the Indian, so different from Bill's decisive step was his stumbling shuffle.

She came out to the fire as he returned with a brimming pail. He looked more swarthy than ever after a night marooned. Bill was opening a can of hash; like Thomas, he showed a dark shadow of beard, but his skin shone as if freshly scrubbed.

"I wish I felt as clean as you look, Bill," Delight sighed. "I'm positively grimy!"

"I left plenty of water in the brook," he smiled. "Why don't you use that pool where we fished? There should be a pretty well tramped-out trail to it by now. If you get lost, sing out and we'll rescue you. This is a de luxe camp, you see —unlimited bathing facilities."

"Don't eat all the food while I'm gone," she warned with a smile for both men. Thomas ignored her; he was kneeling beside the fireplace, arms outstretched, to replace the green limb which supported the kettle over the coals. The action pulled back the sleeves of his jacket so that Delight saw a pink blotch above one wrist. Its unhealthy pallor against the brown skin gave her a momentary twinge of alarm. Some disease—?

The man raised his eyes in time to notice her wide-eyed stare. He straightened, scowling, tugged both sleeves down into place and slouched away to the woodpile.

Even the weak dawn light made the forest less forbidding than it had been in darkness, Delight thought, as she crossed the sand to the edge of the woods. As she walked on, the first rays of sunlight filtered through the trees to transform the drops of rain on branches and bushes to sparkling crystals, to brighten the patches of moss to vivid green. With a startling flash of color a bluejay as large as a crow swooped to a limb above her head and cocked a glittering eye curiously at her. Beyond the violet dusk which still clung among distant trees sounded the tinkle of the brook and a sudden ecstatic burst of song from an unseen bird.

How lovely the world could be, she thought, and how foolish her fears of the night seemed now. But just the same, she fervently prayed that another night would find her at the post rather than here. Her appetite for adventure, had that kind of adventure, had been quickly satisfied, even with two such competent companions as Thomas and Bill Mason.

Bill. What was he talking about last night? What could he have done that ruined his life? And what was the quality in his voice, while he made that heartbroken confession, which called up in her an irresistible longing to comfort him? The memory of that moment flashed little thrills to the tips of her fingers. But he—he must have superhuman restraint. Color flooded her cheeks at the echo of his brusque, "Put your hands under your blanket—"

She came to the edge of the pool still brooding on that rebuff and resentfully threw a stone into the water. It made a satisfying splash. She was wasting sympathy on a man who seemed sufficient into himself—infuriatingly so. Besides, in spite of his evasion, she felt sure that he was in love with a girl in the States, which made her sympathy even more unnecessary.

Well, the only sensible course was to ignore him from now on. But, darn it, her whirling thoughts prompted, what a friend he could be if he would—and how good-looking he is, even with a day's black stubble darkening that square jaw. If anything, it increased his masculine appeal. How different from Thomas was the comparison which popped into her mind; on the Indian the need of a shave only added to his grubby appearance. . . .

Delight frowned in sudden perplexity. Come to think of it, why should Thomas be exhibiting a heavy shadow of beard when Jim, at the spy conference, had stated flatly, "Indians don't have whiskers." Nor did Eskimos, she was positive of that, an odd bit of information which she must have read somewhere.

Once embarked on that line of thought, she began to remember peculiar occurrences which she had scarcely noticed at the time, or perhaps noticed subconsciously. The stumbling, trudging walk of the Indian when she had expected the light, silent tread of a forest animal. Perhaps too many historical novels colored her ideas of Indians, or maybe Bill was right in laying Thomas's awkward progress to weariness.

He had worked hard, when making for this island, in the boat and—the girl's pulses leaped to double time at another memory. In the instant before the first wave from the disintegrating glacier had reached their boat, Thomas had yelled a warning—without a *trace* of his usual guttural accent!

With a shiver of apprehension she faced the only possible explanation. Thomas was not an Indian! He was masquerading. That struck her as too farfetched for even her overworked imagination when her practical mind asked, Why should he? Pondering the riddle, absurd as it was, she knelt at the edge of the pool and rolled up her sleeves. In the nick of time she remembered to remove her wrist watch before plunging her hands into the water.

She caught her breath, but not at the physical chill. It was a mental shock which struck her motionless, crouched beside the pool, staring at her bare arms. On one tanned wrist the removal of the watch had left a small round patch of skin, delicately pink in the surrounding brown.

It was the same sort of mark she had seen on Thomas's wrist just now at camp—seen and dismissed with the rather squeamish reaction that it was caused by some kind of disease. How silly! How utterly childish! His wrist, like hers, bore the mark of a wrist watch—and an unusually large one! An uncontrollable shiver ran through her as Captain Whitaker's words drummed in her ears, "A stop watch, imported, nothing a college boy could afford."

As though a blazing spotlight had focused suddenly on a darkened stage she saw the truth with every detail clear. Thomas was the "college boy" with whom she had talked, the enemy agent who had sneaked onto the airfield, shot a guard and then disappeared so completely that the combined efforts of the post had uncovered no trace of him.

No wonder he had studied her with malevolent eyes when he delivered Captain Pepper's message on the steamer; he must have been afraid that she would recognize him. Small chance of that if her chief memory was of a wispy beard and tinted sunglasses, topped by black hair in an unruly mop. The hair had evidently been combed forward, chopped short in Indian bangs and smeared with grease. Yet there had been a hint, too fleeting for her to grasp, in the swing of his stocky figure when he walked.

With a gasp of consternation Delight sprang to her feet. It was insane for her to stay here mulling over recollections. She must get to Bill—tell him what she suspected at once! She snatched up her watch from a patch of moss and hurried toward the camp.

When she looked up from slipping the watch on her wrist she was dismayed to find herself moving among close-standing trees instead of along the clearer way she had come. Had she missed a turn in the path? She was in the forest! In panic she spun about and ran for the patch of sunlight to her right. Branches whipped her face, tore at her coat. Her foot caught in an unyielding vine and she plunged forward into a tiny glade on her hands and knees.

The shock of the fall brought her to her senses. "Keep cool!" she ordered herself aloud, her heart pounding, for she was sure, as she looked about, that she'd never seen this place before and there was no sign of the trail. "When lost, stay where you are until help comes," she remembered from some book she had read. The humiliation of calling for help was unthinkable. She must be bright enough to figure—

The rapid drum of hurrying feet drew her eyes to the left and relief flooded her. There was the path! One of the men was coming for her.

She glimpsed him through the trees and her momentary comfort vanished under a wave of astonishment. It was Thomas, one hand gripping a stick of firewood like a club. He was heading for the pool where Bill had sent her, perhaps in his haste forgetting to drop the stick. Explanations tumbled in her mind: the ship had arrived—or Bill had been hurt!

Delight started to call out but remembered his true identity in time to check herself. At the same moment Thomas stopped to peer ahead along the trail, his face contorted, teeth clenched; every inch of him breathed menace to her excited fancy. While she watched in breathless suspense, he whirled and went racing back toward the camp.

Still in a turmoil of uncertainty Delight struggled through the underbrush until she found the open path. She started to run for the beach, but forced herself to walk; it wouldn't do to burst out of the woods as though a bear were chasing her. The thing to do was to walk into the camp sedately and make some excuse to get Bill aside while she warned him about "the Indian."

XIX

COMING out of the woods onto the beach, she stopped in midstride and stood paralyzed by horror. Bill Mason lay stretched on his side beside the fireplace, his eyes closed, temple and cheek a crimson smear of blood. Beyond him her dazed brain slowly took in a scene too fantastic to be real.

The tide was high and their boat floated free with no rope holding it to the boulder on shore. Aboard it Thomas hauled furiously on the anchor line astern. The anchor clattered in over the side, streaming muddy water. Thomas sat down and bent to drag the oars from under the thwarts.

Delight's stupor of surprise vanished in flashing comprehension. She had noticed the spy intercept her glance at the betraying spot on his wrist; thinking she recognized him, he seized the moment when he was alone with Mason to strike him down and escape. He must have been coming to silence her, too, then decided against it. That blood—had he killed Bill? A white-hot blaze of fury shook her.

With a hysterical, "Oh, no, you don't!" she raced forward, dropped to one knee beside Mason and fumbled out the automatic covered by his jacket. Her hand shook as she snicked off the safety and aimed above the boat. Gritting her teeth, she willed her hand to rocklike immobility and clicked the trigger. Nothing happened. Muttering at her stupidity, she jacked a cartridge into the breech, aimed and fired.

Thomas ducked at the report and whirled to look shoreward, his mouth open, face blank with amazement.

Delight forced her voice to chill and precise command as she called, "Bring that boat back! Bring it back or I'll shoot again!"

For a long instant he glared across the water, then with a contemptuous laugh picked up the oars. She raced to the water's edge, her gun roared, and a white splinter from the gunwale whizzed past his head. Thomas flinched away and dropped an oar with a clatter. His right hand dove into the wide collar of his jacket.

"Don't!"

Her harsh warning made him hesitate, and the black muzzle of the pistol trained unwaveringly on him added emphasis to the command. He slowly withdrew the groping hand, but his black eyes glared in watchful waiting.

For a moment it was stalemate. The girl wanted man and boat ashore—but not with a weapon. Desperate, she took a chance, knowing that a mishap might be fatal.

"Reach in *slowly* and take out your gun—*slowly!*" she ordered. "Then drop it overboard. Be careful, this automatic is right on you. I'll pump it empty—and I can *shoot!*"

Thomas was past doubting that; her last attempt had been too well placed to be accidental. And even if it *was* a lucky hit, he disliked the idea of being in range when a distraught woman began spraying five or six shots at random.

Like a slow-motion movie his hand crept again to his collar, gradually dipped in and as deliberately reappeared clutching a small pistol. Involuntarily Delight's gun came up an inch, its deadly mouth gaping. With sweat glistening on his forehead, he let his own pistol dangle between thumb and forefinger so that she could see that it was harmless as he held it clear of the gunwale and dropped it. It vanished with a splash.

"Now use one oar as a paddle," the girl commanded, marveling at her cool resourcefulness, "and come in here." Scowling but helpless, Thomas obeyed.

From the corner of her eye Delight saw Mason roll over, struggle to his knees and then to his feet. Alive! Her heart zoomed to the stratosphere. She backed toward him as he stood swaying, legs braced wide to keep his balance, while fingers explored the blood on face and hair.

Breathing heavily he muttered, "What—what the devil got into that fool Indian? I heard him"—his voice became clearer—"in back of me, turned, saw his arm go up—ugh!" He stared from the girl to the boat. "What happened?"

"He hit you all right, Bill, and I—I shot at him—twice."

"Shot at our Indian?"

"Thomas is not an Indian! He's the spy—the man you've been looking for."

"Spy?" Mason felt of his head again. "I don't get it."

"Never mind that now—I can explain later. But hurry, Bill, please hurry and capture him!" Delight's voice shook with anxiety.

"Don't worry. Whoever he is, I'll get him for slugging me!" He shook off the last of his weakness. "Keep him covered." He strode down to the water's edge, circling so as not to come between man and gun.

When the boat touched shore he snatched the bow rope, whipped it into a noose and ordered sharply, "Turn around, hands clasped behind you, Thomas!" As the man obeyed he slipped the noose over the extended wrists, jerked it tight and flung loop after loop around him until he was helpless. Then he hauled him out of the boat and dropped him ungently on the beach.

"Sort of like hog-tying a steer, back on the ranch," Mason grinned at the girl. "Now let's have the dope. What's been going on while I was out?"

"Listen, Bill, *listen!* Isn't that a whistle?" Head on one side, Delight stared hopefully toward the sound. It came again, louder, unmistakable. "It's the steamer!" she cried, running to him.

"About time, too," he agreed thankfully. "They must have

been cruising around here looking for us and heard your shots. Signal with a couple more rounds."

Obediently Delight raised the gun. Then she glared at it aghast and with a laugh perilously close to tears thrust it into his hand.

"Fire it yourself, Lieutenant! I—I hate guns!" she sobbed and slumped to the sand at his feet.

Their return to the ship, via the whaleboat sent in for them, was delayed by Bill Mason's insistence on recovering the spy's pistol. Fortunately the surface of the little bay was like glass, and after some rowing about the gun was located. A gaff, lashed to the boat hook, picked it up by the trigger guard and brought aboard the valuable piece of evidence.

Captain Pepper had lowered a gangway for their reception, they discovered when they reached the steamer. Delight and Bill mounted it under a barrage of shouted congratulations and questions. The barrage fell to a murmur of amazement when two sailors hauled aboard the erstwhile "Indian" still securely bound, and the revelation of his true identity created such a sensation that the overnight marooning of the trio was for the moment forgotten.

Captain Pepper, already unstrung by the result of his bad judgment in allowing the expedition to set out, came close to apoplexy when informed that he had been giving asylum to an enemy agent.

"Aboard my ship?" he groaned. "Lieutenant, I ain't fit to command a rowboat, that's all! I said that when you disappeared, and I've been kicking myself these last fourteen hours while you were gone. But you riled me, Lieutenant, standing there telling me what I knew danged well myself—that it was looking for trouble. And now this on top of it! Taken for a ride by a guy that I should have known was no Indian! But, say," he exploded in grinning relief, "if I hadn't sent you off with Thomas, or whatever his dirty name is, you would probably never have caught him!"

Mason was on the point of suggesting to the captain that it was the spy himself who had proposed his inclusion in the party, but instead he laughed.

"*I* didn't get him—don't think it. I was fooled as thoroughly as you were. But then, neither of us had ever seen the man before. It took Miss Tremaine to spot him." And since Delight had explained in the boat how her suspicion was first aroused and then confirmed, he proceeded to give such a graphic description of her cleverness and courage that her pale cheeks flamed.

"Damn these Indians!" Pepper snarled, recalling a further

indignity. "I took the man on Kasan Charley's say-so. Never gave it a thought. That Kasan! I tell you, you can't trust a Tlingit as far as you can throw him!"

"It's going to be interesting to interview this Kasan Charley," growled Mason. "But right now I'd like to clean up a little and borrow some decent clothes. Mine have taken a terrific beating. Then I intend to ask your Thomas a lot of very pointed questions." When the mate offered him the use of his razor, spare trousers and jacket, he followed the man to his quarters. Dr. Bentley, who had been studying Bill's injury, trotted after them with professional eagerness.

The spy having been already led away, Captain Pepper centered his attention on Delight.

"Miss," he deplored, "I don't know how I'll ever square myself with the major!"

She nodded understandingly. "He must have been frantic when he learned that we had disappeared."

"Major Jim kept the radio sizzling all night!" Bertha Bentley shrilled. "But he wasn't any wilder than we were aboard here."

"That's the truth!" Pepper shoved back his cap to wipe a perspiring brow. "That berg that broke off and swept you away was the biggest I've ever seen come off the glacier in all my years here. Judas, it was like dropping a good-sized mountain into the bay!"

"It surely was!" Bertha confirmed breathlessly. She seemed unwilling to allow Delight a monopoly on dangers endured. "The most terrifying experience of my life! This dreadful ship rolled until I was positive we'd capsize! You can't imagining how frightful it was!"

The captain snorted. "Maybe she can, ma'am. This here 'dreadful ship' as you call it, is a lot bigger than what she was in, and we were a mile or so further from the glacier. So maybe *you* can imagine what it was like for *her*. Why, Miss Tremaine, when I made sure we were O.K. and looked for you—and couldn't see you anywhere—!" He swabbed his forehead again. "I swear my hair turned grayer than it was already!"

"And then not to know what was happening!" Bertha moaned tragically. "My dear, I didn't sleep a wink. And I don't know which was more appalling—the fear that you were drowned or the thought that you might be forced to spend the whole dreadful night in the wilderness with those two men!" Even excitement never dulled for long Babbling Bertha's thirsty curiosity, and she threw the girl a knowing smile. "I can't wait to hear all about it!"

"It wasn't dreadful at all," corrected Delight sharply.

126

"They took wonderful care of me. At least until this morning."

"You were dam—blamed lucky," Pepper announced earnestly, "to have Lieutenant Mason along, miss."

"I think so too!"

"Oh, *do* you?" Mrs. Bentley demanded archly, and edged closer. "He has always seemed so cold and—and distant, don't you know. Was he different with you? Do tell me."

"Please, Mrs. Bentley, I'm really too tired to talk about it."

"Of course you are!" the captain growled, and his long arm moved the inquisitive woman politely but irresistibly aside. "You come with me, Miss Tremaine. We don't have many staterooms on this ship, kinda had to double up last night to take care of the crowd, but I'll fix you up.

"Don't know as a stateroom's just the place for you at that," he rumbled with a shrewd glance at Mrs. Bentley. "Better come to my cabin. I'll have hot coffee sent up in a shake, and you bunk down there for as long as you like—undisturbed. Sleep till we get in to Totum, if you're a mind to. Nobody will bother you, I'll see to that."

The triumphal arrival at Totum drew the largest crowd which the ancient wharf could accommodate, but Delight felt sure that her own adventure was not the cause of the universal interest. In this wild land such mishaps were one of the commonplace hazards of living, worth no more than casual comment at best.

The major greeted her with satisfactory warmth, of course, including a brotherly hug viewed with envy by his subordinates. Then he thanked Mason with quite unmilitary fervor for his care of his sister. For his part, the lieutenant responded briefly and preserved an even more chill aloofness under Delight's own praise.

Just as she expected, she thought indignantly. He was continuing the precise formality he had adopted for the return voyage—maddening formality! Except for that initial burst of admiration for the way she had handled the spy on the island he had been morose, discouraging every attempt on her part to resume the friendly intimacy of their night in the wilds.

Just because he had a girl in the States—and she was positive from his reactions that he had—was no reason to treat her as though she were something dangerously malignant! She punished him, she hoped, with an enthusiastic greeting for the other officers who surrounded her the moment she stepped to the dock.

Captain Steele was in the forefront, his manner as significantly devoted as ever. With a defiant tilt of her chin Delight responded eagerly to his effusive welcome. She hoped this was observed—and condemned—by her late escort.

Disappointingly it was not. Some of the effect of her demonstration probably was spoiled by the advent of the shaggy Husky, who catapulted through the crowd to her side. Igloo paused only long enough to lap her hand with his huge moist tongue before he charged up the gangplank to his shouting master.

But even without that distraction she doubted that Bill would have noticed anything she did. He and the major were deep in conversation at one side of the wharf, oblivious to everything until the captured Thomas appeared at the top of the gangplank. Then all else was forgotten by every onlooker.

This, Delight realized, was the *pièce de résistance* of the day. This was why Jim came to the landing attended by a squad of soldiers, Captain Whitaker and a detachment from the airfield. And it was their grim errand which drew townspeople, fishermen and Indians by the score. The prospect of stark drama here in their own town—a captured spy in the flesh.

XX

AN ENEMY agent! The sort of villain they were accustomed to gape at in the movies as he slunk along the misty streets of some foreign city or raced desperately through the sinister gloom of an Asian water front. Now one was here—in Totum. For this one day they would not view an artificial dream on film, they would take part, if only as spectators, while the long arm of Uncle Sam reached far north into Alaska to pluck a thorn from his side.

The plucking was, after all, disappointingly matter-of-fact. Two Finnish sailors led Thomas down the gangplank, looming over him like twin bergs prepared to crush a bobbing dory. Igloo created a slight diversion by trotting close to sniff the prisoner, who on this occasion was unable to reciprocate the greeting as he had on Officers Row.

The rope around his arms had been replaced by rusty handcuffs which Captain Pepper surprisingly produced from the wheelhouse. His black hair appeared to have been degreased, his face looked less swarthy than for his character as an Indian, and his manner was airy in the extreme. Passing Delight he grinned and brazenly announced, "Sorry to miss supper the other night, ma'am. I'll take a rain check on that invite, eh?"

The outraged sailors lifted him almost clear of the dock as they rushed him away and delivered him, more disheveled than ever, to Major Tremaine. Without ceremony he was installed with Lieutenant Mason and the guards in an Air Force truck and driven off. A few spectators, exhilarated by early morning toasts to patriotism, raised a mild cheer which died away from lack of support. The drama was ended.

Major Tremaine relaxed and strode over to Delight with an apologetic smile.

"Now that he's off my mind, Dee, I repeat wholeheartedly, welcome home!"

Babbling Bertha seized the opportunity to indulge in her secondary passion, the giving of parties.

"We must make it a real celebration. At my house, at seven. I'll invite all our friends who made the trip—and you, Warner, of course!" with a dazzling smile for Captain Steele, which he returned with bored complacence. "And this time you simply *must* order Lieutenant Mason to put in an appearance, Major!"

"Short of issuing a direct command," Jim smiled, "I'll do my best. But don't forget, he has duties."

"You tyrant! You're not going to put him on duty today, after the ordeal he went through!"

Steele uttered a jeering snort. "My dear Mrs. Bentley! You call it an ordeal to be marooned with Delight—"

"Wait a minute!" Major Tremaine interrupted hastily. "I wasn't referring to the lieutenant's regular duties. He has the matter of the spy to clear up with the Air Force, you know."

"You don't think that will take all day and night, too, do you?" Bertha wailed.

"No indeed. I rather think that Captain Whitaker will ship our nosy friend out of here to Air Force Headquarters as fast as he can get a plane off. And I promise to use all my influence to have Bill Mason at your party."

"Thank you, Major. And this time," the lady purred with a sly glance at Delight, "I have an idea that our reluctant lieutenant will deign to accept. At seven, remember!"

There was a distinct resemblance to a gypsy caravan, Delight thought, in the assortment of vehicles which transported the voyagers home from Totum wharf. She rode with Jim in one jeep, Steele and the Kents followed in another. The rest of the party, except for Dr. and Mrs. Bentley, crowded into the ambulance which someone had thoughtfully dispatched from the camp to convey any wounded or weary travelers. The Bentleys scorned assistance, since they wanted "to stretch the kinks out after being on the ship so long," and trudged bravely along the plank sidewalk, while the doctor shouted derogatory taunts at the weaklings who rode.

Jim dropped his sister off at their house and clattered on to camp, with the parting order that she was to rest. Nothing appealed to her more at the moment, and it was annoying to see Warner Steele spring from the second jeep as it slowed and come stalking toward her. How disgustingly neat and energetic he looks! was Delight's envious reflection.

"My personal welcome home!" the captain exclaimed, stepping past her to open the front door with a gallant gesture. "I feel as though I should carry you over the threshold in the approved manner."

"Approved only for my bridegroom," she reminded acidly, "and you are definitely not that!"

His face darkened and his smile disappeared. "You never can tell, Dee. If you knew what I've been through since word came that you were lost—"

"You and me too, Captain!" she retorted tiredly. "I'm a bit unstrung myself, so if you'll excuse me I'll retire, and in Macbeth's deathless phrase 'knit up the ravell'd sleave of care.'"

"But give me a few moments, Dee! There's so much I want to discuss."

"Not now. You'll see me tonight at the Bentleys'."

"In a crowd? That won't do at all! I want you alone, now!"

Delight faced him with lifted chin and smoldering eyes.

"At the moment I can think of nothing I'd enjoy less. If you don't want me in screaming hysterics will you *please go away!*"

There was sufficient evidence of mental turmoil in the last words to warn even the dullest suitor. Captain Steele retreated.

"Tonight, then. I—"

The ungentle closing of the door left him alone.

If Delight hoped for peace by dismissing *him,* she was disappointed. Once in the house she was engulfed in the tumultuous welcome of Tamara Rostov.

"You came back, Miss Delight!" the girl sobbed. "You did come back! I was afraid you were drowned, and I prayed and prayed so hard—and promised—" She choked, flung her arms around Delight and hugged her wildly.

"Don't!" was all Delight could gasp. "Tamara, please, you hurt!" she protested, when she had partially extricated herself from the bearlike grip. She laughed, although tears came to her eyes at the warmth of the Indian girl's welcome. "You really do seem glad to see me, so why didn't you come down to the wharf with all the rest?"

Tamara drew back with flaming cheeks.

"I didn't dare, Miss Delight!" She looked down, scuffing her foot on the rug. "I wanted to—then I thought, No! That Lieutenant Mason would be there, too."

"Why naturally. But I thought you liked him."

"Yes." The girl twisted the bracelet on her arm, refusing to look up. "He's a dream-boat, but—but I couldn't go near him. I—I cheated him!"

"What are you talking about?"

"He asked me to do something for him—we had a secret, like I told you. But I didn't do it. I could have, but I was afraid—afraid to hurt—" She bit her lip in time to stop the stammering explanation and at last met Delight's puzzled eyes.

"I'll do it now, though, Miss Delight! Honest I will! Because I promised the Holy Mother, if she brought you back safe, I'd do what the lieutenant asked. I have to do right, like you told me, even if—" her voice was firm with resignation—"even if I lose my Jed."

"Tam dear, pull yourself together." Delight wondered if she could retain a grip on her own senses. "I haven't the slightest idea what you're talking about."

"You were right, the other day," Tamara continued, paying no attention to the other's protest. "You gave me a good sermon. You told me to remember what Father Darley teaches us—that I mustn't lie or steal or anything—even for Jed. I didn't believe you then, but now I know you were right."

"Of course!" Delight blushed to remember her cool assumption of superiority when she delivered that sermon. "Never mind, Tam, if I preached to you then, you prophesied truly for me. I was amused when you said, 'Just the same, I think you would shoot good for your man.' But it happened!"

As she told of her encounter with the spy her hands trembled at the memory of the cold fury which gripped her when she saw Bill Mason lying bloody and still beside the fire. With an effort she kept her voice from breaking while she ended, "So you see, Tamara, when the chips were down, as they say, I did shoot good. Even," she added ruefully, "if it wasn't for 'my man.'"

The Indian girl, who had listened with open mouth and wide eyes, stood for a moment studying her mistress. Then the beginning of a smile twitched the full red lips.

"You sure about that?" she demanded softly.

Delight could find no answer except an exasperated, "I'm going upstairs to bed!"

At Headquarters Major Tremaine requested Mason to dictate a statement of the events which resulted in the capture of the enemy agent.

"I'm counting on Whitaker flying him to the States for trial," he explained, "and there are reasons why I don't want you dragged along to testify. That might take weeks. I hope your sworn statement will be enough for them."

"I'll run out to the field with it myself when I finish," Mason offered. "They might have some questions. And I can show them the lump on my head, too," he chuckled.

"That's what worries me, Lieutenant. So far, all they can hold the man for is assault on you, the rest is guesswork. Unless his pistol matches the bullet our surgeon took out of Corporal Fanning, we have nothing but the corporal's *impression* of his attacker—in the dark. And bullet testing will have to be done in the States. They might take their time about that and other things and hold you there indefinitely."

"How about his attack on Kasan Charley?"

"Where's the proof?" Tremaine demanded. "Charley saw nothing but a lot of stars when he got it. A couple of buttons and a wisp of charred cloth which Chief Peter *thinks* came off a yellow coat worn by a white man. A smart defense lawyer would have a field day kicking such evidence to pieces." He shrugged. "Make your statement as detailed as possible; we'll hope that it will satisfy the Air Force."

Because the only available clerk who knew shorthand was sadly out of practice Mason was obliged to dictate his story at a snail's pace. In addition he discovered that reliving the time on the island with Delight made it difficult to preserve the officially impersonal tone suited to such a report. But he finished at last and then waited with the major while the clerk transcribed his notes on a noisy typewriter in the next room.

They were reading over the statement before Mason signed it when Captain Kent appeared in the doorway.

"Am I interrupting, Major?" he asked.

"Come in, Captain. We are working up a report to go to the Air Force on our spy capture."

"Need any help?"

"We could use plenty," Tremaine confessed. "I'm not happy about this, Kent, afraid we may lose the lieutenant as a necessary witness for Lord knows how long. His dented skull is about the extent of our tangible evidence against the man." He looked up with sudden hope. "Unless you've dug up something."

"Not I." The captain was sober except for a twinkle in his eye. "But a couple of my operatives may have—er—unearthed something you can use." He spoke over his shoulder. "Bring them in, Sergeant!"

A thickset noncom solemnly escorted Kent's son to a place in front of the major's desk, meanwhile keeping a restraining hand on Igloo's collar. The dog sank on its haunches beside Harry and grinned wolfishly at Tremaine.

Harry Kent, pink with embarrassment and excitement, silently laid on the desk a pair of red canvas shoes crusted with dark brown earth. The major exchanged a look of stunned amazement with Mason.

"Tell it, Harry," Kent prompted.

"Sir!" The boy gasped, swallowed loudly. "Those look like the shoes that spy had on when I saw him—when he was talking to Miss Delight. Lookit! Red, and with thick soles of that white rubbery stuff."

"Where in the world did *you* get them, Harry?" asked Tremaine.

"Out by Charley's shack, sir! As soon as I heard about him I went over there to see where it happened—you know, his getting conked—and I was just looking around." He darted an apprehensive glance at his father and defended, "Chief Peter told me I could, Pop. He was right there all the time. And Igloo"—he dropped one hand on the massive head—"Igloo poked and sniffed around and then he started digging for something—and he dug up those shoes."

"This was near the shack?"

"Sure, right close to it, in a hole under the back wall. Not very deep either, sir!"

Tremaine leaned back in his chair, smiling at Mason.

"We're not as lacking in evidence as we thought, Lieutenant. The attack on Kasan Charley should be enough to hold your young friend, without your presence, until they have time to pin the espionage angle on him." Tilting forward again until he could rest his elbows on the desk, he nodded at Harry Kent.

"Nice work, soldier, your father should be proud of you. As a detective, you're tops! Our enemy agent seems to have tripped over you more than once, because if you hadn't reported his meeting with my sister we might never have suspected him."

He reached across the desk and gravely shook hands with the boy.

"You may not rate a decoration for this, Harry, but you've earned the gratitude of the whole outfit."

Harry stood first on one foot and then the other, self-consciously.

"Well, gee! I'm glad we helped," he mumbled. "I guess— I mean—" He hesitated. "I know I mustn't talk about this to anybody," he admitted sadly. "But it would be entertaining to tell—"

"We'd rather you kept it under your hat, Harry," was Tremaine's quiet suggestion. "I think you know why."

"Yes, *sir!* And anyway I can make up stuff just as exciting, I guess." Filled with the importance of a secret Harry went out, his head high and Igloo pattering faithfully alongside.

"That," Captain Kent sighed, "was no idle boast, Major!"

XXI

THE BENTLEY dining room had seldom contained a gayer congregation than the guests who enjoyed Bertha's Welcome Home Dinner. The hostess, doing honor to the occasion and violence to her complexion in an off-the-shoulder dress spattered with blatant orange poppies, set the pace by her unconcealed excitement over the presence of the elusive Lieutenant Mason. It was plain that she foresaw all sorts of intriguing developments with Delight also on hand.

Her expectations were dashed by the cool formality of their meeting. Delight wore the same pink sheath she'd chosen for her first dinner party, and her glowing beauty set Mason's heart racing, but for all the sign his tanned face gave she might have been still enveloped in the tattered blanket.

Although the girl seethed inwardly at his apparent indifference, she gritted her teeth and met it with equal calm. When she had exchanged a polite word or two with Bill she moved on to greet Susan Kent, her captain and the other guests.

One of Mrs. Bentley's exotic dinners, following the round of cocktails, warmed the assemblage to hilarious comparisons of their various hardships on the glacier trip and during the night of anxiety in the crowded sleeping quarters aboard the ship. But Delight took little part in this discussion. Until now she had not realized, or at least had not admitted, that she was utterly worn out, in a daze of weariness, both physical and emotional. This meal began to seem only a continuation of that first dinner party, as though she had been dozing in her chair and dreamed all the excitement of these last days, and was now awake again.

Almost the same roster of guests was present as before, augmented by the townspeople who had been on the trip. Well, of course Bill Mason hadn't been present last time—hastily she stifled the thought of him. Anyway, the same ruddy sunlight flooded through the broad windows to drown the paler glow of candles and turn the cedar-paneled walls to shining amber. With a twinge of alarm she wondered if Babbling Bertha would shortly pierce the din of conversation with that shrill laugh and a demand for the name of Delight's "fiancé."

This time, however, it was Dr. Bentley who interrupted, by tinkling a spoon against his glass for attention. With portentous gravity but twinkling eyes, he announced:

"I believe, Major, that we have been forbearing long enough to satisfy all the conventions. So now, for Heaven's sake, tell us what we're dying to hear. And I charge you, in Othello's words, 'a round unvarnish'd tale deliver.' What about your spy?"

The instant silence testified to unanimous interest. Jim laughed.

"Correction, please, Doctor! Not *my* spy; I haven't the slightest claim to glory in that operation. But certainly there's no reason why you should be kept in suspense about most of the details, so I'll request Lieutenant Mason to bring you up to date."

Bill leaned forward, hands clasped in his lap, and surveyed the circle of expectant eyes.

"I can't claim the glory either. You all know who actually caught the spy." His look at Delight startled her with its warmth.

"Please don't go over that again!" she begged. "Actually, I'm not too happy about it."

"You regret defeating the enemy?" he asked, amused.

"No, but it isn't pleasant to—to hurt a young man, whoever he is. They won't shoot him, will they?"

"Not a chance. Don't lose any sleep over him. Actually, you see, you did him a service when you nabbed him. I haven't much to brag about in the affair, but I did make a few right guesses. One was my suggestion that this lad, whose real name nobody needs to know, was *forced* into espionage.

"It seems that his parents left him several years ago to finish his education in the States, while they paid a visit to their old homeland. You may all have three guesses as to the homeland," Bill offered, with the wry warning, "but I won't tell you if you are right. Anyway, you know how these things are worked; the government there grabs father and mother and suggests to son—the young man we are discussing—"

"Call him Joe College, if he must have a name for your story," the major suggested helpfully.

"O.K. Joe College is informed by that—er—unfriendly
135

government that he can make sure his folks go on living by signing up with their Intelligence Department. I suppose he hadn't much choice, really; if he was noble enough to refuse and sacrifice his parents, they'd hardly let *him* live to go around bragging about it."

Mason scowled at his plate. "Sounds fantastic in this day and age, but believe me, I've known of such things happening. Anyway, the boy, Joe College, plays along, takes all the special technical education and other training they order—until they have this chance to use him."

Warner Steele swung in his chair to face Bill.

"I take it that *he* told you this. What sort of strong-arm methods, dredged from your foreign service we've heard so much about, did you use to break him down to a confession?"

"He didn't break down, Captain." Mason ignored the sneering tone. "In fact he's about as jaunty a captured prisoner as I've ever run into." With a glance at Delight he asked, "Did you notice his rather flip remark to you on the wharf?"

"Yes, but I didn't think *you* did." Her cheeks grew hot as she realized how her answer betrayed a keen interest in Bill Mason at that time and she made quick diversion. "It was exactly the way he acted when I first met him—as though he hadn't a care in the world."

"He's keeping up the act—if it is an act. As soon as he made sure that we would put him away where his—his employers—can't get at him he cooperated with apparent pleasure. All he asks is for us to let the word reach those employers that he's securely jugged."

"Why tell them anything?" demanded Mrs. Bentley indignantly.

"Because then they'll have no reason to hold his parents any longer, we hope. And in that case, with them safely back in the U.S., we might find him very useful ourselves. As I predicted, he is an unusually brilliant electronic engineer."

"He's a brainy cuss in many ways, I judge," said Captain Kent. "Witness the way he dodged us for two days."

Bill nodded. "Quite a performance. Knowing the country well he had no trouble in hiding, first in the woods and then in Kasan Charley's cabin. By the way, Dr. Bentley, you examined Kasan and agree with our medic, I understand."

"Absolutely. That Charley has a remarkably hard head, even for an Indian. He'll be up and around in a few days."

"Our spy acted relieved to hear that verdict, and I think he was sincere. He apologized for having to whack the old man." Mason grinned. "No apology to me or Fanning, the wounded guard, though. As Army men we're supposed to expect such treatment in the course of duty, I guess.

"But getting back to our spy's escape; he got a real break when he chose Kasan's shack for a hideout. With the Indian away it not only gave him a chance to shave off his beard and swap his rather noticeable costume for some Indian clothing, but let him intercept Captain Pepper's message about the glacier trip. That offered a perfect chance for him to get out of town and rejoin the ship that dropped him off here."

"Then he did come from that strange ship we heard about?" Steele snapped. "We ought to alert everybody again and find her!"

"Too late for that," Bill said. "Noon today was the deadline for his returning to her. After that she pulled out for good."

"He told you that, and you *believed* him?" Steele growled.

Major Tremaine waved him to silence. "It doesn't make much difference, Captain, we aren't going to hunt her down. What could we do if we found her? Ask impolite questions, or send a boarding party to capture her? Neither of which would improve relations with her country. Go ahead with your story, Mason."

"You all know the rest. The spy snapped at the chance to leave the steamer by piloting us ashore. He intended to run out of sight of her, land us on some beach where Delight could hunt for fossils, then take off in the boat. My ordering him back to King Crab Beach, in plain sight of the ship, he says, made that a little riskier, but he was still determined to try it.

"The tidal wave was what licked him. He didn't dare risk leaving our island in the fog, and during the night when it cleared up a bit, he couldn't because the tide left the boat high and dry. In the morning he grabbed his first opportunity, laid me out with no trouble at all and took off.

"He'd have made it, too, if he hadn't overlooked one factor —that our heroine can shoot like a sniper!" Bill gave Delight an admiring bow. "He didn't bother with my forty-five because I was *out*, and he'd never seen a woman who could hit a barn door with such a heavy gun. He says the slug that knocked a hunk out of the gunwale beside him was the most staggering surprise of his young life."

The major snorted. "Surprised me to hear of it, too! Have you been practicing secretly, Dee?"

"Of course not! I don't know what made me suddenly so expert, except that I had the most awful feeling he *must* be stopped." That, she thought, was only half the story, and she shuddered at the recurring picture of Bill Mason's face smeared with blood. Anything to banish that nightmare! "You haven't told us, Bill," she urged hurriedly, "whether the spy found out any secrets at the airfield."

"He denies it, says he was on his way *into* the hangar when the guard jumped him. That's an additional reason for him to want to stay safe in our jail and not rejoin his friends —as a failure."

Mason frowned doubtfully. "On that one point I'm not sure I believe him, since he *did* try desperately to regain his ship. But it doesn't matter." He grinned, with a look at his watch. "Right now he's on a plane for the States, and any information he *did* get won't be of much use to him where he'll be for the next few years."

"That," Tremaine said, "would seem to wind up what mystery writers would call 'The Affair of the College Boy.' And its successful conclusion offers a fitting occasion for an official announcement." He left his chair to shake hands with a mystified Bill Mason. "May I be the first to congratulate you, Captain Mason?" Jim asked with a broad grin.

"Captain!" Bill repeated, flushing.

"Yes, Captain, your promotion arrived with other official mail on the plane this afternoon." He resumed his seat and waited for the excited chorus of approval and congratulations to subside, then addressed Mason again. "This has no connection with our recent spy hunt, by the way. It's long overdue."

He cleared his throat portentously and glanced about the table.

"I have another piece of news which may interest you. Some months ago I was sent here with Captain Kent to put this task force on a more efficient basis. Apparently we have succeeded—at least to the satisfaction of Headquarters—as both of us are to be assigned elsewhere. Together, I hope," he interpolated with a smile for Susan Kent. "Anyway, I was directed to suggest the officer best qualified to take over here in Totum, and I had no hesitation in naming William Hamilton Mason."

There was a brust of laughing applause to which all but Steele contributed. The major raised his voice above it.

"You will be glad to hear, Captain Mason, that your experience and qualifications are so well known to the general commanding this area that he didn't consider my glowing recommendation in the least overdrawn. When I leave here after the first of the month I shall take great pleasure in turning over this post to you as commanding officer."

This time there were cheers with the applause, cheers which

stopped short as Mason leaped to his feet. Tremaine laughed.

"Got a speech of acceptance all prepared?" he joked.

There was no answering smile from Mason. His face was ghastly in its pallor, with deep lines slashed about eyes and compressed lips.

"No, sir, no speech," he muttered and then burst out in a choking, husky voice. "Major Tremaine, I must talk to you! I can't let this go on. Sir, could we go to your office at once?"

Tremaine had not been a commanding officer for years without learning to read faces and emotions, to recognize a crisis of nerves. He nodded agreement, then turned to Mrs. Bentley.

"I know you will excuse us, there seems to be official business which requires immediate attention." He followed Mason, who, with a muttered apology, was leaving the room. Over his shoulder he said, "Someone will see you home, Dee, if I'm not back before this party breaks up."

"Escort duty accepted with pleasure," announced Warner Steele before anyone else could offer.

Delight silently vowed she would make other arrangements more to her taste, but she counted on a little time for that. She had none. Dinner being over, the departure of the two officers for what was obviously destined to be a painful discussion brought the party to an untimely end. Although she was glad to leave, she took no pleasure in descending the Bentley steps with Steele's hand firmly under her arm.

The aroma of numerous cocktails still clung about him and she gently disengaged her arm and moved aside.

"This is unnecessary, Captain," she said smiling, and to disguise the reason for her avoidance of his grasp waved at the sky. "We're not treading a dangerous path in the dead of night, you know. Did you ever see a more glorious sunset? The islands stand out against the golden bay like great heaps of sapphires and emeralds. Really, I don't need an escort in broad daylight."

"Never let it be said that a Steele allowed a lovely lady to walk home from a party alone, daylight or not," he protested. However, he abandoned his effort to link arms, but persisted in accompanying her. "I consider it my lucky night, since your brother and Mason put the kiss of death on Babbling Bertha's soiree."

"Poor Mrs. Bentley was disappointed, wasn't she?" The girl tried for a casual air. "But I think everyone there was as tired as I." She would have welcomed the walk home through the crystal evening air alone with her teeming thoughts, and she resented the heavily affectionate interruptions of her companion.

They had almost reached the bridge on the road from town to the camp when she heard hurrying footsteps behind them, turned and recognized a possible savior.

"Why, here's Tamara!" she exclaimed eagerly. "She will go with me, Captain, so you needn't bother." As the Indian girl overtook them, Delight asked, "Going my way? I'll be glad of your company."

"No, please, Miss Delight!" Tamara gasped. "I've got to go to the camp quick!" With a breathless sob she broke into a run.

"Tamara! What's the matter? Has something happened to Jed?" When there was no answer Delight looked up anxiously at Steele. "Have you heard anything about trouble there?"

He shrugged. "Don't bother your head about her. These natives go haywire without the least excuse. Seem to enjoy it."

"Tamara doesn't." Recalling the girl's abysmal despair after that other visit to Crane she shivered in sympathy. "This night is full of *yek*, isn't it?" she asked absently.

"How's that again?" On the pretext of not hearing, he moved closer and again took her arm.

"Just an Indian superstition." Delight gave up trying to avoid him and let him talk, but with no understanding of what he said. Almost walking in a trance she came to her front steps and automatically turned to him. "Thank you for seeing me home. Good night."

As she went across the porch he followed.

"Mind if I come in for a minute?"

She definitely did mind, but she tried to discourage him without actual refusal.

"It's rather late, Captain, and I've had a long day."

"I know, but I want to talk to you." Stubbornly he followed her inside, tossed his cap on the table and faced her, hands on hips. "We haven't had a moment alone since you got back from that damned fool glacier trip with Mason!"

The contempt in the words was unmistakable and Delight's anger kindled at it.

"That's not the way you described the expedition when *you* planned to go."

"If I had been along it wouldn't have mattered that you had to spend the night on that island with me—"

"*Mattered?*" she broke in sharply. "What do you mean by that? Are you being mid-Victorian," with an ironic laugh, "suggesting that my good name has been ruined because I spent that night with Bill?"

"Of course not! But it was unfortunate that Mason was the one."

"I think it was most fortunate! No one could have been
140

a better companion." At the memory of his tenderness her eyes filled with tears. She turned away and in an attempt to hide her emotion jeered, "If your delicate sense of propriety is outraged, remember that we were chaperoned by the spy."

Steele caught her shoulders and swung her to face him, his blue eyes burning into hers.

"A good companion, was he? Who wouldn't be good to you, Dee? I would! I'm crazy about you, have been since you landed here. But you won't give me a chance—"

"You'll *never* get that chance!" She made no effort to throw off the hands gripping her but stood rigid, only her voice shaking with resentment. "Let me go, Captain Steele!"

"I'll never let you go, Dee! I made up my mind to that the first day I met you. Darling, you've got everything I want in a wife—beauty, brains, spirit. Forget that tramp Mason—"

Her stinging slap, as she twisted away from him, rocked him back on his heels. White-faced, he glared at her, a vein in his forehead swelling and throbbing. Something in her eyes betrayed her and he swore in a savage whisper, "By God, so that's it! You're in love with him!"

She pressed her hands against her face, her whole body shaking. Desperately she struggled to utter a denial, but the words would not come.

"You've fallen for him!" Steele rasped, towering over her, his fists clenched. "That rotten bounder, making love to you, when he—"

"He never has!" At least she could deny that with truth, even though, worn to the breaking point with hours of strain, she knew it sounded as a forlorn wail. "He's ignored me as though I were—were nothing! He has a girl back home."

"*A girl?*" Steele's laugh was scornful. "He told you that? I can tell you a lot more."

"I won't listen! Bill was afraid you'd told me lies about him!"

"He was afraid I'd tell you the truth!" Rage lifted his voice to a near shout. "I ought to know, I was there in Washington with him. Damn it, *I* was the one who went out in the rain and picked a girl off the street for him—for a thousand bucks—and brought her in! I can tell you—"

He stopped, the horror in her eyes piercing through his anger.

"Don't look like that, dear. When you know the whole story—"

"*I know now!*" Delight whispered, shrinking away from him. She felt the wall against her back and spread her arms to brace against it. Steele's figure wavered before her in a swirling crimson haze and his voice still seemed to hammer in her ears.

This was a thing far outside Warner Steele's experience. He shifted uneasily, his anger dulled by alarm. He put a tentative hand on her arm.

"Sit down, Dee, take it easy. I shouldn't blow up that way when you're tired."

He gave up the attempt to calm her when he realized that she did not hear him, was not even aware of him standing there. Her dilated blue eyes looked through him, beyond him, like a sleepwalker's vacant stare.

"Dee, I'm leaving. Sorry I picked a bad time." That haunted glare shook his nerve and he retreated to the table. Snatching up his cap, he hurried to the door. The girl did not move. He went out, cursing his jealousy-driven tongue.

XXII

SEATED at the desk in his office Major Tremaine waved at a chair.

"Sit down, Lieutenant—excuse me, *Captain*. Smoke?"

"No, thank you." Declining both invitations, Mason stood at ramrod attention and came to the point at once. "Sir, I realize that your recommendation must have had a lot to do with my getting promoted at last, and you'll think my request is rank ingratitude. But I must ask you to use your influence now to have me transferred."

Tremaine took out a cigarette and lighted it carefully as his eyes studied the haggard lines etched deeply in the younger man's pale cheeks.

"Transfer to another post?"

"To the States."

"Oh?" Jim lifted a humorous eyebrow to take the sting out of, "Dreading a winter up here?"

Mason's flush relieved some of the strained look. "No, sir, of course not. I have to go back—to—to attend to some personal business."

"You're passing up a chance to command this post, a boost toward your majority?" Tremaine concealed his amazement by leaning forward to drop some ash in the tray on his desk. "You're out of your head, man! Why not attend to your personal business from here?"

"Because I can't stay here! I—" Mason hesitated, clenched his hands and relaxed them. "I've got to get away—because I'm in love with your sister."

142

The major kept his position, elbows on desk, one hand tapping the cigarette on the tray. He watched the ashes fall as he asked quietly, "Said anything to her?"

"No!"

"Not going to?" Jim persisted, eyes still on the monotonously tapping cigarette. "Shouldn't she have a chance to decide whether you stay or go?"

"Don't *you* tempt me, sir! I've been through the tortures of the damned these last forty-eight hours. I can't stand much more." He ground one fist into the other palm. "You know Delight is engaged to a man in the States, but even if she wasn't—if she were free—I couldn't ask her." He leaned forward suddenly, planting his hands on the desk. "Sir, *I'm* not free!"

Tremaine looked up under heavy brows. "Do you care to explain that?"

"I'm married!"

The major nodded slowly, twisted in his chair and reached toward the safe behind him. Then he withdrew his hand, swung back and picked up the cigarette he had laid down.

"So you're married," he said evenly. "That isn't entered on your records, Captain Mason, and I believe you've never mentioned it before. Suppose you tell me about it."

Mason drew a deep breath and straightened.

"That's what I want to do, sir, but it was such a miserable piece of—of damned foolishness that I'm ashamed to talk about it. I've hidden it all this time, run away from it, until something Dee said—" He shut his teeth on the explanation. "Something changed my mind, and I'm going to face it—right it if I can.

"It happened years ago, just after I'd received my commission at the Point. Four of us got together in Washington at a hotel to have a real wingding of a celebration and dazzle the world with our new uniforms." An angry flush drove the pallor from his face. "Warner Steele crashed the party with a couple of civilians. I didn't want him, never had liked him at the Point, but I couldn't very well throw him out—we were classmates."

"I know that," said Tremaine.

"Yes, sir. And you know—well, you mentioned that there wasn't good feeling between us." Bill strained to keep his voice under control. "That's putting it mildly; we never got along from the first—had a few real set-tos." He bit his lip and changed the subject. "Anyway, Steele horned in that night. We had dinner in a private dining room at the hotel, and because I had more money than the rest—at twenty-one I came into a large income from my parents' estate, sir—I insisted on throwing the party, the whole thing.

"So, since I'd closed my local checking account when I left the Point I had considerable cash with me, and the party turned into quite a blowout, with liquor to burn."

He paused to rub a hand over his chin, and when Tremaine waited in silence, he went on doggedly.

"I'm not trying to apologize for my actions, Major, but honestly, I'd never been much of a drinker. That night, though, with four years of training finished, and with the others whooping it up, I kept pace with the best of them—or the *worst,* I suppose. Along toward the end of the evening we were all high, yelling, kidding each other about the times we'd slipped one over on the O.D.—or hadn't—bragging about how we'd show the Army what new blood could do. You know how it was, sir."

"I know," Tremaine agreed wryly.

"Well, the talk got around to women, of course, and there was more bragging, climaxed by Steele's announcement that *he* didn't intend to struggle along on Army pay. He was going to grab off a wealthy wife to keep him in style. Said he went to West Point because an officer's uniform would be a big help in that project.

"That burned me, sir. All my life the uniform has meant a lot to me. I made some remark about Warner being just the type who'd use it to feather his nest—and the trouble started.

"He staggered upright at his end of the table and pointed at me. I remember how his arm wavered and every word he said. 'Sour grapes, Mason! You'll never do that, will you?' he shouted. 'No, because you're yellow—afraid of women!' He let out that sneering laugh of his. 'I'd bet a thousand dollars you'll never have nerve enough to get married!'

"Everyone roared at that and started riding me, because it had been sort of a standing joke at the Point that I was painfully bashful. I never took a girl to any of the parties—never went to them, in fact—always managed to have duty somewhere else. So I really took a beating from the crowd, although I noticed Steele was too busy whispering with one of the civilians to make any more cracks.

"But I was too far gone that night to be bashful; all I knew was that Steele was questioning my courage and I couldn't stand for that. I pounded a bottle on the table and called him a liar.

" 'I'm not afraid of anything!' I shouted. 'I'll marry anyone —if she's young, white, and looks clean!'

"Warner weaved around the table to me and roared, 'Is it a bet, Mason? For a thousand bucks?' and I shoved him away and said, 'No bet, Steele! I won't take your money, it's probably as dirty as you are! But you produce the girl and I'll give *her* a thousand to marry me!' "

Tremaine's eyebrows arched. "You wouldn't bet, but you'd pay out a thousand dollars? For what?"

"To prove my courage—can you imagine a more stupid gesture!" Mason exclaimed bitterly. "Drunk as I was, it seemed as though I must prove beyond a doubt that I was a real man! The money meant nothing to me, especially in my condition that night.

"There was a real riot then, with the whole gang hooting and razzing me. Steele and one of the friends he'd brought in, name of Goddard, got in some nasty cracks until I was fit to murder them." Mason paused, scowling, to wipe his sweating face. "This Goddard, a cousin of Steele's and the one he'd been whispering with, I'd met before and never liked much, and by now I was hating him. Anyway, I took him and Steele by the scruff of their necks and slammed them together to silence them. 'You two lay off!' I yelled, or something like that. 'I've made my proposition; now you put up or shut up!'

"Major, I nearly dropped when Goddard pulled a bunch of papers from his pocket, slapped one down on the table in front of me and laid a fountain pen on it. It was an application for a marriage license, and he slid a blank license alongside it. I remembered then that he was some kind of a city magistrate. 'Sign here, Mason,' he jeered. 'If we can dig up a girl I'll tie the knot.' I guess that sobered me enough to be able to think for a minute, and I laughed. 'Ever hear about blood tests and waiting periods?' I asked cockily, and to show I wasn't worried I gulped another drink.

"That one knocked me off base again and in a daze I heard him yelping that the District of Columbia didn't require a blood test and he had pull enough to get the three-day wait fixed up afterward. The next thing I knew I'd signed the paper and Steele went charging out to find a bride for me."

Mason had to stop to clear his throat and brace trembling hands on the desk. Tremaine pushed back his chair and walked thoughtfully over to the window. Hands clasped behind him he stood looking out, with the sunset-crimsoned sky glowing on his face and the gold leaves on his shoulders.

"Shall I go on, sir?" Mason asked thickly. "It's not only disgusting—it must seem unbelievable to you."

"Better get it over with," Tremaine advised without turning around.

"Right, sir! Well, some of the fellows had sense enough left to try and talk me out of it while Steele was gone. Not Goddard, though. He kept needling me. 'Losing your nerve, eh?' he taunted. 'The yellow's starting to show, soldier!' Stuff like that. If they hadn't held me I'd have socked him."

Mason paced across the room and back, pounding his fists together as he talked.

"He and Steele must have cooked the thing up while the others were riding me. Maybe Goddard mentioned that he had the necessary papers with him, and Steele grabbed the chance to make a sucker of me, to the tune of a cool thousand. We were all drunk, but that doesn't excuse *me!*"

He halted and faced the major.

"Steele came back about then, and he had a woman with him. I can still feel the disgust that shook me when I saw her—a hat pulled low, dark glasses, a long brown coat, and all of it shining wet. It must have been raining like the devil. Steele's hair was plastered down and his uniform soaked, but he swaggered in like a general. 'Here's your bride-to-be,' he announced with a drunken leer. 'She'll marry you for a thousand and agree never to see you again.'

"Goddard took her off in a corner, asked some questions, wrote things on the papers and had her sign. Then they lined us up. Steele trying to keep me on my feet, and the woman shivering so that she could only mumble her answers, while Goddard—Goddard married us!" Mason's voice trembled as he relived the shadowy scene.

His abrupt laugh was harsh with contempt. "I used the ring I always wore—a seal ring that had been my father's. I wonder that his spirit didn't strike me dead! Then I hauled my roll out of my pocket, but I couldn't manage it. Goddard had to count out the thousand dollars for the woman. He gave her the money and the certificate he'd made out, and she left. I never saw her after that."

He wiped his forehead again and took a deep breath.

"There it is, sir, the whole miserable story. I was a fool to get drunk—the first time in my life and the last, believe me —and more of a fool to think I had to prove my courage that way. But I've paid a price for it. I turned a clean page in my life when I woke the next day, and I've kept it clean, but I'm still paying." He shook his head like a punch-drunk fighter. "I crossed Steele and Goddard off my list for good— after it was too late."

Major Tremaine turned from the window and became a dark silhouette against the fading sunset glow. His voice seemed to come from far away.

"Who was the woman?"

"I don't know. Neither her name nor what she looked like."

"You must have realized that if that marriage was legal it had to be recorded. A check at the registry there would have given you her name."

"I didn't want to know," Mason admitted wearily. "My

146

orders took me out of Washington the next afternoon, and ever since then I've been overseas, on one assignment after another, until I came here. Occupied Germany, our embassy in Russia, then Korea and the Far East—but you know all that, sir.

"It was my own choice; I was running away from my disgrace. Now I want to 'face up to it,' " he quoted softly, "and hope it may disappear like—" He stopped short, flushing, and switched to a firmer tone. "If I can get within striking distance of Washington I hope to trace the woman and straighten out this mess."

The major sat at his desk, chin on hands, and eyed the younger man coldly.

"How about—eh—Goddard? He must have the facts. You never contacted him?"

"*He* contacted me!" Mason snapped. "Got track of me after a while and wrote that the woman wanted money—five hundred dollars—and she wanted it paid through him, so I couldn't bother her. I had a flash of hope then, because a lawyer I talked to said the marriage might be annulled if I bought her off.

"I wrote back to Goddard for her name and address, explaining why I wanted to get in touch with her myself."

"You say this correspondence was *after* you went overseas?" Jim asked frowning. When Mason nodded, he took out a cigarette and tapped it gently on his thumb, seeming buried in thought. "But you didn't get in touch with her?"

"No. Goddard replied that the girl was perfectly satisfied the way things were, provided she got the money. And if *I* wasn't satisfied she was ready to live with me! Lord knows that was the last thing I wanted, so she had me cold. Besides, I knew I deserved everything I got. As I had plenty of money and no family left, I decided to pay for my folly. So I sent the five hundred."

He stared gloomily at the major. "I don't need to tell you that I started something with that payment. Fifteen hundred and a gold ring wasn't enough for her; the demands have been coming pretty regularly ever since. Wouldn't blame you if you laughed at me! Believe me, when I get in a mess I go the whole hog!"

Tremaine did not laugh. He rolled the cigarette back and forth on the desk, watching it soberly.

"Any proof that she ever received the money you've been sending?"

"No. If I can get a transfer I'll make it my business to find Goddard, pry out the information I want, if I have to strangle him, and try to get this woman off my neck. I'd force

147

it from Steele but I'm sure he doesn't know anything or he'd have tried to sell it to me. Maybe he bribed Crane, hoping to get a lead from my mail he could cash in on."

The major leaned back and shook his head.

"I'm sorry for you, Mason. You got a raw deal, no matter how much you were to blame. I don't see how I can help you about a transfer, now that you are slated to be commanding officer here. I feel—"

A knock on the door stopped him. Tremaine flung an impatient *"Come in!"* that rattled the windows.

A noncom eased his grizzled head cautiously past the half-opened door.

"Excuse me, Major, but that Tamara dame wants to see Lieutenant Mason. At once!"

"Sergeant, I told you not to interrupt us!"

"Excuse me, Major, but she's been ramping around out here quite a while, waiting, crazy as a coot. She's sort of—hysterical, sir."

Mason, suddenly remembering, spoke quickly. "Sir, I asked her to have a talk with Crane about that matter of the mail. I gave her a pass to get in here with—perhaps you should hear what she has to say."

"Send her in, Sergeant," sighed the major.

Quick, soft footsteps in the hall. The Indian girl came through the doorway, saw the major at his desk and with a dismayed gasp backed against the door. Reddened eyes in a tear-stained pallid face flashed to Mason.

"Please—please, Lieutenant, sir," she stammered, "I must see you alone. Jed told me to see no one else."

"It's all right, Tamara. The Major will have to hear the whole story sometime, you know. You did see Crane after all?"

She nodded, clamping her lips in a thin line as though to withhold any details. Then with a sob, she confessed, "I saw him that same day, but I didn't tell you. I—I thought if you never knew what he said, it would save him. But it's no use to try and help my man by hurting someone else, is it?"

She fumbled in her blouse and held out the ivory flute.

"Here, take it, Lieutenant, sir. Jed said to give it to you. I wasn't going to, and I hid it in the church, and then Miss Delight and you were lost and I knew it—it was because of what I'd done!" She was crying and panting now. She thrust the flute into Mason's hands. "Take it!"

"What's this?" he asked, puzzled.

"The letter's inside—pull off the end! It's the only one Jed kept, he swears that. Somebody hired him to watch your mail, just like you thought."

"Who?"

"He won't tell you!" Tamara stamped her foot for emphasis. "You can kill him but he'll never tell. But he didn't show it to—to that other man. He said he was through, it was too dirty business for him. And he's sorry, Lieutenant, sir!" Her tone softened to pleading. "He *is* a good man. Won't you let him go?"

Mason twisted off the end of the carved flute and pulled out a crumpled envelope.

"Addressed to me, postmarked Washington," he told the major.

He nodded to Tamara and even managed a kind smile.

"Thank you, you came through for me when I trusted you and I won't forget that. I think you've helped Crane, too. I agree with you that he's a good man, much too good to waste. Let me talk to Major Tremaine, Tamara; we'll see what we can do, and I don't think you need to worry." He opened the door for her and closed it on her sobbing gratitude.

"Sorry for the interruption, Major, but—"

"What we were discussing was important," Jim interrupted, "but if that letter's too hot for Crane, then it may be important, too. Better see what it is."

Mason unfolded the single sheet of paper in the envelope, read a few words and with an exclamation turned the letter over to look at the signature. Angry color flooded his face as he went back to the beginning and read it through. He looked up at the other and tried to speak, but his dry lips could form no words. With a shaking hand he laid the paper on the desk in front of his commander.

"Read it," he muttered hoarsely and went over to the window to stand staring unseeingly at the purple mountains. "It's from Goddard."

Tremaine picked up the letter.

DEAR MASON:

This is practically a voice from the dead which is probably all right with you. Just came through my second heart attack here in the hospital and the next may be my finish. Don't want to face whatever God there is with a dirty conscience, so this letter. Corny, eh? But I mean it.

About that marriage, Mason—it's legal all right. I took care of that when your *pal,* Cousin Warner, talked me into it. He always hated you—envy, I guess.

Later on I was hard up, remembered how flush you were, so put the bite on you for "payments" to the girl—and kept the money, of course. You sure were an easy mark. Sorry; things look different to me now.

Sure, you can get the marriage annulled if you locate the woman. Don't remember her name but it is on the record

I filed. I do remember being surprised when she gave her address as the Hotel Gleason, where you were throwing the party and—

Tremaine slapped the letter on the desk and stood up. At the sound Mason turned, his face drawn and gray, eyes blazing.

"Finished, Major? I'm going to find Steele and by God—"

"Hold it!" Tremaine snapped. His usually ruddy cheeks were as pale as the other's. He swung to the safe, removed a small metal box, and unlocked it with a key from his pocket. He pulled out a folded paper and a small object which he tossed on the desk, where it rolled in a slow circle before it came to rest.

"Is that your ring, Mason?" he demanded harshly.

XXIII

BILL MASON leaned across the desk, staring at the circlet of gold as though it were a ticking bomb. Slowly he put out a hand to pick it up, twisting it so that the light brought out the coat of arms engraved on its seal. His lips tightened to a grim line as he raised his eyes to the man who sat tensely watching him.

"It is—it *was* mine, sir. But where did you—how—?"

"Where did I get it?" Tremaine took a moment to light a cigarette and tip back in his chair. His voice had regained its normal quiet but decisive tone when he answered the breathless question.

"Six years ago I came back to Washington from Formosa duty and found my wife dead and my sister desperately ill." He looked away from Mason's sympathetic eyes. "Gerry, my wife, had been picked up out of—of the gutter near the railroad station at daybreak. The police thought it was assault and robbery until—" He wet his lips.

"She was too badly smashed up for that—it must have been a hit-and-run accident—and she had a thousand dollars in large bills in her purse." At Mason's sharply indrawn breath he held up a silencing hand.

"That same morning the maid found Delight unconscious on the floor in their living room at the Hotel Gleason, with this note in her hand." He lifted a wrinkled slip of paper from the box and read with stoic composure:

I lied to you, Dee. I was going to ditch Jim even if we raised the money. Now that I have it, I'm off.

GERRY

Mason broke in, unable to restrain himself. "Good God! You think the woman I married was your *wife?*"

Again the major held up his hand for silence and the cold voice went relentlessly on.

"That ring was on the living room table in the suite my wife and sister shared. Beside it was this." He opened a folded paper and laid it deliberately before Mason. "A marriage certificate naming William Hamilton Mason and Geraldine Tremaine." He pushed the paper away with his fingertip as though it were too loathsome a thing to touch.

Staggered by the revelation and by the release it meant for him, Mason walked to the window and rested shaking hands on the sill.

"Sir!" he said hoarsely. "Do you realize what this means?"

"Do you think I've realized anything else for the last six years?" Tremaine groaned, for a split second losing his self-control. "The last shred of faith in my wife—" He clamped his jaw shut and scowled down at the marriage certificate.

The suffering in his face shocked Mason from preoccupation with his own situation.

"Major Tremaine!" he muttered. "There's nothing I can say that would be anything but empty words. My God, what rotten chance landed me in your command?"

Jim looked up with the ghost of a smile. "It wasn't chance, Captain, nor even the War Department, unassisted. For six years I have wanted to find out what sort of man this Lieutenant Mason might be." His hard eyes raked over the younger man, but he held to an icy monotone.

"It was easy enough to keep track of your career although our paths never crossed. But I wanted to *know* you. Then I took command of this post and was able to have you assigned here. I never expected—"

There was a commotion in the hall. The muffled but outraged protest, "No, Miss! Wait—"

The door burst open and Delight Tremaine rushed in, slammed the door and leaned back against it. Gasping for breath, her eyes enormous in a waxen face, she appealed to her brother.

"Jim! I know I shouldn't come in like this—but—Oh, *Jimmy darling!*" she moaned.

"Steady, Dee! Take it easy," he soothed, jumping to his feet and moving toward her. "What's the trouble?"

Outstretched hands gripped his and she pressed close, hiding her face against his shoulder, while shudders racked her slender body.

"Oh, Jimmy!" It was a muffled wail. "I *remember!*"

Gently he led her to a chair and stooped over her, his hands still holding hers with comforting strength.

"Don't take it so hard, dear," he begged. "We knew this would happen sooner or later, didn't we? Knew we must face whatever your memory brought."

"Yes—but," she sobbed, "this is horrible!"

He stroked her hair with one hand tenderly.

"Come on, sweetheart, get a grip on yourself and tell your big brother about it. What made you remember?"

"Captain Steele!" she gasped. The name brought a convulsive start from Mason at the window, but the girl did not realize that he was in the room. She had eyes only for her brother, drawing strength from his grave face so close to hers. "Captain Steele made me remember everything. It—it was as though something exploded in my head."

Her fingers locked and unlocked ceaselessly as she talked, her knuckles white with the desperate pressure.

"He took me home from the Bentleys'," she continued more evenly, "and came in. I didn't want him to, but he came in and talked. He was furious about that glacier trip —that Bill Mason was the man with me on the island. He said things about Bill—"

She lifted a trembling hand to her mouth and bit a finger, looking up at Jim in pathetic appeal.

"I hit him—as hard as I could," she confessed in a hoarse whisper.

"Good for you, sis!" was her brother's comment. She seemed not to hear.

"He threatened to warn you against Bill when you assigned him to the trip, and tonight he—he told me about that time in Washington—that he was the one who went out in the rain to get a girl for a thousand dollars!"

"I know, Dee."

"You *don't* know—you can't!" She brushed a hand across her eyes and stared at the blank wooden wall of the office. "When he said that, in a blinding flash the cloud which has covered those last days with Gerry split open and the whole hideous memory swept over me." She shivered.

"I remember our last evening, when we expected you and you didn't come. It had been a heartbreaking day for me. For weeks Gerry had been more and more restless, threatening to run away. But she owed someone money—she wouldn't tell me what for—and—and, Jim, there was a man she wanted to go away with!"

Delight choked and stammered, "I—I tried to hold her

—begging her not to hurt you so, pleading with her to wait until you came. And then—then you didn't come!"

"I couldn't, Dee. There was a bad plane crash where I was stationed. They needed me."

"I knew you'd come if you could, I told her that. I even promised to try and get the money she needed so desperately —get it somehow—if only she'd wait for you. I was nearly out of my mind, I couldn't bear to have your heart broken, Jim."

He pressed her hands in his, but she did not turn from staring at the wall, as though it were a screen where she saw past events exposed in terrifying sequence.

"I took all Mother's rings, the diamonds and even her plain gold wedding ring. I put on my oldest hat and coat, and a pair of sun glasses that Gerry had left on the hall table."

At that Mason took a shocked step forward, but Tremaine's look halted him in his tracks. The major's face was twisted with pain.

"I don't know why I wore the glasses," Delight muttered, "because it had been raining all evening. For a disguise, I suppose, when I went to the pawnshops within walking distance of the hotel. All of them. I tried them all!" she repeated wearily. "But no one would even *talk* to me, after they saw what I had. Suspicious. I don't blame them. I was nervous, shaking all over and stuttering when I tried to explain. And the diamonds were so valuable.

"Then finally, when I was coming back to our hotel, a man stopped me. He was very polite, but I was frightened. It was so dark I couldn't see him very well, and anyway I had on those sunglasses, but he was a second lieutenant and I thought perhaps he knew me, someone I'd met at an Army party. He didn't speak clearly—he'd been drinking—and he wanted me to come with him and do something to help another officer.

"I couldn't understand what he wanted, and we stood there in the rain and he talked about a thousand dollars. A thousand dollars to go through a marriage ceremony with an officer friend to—to save a huge fortune."

"You?" Tremaine whispered.

Delight paid no attention to the interruption. " 'A thousand dollars, a thousand dollars.' He kept saying it, and that was what Gerry needed. I couldn't think of anything else after that—Gerry needed it! You've always been so wonderful to me, Jim," she whispered with a sob, "and your heart would have been broken, and mine with it. I said I'd do it! I was out of my head by then, and I was only eighteen. I didn't think or reason. I just felt!"

She rubbed her fingers across her streaming eyes and choked.

"He hurried me into the hotel—my hotel—and into one of the private dining rooms. It was foggy with tobacco smoke and there were some officers standing around, arguing in loud voices. They stopped when we came in, but I didn't look at them, I kept my head down. A man in civilian clothes asked me questions and had me sign a paper he had filled out, and then he—he married me to one of the officers. I didn't look at him either, not even when he put a ring on my finger. Someone handed me a piece of paper and a roll of money and I went out. It was very quiet in the room, I remember, when I left."

It was quiet in the major's office, so still that she might have heard Bill Mason's harsh breathing. But she was years away, mesmerized by the haunting pictures she saw on the wall before her.

Tremaine said gently, "Go on, dear."

"I was in a fever to get back to Gerry, give her the money. She was in our living room and—and I threw the bills I had in my hand at her and said, '*Now* will you wait for Jim!' and I wanted to slap her face when she laughed. I went into my bedroom and locked the door for fear that I *would*.

"I lay on my bed, and must have fallen asleep with my clothes on, because in the morning I realized that I was fully dressed, even to the coat. And—and I opened my door and there was a note from her lying there. It said she'd gone!" Delight bit her lip and shook her head slowly. "That's all I remember—everything is a blank—until I found myself in a hospital bed and you there, Jimmy!"

She clutched his arm and shook it.

"It was *all* a horrible dream, wasn't it, Jim? I must have been delirious and had a nightmare. It isn't true, is it!"

Without a word Tremaine reached for the marriage certificate and handed it to her.

" 'William Hamilton Mason and Geraldine Tremaine,' " she read in a strangled whisper. "Why—" She stood up, gripping the chair back, and for the first time saw Mason as he stepped forward, haggard with strain, the veins on his forehead and neck standing out like cords, his gray eyes dull with pain. Hers turned from suffering to contempt, darkened to blazing indigo as she accused, "So, *I* am the girl you—you married to save a fortune!"

"So it seems," he admitted levelly. "But not to save any fortune. It was a thousand-dollar dare."

"You must be very proud of yourself!" she cut in, anger fast driving out her former emotion. "Well, what have you to say?"

154

"Nothing—now."

"Nothing!" she mocked. "The strong, silent lieutenant—I beg your pardon, *Captain* Mason!" Impatiently she whirled on her brother and held out the certificate. "This—this miserable thing isn't legal, is it, Jim! It can't hold me, can it?"

"Dee, darling, I'm afraid it can." He rubbed his face with the familiar gesture of indecision, battling to submerge his own tumultuous thoughts and answer her plea. "We have it direct from the official who performed the ceremony that it was all according to Hoyle. But probably it can be straightened out somehow, if you both want it."

"*Want* it?" she echoed shrilly.

Jim shook his head, trying to clear his numbed brain.

"Please, dear, I can't stand much more." He stared past her, seeing a ghost from years gone by. "Gerry didn't do it!" His voice was a tortured murmur. "And for six years I've believed she—" He closed his lips on the accusation and shook his head again. "Dee, I'm in no condition to think clearly, to give you any help. I'm sorry, but I'm just plain beat. I'm getting out. For God's sake, Captain, *you* talk to her!" He crossed to the door and fumbled for the handle.

"I won't stay here!" Delight cried wildly.

"You must." Jim spoke without turning. "This is something only you and Bill can settle, settle between you. Get it done now, there will never be a better time." He went out and shut the door, and they heard his slow-paced departure down the hall.

Head up, eyes stormy with outrage, Delight dared Mason to speak. As the silence lengthened she clasped her hands tightly to hide their trembling.

"Still nothing to say?" she jeered in desperation.

He stood looking down at her with a face carved from lifeless bronze, but deep in the gray eyes glowed a fire that made her heart pound suddenly. Breathlessly she snatched at the first thought that offered.

"Why, how stupid of me," she stammered. "You don't want this frightful mistake to continue any more than I do! You want to be free to marry that girl at home and I want— I want my freedom."

"Weren't you going to say, 'I want to marry *himself*'?" Mason suggested with an ironic smile. "Life is queer, isn't it, Dee? Here I've been crushed under a mountain of regret for years, but when I take Grandma Tremaine's advice and face up to it, it disappears. Because I've changed my mind, Dee. I don't want my freedom."

The horror of her awakened memory was still so strong that she faced him with white face and blazing eyes.

"You wouldn't hold me to this! You made a beast of yourself once, have you forgotten that so soon? Or do you think a thousand dollars was too much to pay for a drunken joke? You can have it back!" Hysteria threatened in the rising voice. "Jim will pay you the money you gave me. Take it, and let me go."

"Delight, listen to me." Mason put a hand on her arm, but she shrank away. He clasped his hands behind him to reassure her, and spoke without a trace of his former lightness. "You're making a tragedy out of this, but there is no tragedy. You'll see that when you've had time to get over this shock. Believe me, dear, you have nothing to fear from me.

"When you go back to the States with your brother it will be simple to have this marriage annulled. I won't contest it, I'll do all I can to help. Get a lawyer, have him call on me for anything necessary, and of course I pay for everything." The joy in her eyes hurt him and he added quickly, "There's just one more thing I must say to you."

"Don't—don't say any more!" she begged. "You've promised me my freedom. That is all I want."

"You must hear this, too." He put his hands gently on her shoulders, forcing her to look at him. "Delight, I want you to know that I love you. I've loved you since I saw you step from the plane that day you arrived in Totum."

Amazement held her breathless for a moment, and then, before she understood the quickened beating of her heart, resentment and injured pride urged her to hurt him.

"Do you expect me to believe that?" she demanded scornfully, and shook off his hold. "*You*—a man who marries a girl he has never seen before at the drop of a hat. How many other women have you married to win a thousand-dollar dare?" she jeered.

"How many other men have *you* married for a thousand dollars?"

She put her hands over flaming cheeks and stared at him like a slapped child.

"I—I was too ill to know—"

"And I was—" He checked the excuse and his own face flushed. "Forgive me, dear, for that unpardonable remark." He laughed softly, without a trace of amusement. "A perfect demonstration of the old Mason temper on the rampage. Something you'd have to learn to live with if—"

"I have no intention of living with it," she reminded hotly. "I'm leaving you now, and as I never want to speak to you again, I must ask you to return my ring." Her eyes snapped from the seal ring lying on the desk, as she explained quickly, "The ring I asked you to hold for me when we were fishing."

Involuntarily, as Mason remembered the incident, his hand went to his pocket.

"Oh, sorry, it's in my Windbreaker. I'll bring it to you—"

"No, *send* it, at once!" she ordered as she turned toward the door.

The cool dismissal angered Mason again. There was a white line about his lips as he caught her arm and swung her about. His hot eyes bored into hers, but he said evenly, "On second thought, you don't get your boy friend's ring back until your lawyer notifies me that the annulment has gone through."

"You have no right—"

"Hold it!" He could have been barking an order at his men from the tone, but there was a glint of amusement now in his eyes. "My wife cannot accept jewelry from another man!" With a bow he released her arm and started for the door.

"I want that ring!" she blazed. "If you don't return it at once—I'll—when I get home I'll make trouble! I'll have you transferred to—to some horrible place!"

Mason laughed, suddenly turned on his heel, and came back to her.

"You'd banish me?" he asked with a reckless grin. "All right, if I'm to be sent to the ends of the earth, I'll kiss my *wife* good-by. Before the startled girl could move he crushed her in his arms and kissed her full on the lips.

XXIV

DELIGHT sat before the mirror in her bedroom, elbows propped on the bare bureau, chin in hands, while she studied her reflection. This was what she had done, she thought, on the night of the Bentley dinner party, when she first arrived in Totum. How much had happened since then, and how different this face from that carefree one which had smiled confidently back at her so many weeks ago.

She lifted her chin defiantly, as though she challenged the world to find her changed. But in her heart she was forced to acknowledge that the lips which had been gay were grave now, and the violet eyes had known more than their share of tears.

With an impatient exclamation she whirled and looked around the room. It was stripped and as bare as it had been when she arrived. All her personal belongings, except those she would need tonight, were packed, waiting to be transferred to the plane which would depart tomorrow.

Tomorrow! How fast the first few weeks had flown, and how these last had crept in petty pace from day to day. Tomorrow she would be glad to go, eager to take the first step toward her freedom, relieved to quit the place where every day had become long hours of uneasiness.

Constantly with her was the fear that somehow a hint or whisper would disclose the secret of that sordid marriage ceremony. More than once she had shivered when she caught the sharp eyes of Babbling Bertha peering at her ringless hand in calculating suspicion.

She gave a scornful shrug. Only one more night! They were all welcome to anything they could discover after she was safely away. Restlessly she paced to the window.

The sun was dipping below the horizon. After the almost endless summer light, how short the days were growing. Wind with a chill in it swept long rollers up the wide beach already littered with refuse from the increasing tides. Near the town, and even dotting the hillsides of blue-gray pines, a few trees showed their autumn foliage. No flaming crimsons and dazzling yellows here, but only varying shades of russet and umber, as though even the trees felt the depressing approach of winter.

Winter at the post would be desolation, Delight thought with a shiver. What if there was gay talk of frequent trips to the cities only hours away by plane, of festivities planned by those who would remain in Totum and at the post? What pleasure would there be in any of that without companionship, without—Hurriedly Delight moved from the window to stand beside Tamara, who was on her knees tugging at a trunk strap.

"I'll miss you, Tam!" she sighed. "Are you quite sure you won't come with me? Think of Hawaii! Now that my brother is a colonel and assigned to staff duty there, *I* can think of nothing but exchanging Alaskan winter for perpetual sunshine and soft breezes. I can hardly wait! Better come along. It isn't too late to change your mind, even now."

The Indian girl sat back on her heels and looked up with a serene smile.

"Go—and leave my man? Not a chance! Everybody says Jed's a fine guy now. Just what I told you long ago, Miss Delight. He's very happy to be out of that terrible mess, and he doesn't shine shoes for that awful—for Captain Steele any more."

"I'm sure he'll make a good soldier now, Tam."

"And it was Lieutenant Mason who put him in charge of that new rocket gun—er—bazooka—they have in Baker Company," Tamara declared eagerly. "He said Jed was wasting his time just being a rifleman!"

158

"That's fine," Delight agreed absently, turning to the mirror to give her hair a final pat. "Haven't you finished with that trunk yet?"

"Yes'm." The girl was not to be detoured from a subject so dear to her heart. "Father Darley says Jed's turning out better than he hoped." She giggled. "He guesses he's got all his wild oats planted now that he's marrying me." With a quivering sigh she whispered, "I really love that guy, Miss Delight! And like I told you, we're going places!" Light-heartedness overcame the moment of solemnity and she laughed. "In the Army is where you really *do* go places, don't you? Maybe, when we get to traveling, we'll meet you somewhere—eh—maybe?"

"Wherever it is, Tam, I'll be glad to see you. And I *am* happy that things have turned out so well for you and Jed Crane. I'm going to miss all you people dreadfully."

"Then why go?" the girl demanded. With a grin at Delight's back she quoted, " 'It isn't too late to change *your* mind, even now.' We're all crazy about you. We're sorry to see the major go, too, but we like Lieutenant—I mean *Captain*—Mason very much. It's so confusing!" she sighed. "I called your brother the major, didn't I, but he's been promoted. His golden leaves have turned to silver and he's a *lieutenant* colonel. But Captain Mason *was* a lieutenant before *he* was promoted!" She giggled. "No wonder Jed laughs at me. I never can get all these officers lined up right."

"You'll learn in time," Delight encouraged. "Remember, you're in the Army now, so you'll have to."

"Yes'm, I will! I saw your brother's silver leaves today. My, they're pretty! Jed says, 'Hooray for Washington, for once they're giving the right guys a shove up the ladder.'

"It's funny, though," she mused, "Captain Mason doesn't act pleased with his new job at all. He used to smile so nice, once in a while, but he never does any more." She slanted another glance at Delight, who was very busy with her hair. "Do you suppose that girl in the States, the one he's in love with, really doesn't love him after all? She must be crazy, not to know a dream-boat when she sees one, don't you think?"

Delight glanced in desperation at her watch.

"I'd better go now. My brother will be getting impatient."

"It's going to be quite a party," Tamara remarked casually, but with an impish grin. "Now that Mrs. Bentley's sister has arrived maybe Captain Mason will perk up a bit. My, but she's pretty, Miss Delight. A real dish, Jed says. I helped her unpack, and she's just back from Paris, France, with the most beautiful dresses and things! I'll bet she'll make Captain Mason stop working all the time and have some fun. He's looked sort of tired and white lately, ever since that trip—"

"Tamara, please get my short yellow coat from the closet. I mustn't keep the colonel waiting."

"You going to put on a coat and cover that lovely dress?" Tamara protested indignantly. "It's so white and soft." She touched the tulle scarf at Delight's throat. "Hot dog! You look like a bride tonight. That's the same as the veil in those wedding pictures in the magazine I saw downstairs."

"Well, I'm not a bride!" Delight said severely. "If I look like one in this dress I'll take it off. You'll have to get out my yellow one, Tamara, the evening dress I've never worn here. It seemed too definitely formal, but tonight—" her cheeks began to glow "—since it is my last appearance in Totum, I might as well try to leave a good impression."

"The colonel's waiting and—"

"It won't take long, Tam, and I want to leave that Paris-gowned Bentley sister something to live up to."

"But Miss Delight! That yellow dress is all packed, and I had to jump on the trunk to shut it. It will be an awful job to—"

"Never mind that!" Delight's chin was set defiantly. "Get out that dress! It's your fault, anyway, for criticizing the one I have on. And I'll need the gold slippers," she added, with her first smile in many days, even though this smile had more of anticipation than humor. "If I'm going hog-wild I might as well go!" she muttered. "Nero-fiddling-while-Rome-is-burning stuff."

Colonel Tremaine called to her twice before she was ready, the second time in a fair approximation of his parade-ground bark.

When she finally hurried downstairs to the living room, where he was pacing the floor, he complained, "We're going to be late—" Then he saw her costume, did a double-take, opened his mouth to exclaim, then changed his mind. In silence, but shaking his head, he followed her to the door.

As they walked down the hill toward the river, one glowing segment of the crimson sun still peered between two islands far down the bay, like a red-hot coal caught in the bars of a grate. A moment later it slid from sight and cool green twilight descended over the sea and the town. Overhead quivering gold and vermilion painted every cloud, with deep purple shadows throwing the swelling billows into sharp relief.

Tremaine glanced sidewise at his sister, noting that the sunset put a flush on her usually pale cheeks. Sunset, or some secret plan for that evening? The unaccustomed, almost exotic splendor of her costume suggested that alternative and even a possible objective. Uneasily he wondered how to approach the delicate possibility without open questions.

Delight had not spoken of Bill Mason to him since that

harrowing night at Headquarters, when her awakened memory struck at her like a coiled serpent. Once or twice Jim had brought up his name, only to be rebuked with a bland, expressionless stare and a quiet, "Captain Mason and I have come to an understanding, Jim. Please let it go at that."

But Tremaine had not become a colonel by dodging disagreeable tasks. Resolutely he made another effort, calling on all the tact he could summon up.

"I'll probably have to leave before the party is over, Dee. Father Darley is coming to Headquarters for a last talk with me. He'll send word to the Bentleys' when he can make it. And then I'll want to go over a few details with Mason. As post commander he's running things rather shorthanded until they send in more officers. With Kent and myself out, and Steele gone, it throws quite a load on those that are left."

"So Captain Steele has moved on," Delight murmured. "I wondered, but was relieved that my pet hate in Totum hasn't bothered me since that—since *lately*," she amended hastily. "Where is he now?"

"Far away." Jim relaxed at her undisturbed acceptance of the forbidden subject. "As you can imagine, Bill Mason was in a mood to have his blood, so I ordered Steele to Anchorage the next day. A top-secret mission," the colonel grinned. "So top secret, in fact, that even I didn't know what he was to do there until I invented something at the last minute.

"Anyway, it got him out of camp until I shoved through his transfer in record time. He is now somewhere in Texas, I believe, and if I'm not to be quoted, good riddance!"

Delight took a long minute to put into words a question which had tortured her for days.

"Do you think he—he knew or even suspected that I was the girl that night in Washington?"

"He hadn't the least suspicion, Dee. Bill and I are both positive of that. From what Bill has told me about him, and from what I've noticed myself, I would bet that Steele is the type who would have used any such knowledge if he had it, even if it was only to make trouble."

Tremaine kept his voice to matter-of-fact calmness as he went on, "I'm glad this has come up, Dee, because there are one or two things I've wanted to say. They must be said," he insisted at her murmured protest. "Don't shut me out of your life any longer, Dee, I—"

"Jimmy dear!" Her voice broke as she protested. "I never meant to shut you out! I—I just couldn't talk about it. At first my heart—my brain—felt numb, as though they had been beaten into insensibility. And then—then they *hurt* unbearably, as if they were torn to raw, quivering flesh!"

Jim patted her shoulder sympathetically.

"I know it must have been hell, dear, but have you ever stopped to remember that you aren't the only one who has suffered? Don't let your feelings dope your sense of justice. I'm not defending Bill Mason, God knows, but before you condemn him—"

"You *seem* to be defending him!"

"No, Dee, I only want you to be fair. We mustn't forget that Bill didn't *make* you marry him. You were offered what amounted to a business proposition—never mind his motives or his mental state—and *you* accepted it. You were *paid* for it."

He stilled her protest with a raised palm and his voice choked with feeling.

"Don't get me wrong, child! I realize that what you did was a gallant attempt to help me. I'll never come close to settling the debt I owe you for that—trying to help me and Gerry. When I found that marriage certificate and the man's ring, and then her note to you, I—well, I thought she had—"

He paused and cleared his throat. "You were out of your head, you know, apparently had been ill for some time and could tell me nothing. Even when you recovered, you couldn't help fill in the blanks of that last day and night."

"Jimmy, how you have suffered!"

"Forget me! Do you think these years of uncertainty and remorse haven't hurt Bill Mason? Paying out blackmail money, that's what it was, you know; and always the threat of that unknown wife and whatever deviltry she might cook up hanging like the sword of Damocles over his head.

"Play fair, dear. Actually you were as much to blame as anyone else, but you didn't have to suffer and worry all these years because you had no memory of the business. Bill Mason has paid the full price, perhaps an exorbitant price, for an act of folly which, as far as I can find out, was his first and his last. Don't treat him as though he were a pariah."

When Delight remained silent he offered a final argument.

"I told you that I got Captain Steele away without bloodshed. Bill Mason would have been at his throat in a minute if I had not made him realize that any such move could conceivably break the secret wide open and drag you into the spotlight of publicity. So, like the gentleman he is, he left Steele alone."

Delight sighed, took a few silent steps, and then quoted, " 'You never know what stuff a person is made of until he comes to the great crisis of his life.' Do you remember when you said that, Jim? Well, when I came to mine I—I made an awful mess of it, didn't I!"

"My dear girl, that wasn't the crisis of your life, it was only a dramatic climax to one chapter. There is another thing you should know," he added hurriedly, as they approached a group of officers standing in front of the Bentley home. "That night, after the party celebrating the safe return of you and Bill from the ice fields, he begged me to arrange his transfer as soon as possible. His reason—he was so in love with you that he did not trust himself to stay here."

XXV

THOSE last words from Jim echoed over and over in Delight's mind while she danced and laughed her way through an evening which seemed as though it would never end. Fortunately she was allowed no moment to herself or she might have become lost in conflicting anxieties and desires. Her choice of the daffodil-yellow dress and its attendant accessories to create a sensation proved sound. The men swarmed around her, even Dr. Bentley succumbing to the extent of a brief waltz with his guest of honor.

"The belle of the ball," he smilingly assured her, puffing from the unusual exertion. "Sister Grace, as B.B. persists in calling her, will have to wait till you leave if she hopes to make any conquests here."

Delight resolutely crushed an impulse to look across the room where the lady in question was sipping punch—and laughing up at a tall officer with captain's bars on his broad shoulders. All evening, it had seemed to her, wherever she glanced, there was Captain Mason devoting himself with convincing thoroughness to the tiny and vivacious girl from Paris.

Was it the striking black hair and the ridiculously long black lashes which alternately veiled and revealed dancing black eyes, or that almost indecently low-cut, clinging dress from some master *couturier* on the Rue de Something or Other that drew him? And why should she feel a numbness in her heart each time she glimpsed that twosome, and an impatient jab of resentment at the complacent smile on Babbling Bertha's face while she kept tabs on the progress of their very evident mutual interest?

Delight snapped out of her absorption to find the gray-green eyes of her partner studying her with amusement.

"Grace would hold her own in any company," she said hastily.

"Seems to have made *one* conquest this evening," the doctor pointed out with a broad grin.

Delight shut her lips firmly on a tart answer and greeted Lieutenant Peck, when he cut in, with a smile that rocked the young man to his heels. He was blissfully unaware that the smile expressed unbounded relief at being rescued from the doctor's disturbing remarks, and he accepted it as a tribute to the pleasure of his company or perhaps to his dancing skill.

As a reward, and to convince her that she was wasting time in a sedate dance with an elderly retired medic, he whirled her through the maze of what turned out to be as near a jitterbug performance as the crowded room allowed.

Partner succeeded partner, with only Mason staying too pointedly outside her circle of admirers. Well, she had told him bluntly that she never wanted to speak to him again, hadn't she? He was being the perfect gentleman by respecting her wish—*darn* him! In desperation she pleaded exhaustion and forced a disappointed cut-in to sit out the dance while she tried to compose herself.

It was useless. The confusion of talk, laughter and music, the stifling closeness of the crowded room—although the windows stood wide and a breeze from the sea stirred the long curtains—above all the ceaseless combat of warring emotions grew unbearable at last. And when someone commandeered the record player and put on a series of haunting love ballads to replace the tunes to which they had been dancing, her endurance was strained to the breaking point.

With the songs came a flood of memories: the night on the island and Bill's tender care of her, the paralyzing terror of the cry which came from the forest and the peace found close by his side, the stern voice that quivered with unspoken tension while it ordered harshly, "Put your hands under your blanket—they'll be safer there." The mere remembrance swept hot blood to her cheeks and set her heart thumping until she felt that she must either scream or rush out of the house into the empty night.

She did neither, thanks to a father and mother, grandfathers and grandmothers who had bequeathed her their priceless ability to meet life as it came, head high and with bravely smiling lips. Instead she walked steadily across the room to where her hostess stood talking to Bill Mason and his lively partner.

Bill turned to meet her with a smile, but Delight ignored

him as she had ever since that world-shaking scene at Head-quarters.

"Good night, Mrs. Bentley—and Grace." She was able to give the sister a smile which held nothing but friendliness. "It's been nice to meet you, if only for a day. And I've loved this party, it makes the perfect final memory of Totum to take away with me. I have to finish some packing," she improvised quickly, with a sigh, "and Jim made me promise to go home early and get it done."

"Oh, my dear, must you?" Bertha's smile had spikes in it. "You're leaving Grace to shoulder the whole burden of entertaining all these nice young men, you know." There was an unmistakable undertone in the regret, indicating Bertha's opinion that her sister was more than capable of carrying out the assignment. Perhaps fearful that she might be offering an inducement for Delight to stay, she gushed, "But you do look tired, my dear, your face is quite gray. You have never been quite the same since our trip to the glacier, have you!"

From under lowered lids Delight saw Bill Mason frown and make an impatient movement as if he would speak. She knew he must be thinking, as she was, of how much more she had borne than a mere adventure in the ice fields. But she allowed him no opportunity to make any protest, saying lightly, "How silly I must seem to all you old-timers, to let a little thing like a night in the wilderness get me down!"

"Old-timers!" Babbling Bertha exclaimed indignantly.

"I meant old-timers here in Totum, of course," Delight assured her sweetly. "Perhaps I should have said 'veterans'?" She caught Bill's repressed flicker of a smile, but refused to answer it, listening gravely to her hostess.

Mrs. Bentley clasped her hands in dramatic despair. "She isn't much like the radiant girl who proposed a toast to her fiancé at our dinner party, is she, Captain Mason? Oh, but I forgot—you weren't here, were you? Too busy! Perhaps as our new commandant," she suggested, linking arms with Grace and sending an arch look from her to Mason, "you may find that you have more time for us civilians."

"I'm sure he will," agreed Delight coolly. "He's had a wonderful time tonight, haven't you, Captain?" she demanded with a knowing glance. "Remember, when we first met I told you that you only needed practice to become a charming companion."

"I remember it very well." His look spoke louder than the words. "And I practiced every chance I got." He smiled. "You see the result."

Mrs. Bentley intervened. "Grace and I—all of us—are

planning to be at the airstrip tomorrow, Delight, to give you a royal send-off. But my dear! I imagine our poor efforts won't be a patch on the welcome you'll receive at the other end from the happy man!"

"Happy man?" growled Dr. Bentley, who had joined the group. "*Lucky* man, you mean, to be getting her back at all! Delight, I'll tell the world that letting you leave Totum proves the young men here have about as much snap as there is in a dead Martini! If I was fifty years younger—!" Laying a hand on the breast of his white dinner jacket and rolling regretful eyes to Heaven, he heaved a noisy sigh of resignation.

"*Fifty?*" Delight laughingly rejected that figure. "Make it forty, Doctor, and then——" Her duplication of his sigh brought a delighted chuckle from Bentley, but her smile faded as she found Bill Mason's eyes fixed on her with an intensity which set every nerve tingling. "And now I really must run along," she gasped.

Mason nodded. "I'll see you safely home, Delight, whenever you are ready to leave."

"But you needn't—"

"The colonel asked me to," he explained easily. "He and I still have a few matters to discuss in connection with the transfer of command."

"But there's no reason to——" This time Delight interrupted her own stormy protest when she caught a ferret look on Mrs. Bentley's intent face. "If it's an order from the colonel, I suppose that settles it." She hoped that what she meant for a lighthearted smile appeared so to the others.

"I would feel terribly guilty, Mrs. Bentley, if *I* were responsible for taking away the lion of the evening. But you lucky people are going to have him all winter," she reminded, "so you won't begrudge me these last few minutes, will you?"

She was overdoing the lighthearted affection act, she realized in alarm. Voice and words were too gaily challenging; she had twinkled her eyes too merrily at Bill Mason. She heard his quick indrawn breath before he turned to bid a formal good-night to the Bentleys and Grace, and she felt tension like a charge of electricity building up in the atmosphere as he guided her through the protesting guests to the door.

Walking down the hill beside him she sent a frantic S.O.S. call to her benumbed brain for some trivial remark which would shatter the taut silence, a stillness presaging a storm. She sent a questing look around the bay and the camp for inspiration. No help from that dreary scene, where she had been so happy until—Without warning, tears flooded her eyes and she stumbled.

Instantly Mason's hand was under her elbow. His fingers closed warmly strong and steadying.

"All right?" he asked in a whisper choked with repression.

The girl had to wait a moment to steady her voice before she said, "Perfectly all right, thanks." She couldn't stop with that sufficient answer but chattered on, she thought wryly, with Babbling Bertha inanities. "It's—it's these tricky spike heels which I put on to impress the natives. I've worn loafers so much that when I step out in style the high heels are apt to throw me."

Silence again. His hand still held her arm lightly, and not for the world would she have drawn away. She looked around again. The moonlight made the bay a mirror of glistening quicksilver and flung its glamour even over the drab barracks of the post and the bleak white houses of Officers Row perched on the hillside above the parade ground.

Beyond them, the soft purple hills rolled back like waves, ridge after spruce-clad ridge, to the gigantic snowy peaks of the mountains silvered by the moon. A dreary scene? Nonsense! Wherever she looked she saw only breath-taking beauty, beauty now so familiar that she would forever miss it when she was far away.

They crossed the bridge and started up the long slope toward her house. From the deep shadow of the camp entrance a dark figure stepped with a click of heels, and moonlight gleamed dully on his helmet, dazzlingly on his bayonet, as he presented arms. Mason snapped a salute and went on, still silent.

Delight felt herself slipping back into that stunned, almost comatose state where speech would not come and even to breathe was a herculean labor. How different this was from her walk home with Captain Steele after the other Bentley dinner, when his complacent chatter only added to her dislike of his blatant vanity. If Bill would only *say* something —anything—instead of stalking at her side in this portentous silence like Fate approaching a mortal with impending doom.

It was unbearable! "What a live wire Bertha's sister is!" she exclaimed suddenly. "Totum won't be dull this winter with her on hand!"

"I should say not!"

Delight stumbled again but caught herself in time to conceal it. Did he have to be so darned enthusiastic? With immeasurable relief she discovered that they were at her door.

"Thanks, Captain—"

"I'm coming in." At her automatic protest he raised his eyebrows in pretended surprise. "I assure you I only want to see what furnishings I'll need when you move out."

She felt herself blushing as she led the way into the partially dismantled living room and watched him survey it slowly. That same dreadful paralysis was creeping over her, threatening to deprive her of the power of speech.

"You see I've left our rose-colored curtains for you," she murmured idiotically. She tried again. "Jim did tell me that as commandant, you would be moving in here, but somehow I just can't imagine a bachelor captain of infantry basking in such very feminine color."

"I'm not a bachelor."

The curt reminder was shocking as a dash of cold water and she caught her breath. Then she recovered and answered with a flippant laugh, "Cheer up! Once I reach the good old United States proper you won't have a ball and chain around your neck for long." Even as she spoke and saw his eyes smolder a surge of passionate longing shook her body with a force that frightened her.

And I will never see this man I love again! she told herself. Aloud, she gasped, "As for the color of the curtains, I'm sure Bertha's sister—"

"Stop calling her 'Bertha's sister'!" he snapped. "You know her name!" His face was white, drawn and lined with strain as he glared down at her. "And—don't play with fire, pal!" he warned through tight lips.

In her turmoil of emotion she hardly knew what she was saying, only panic drove out the words in bitter scorn.

"Why, you must be in love with her already for such an angry defense! I thought so when you monopolized her all evening—to the envy of the other guests. All right, when I go—"

She never finished the sentence. Bill gripped her shoulders. Even his lips were white as he groaned, *"When you go!"* His fingers tightened. "Do you realize that I have the right to keep you here? *Here*—in this house—*with me?"*

Her face was as colorless as his, so close above her. Desperately she longed to wrench free, but she could not move. She stared into his glowing eyes.

"Do you mean—" She tried to force the tremor from her voice, but failed. "You don't want me to go?"

"Want you to go? Good God!" In a sudden surge of passion he caught her in his arms and crushed her close, kissing her eyes, her lips, her throat. He let her go then and stepped back. "That ought to show you how much I want you to stay!"

He heard her stifled sob as she leaned against the table and the reckless light died in his eyes.

"Don't be afraid, Dee," he muttered, ashamed of the outburst. "I swear that won't happen again!" He swung on his heel and strode to the door.

Delight struggled to speak, to still a heart that pounded until it deafened her. Through stiff lips she could utter no more than a pleading, "Please, Bill!"

When he wheeled, gray eyes again turbulent and flaming, her courage almost failed and a barely audible whisper framed the words. "Before you go—won't you please give—give me my ring?"

A flush of resentment darkened his face. "I told you that you could have your ring back when you are free of me—and not before," he reminded coldly.

She could not raise her eyes from her nervously twisting hands. Faintly she murmured, "I—I didn't mean *that* ring."

She heard the quick tread as he moved close to her and saw his hands clenched at his side, but still she could not look up.

"What are you talking about?" he demanded hoarsely.

For an instant she lifted her eyes to his.

"Why, the—the ring with the coat of arms—my wedding ring, in case you've forgotten. I—I think I would like—" The violet eyes dropped from the mounting fire in the gray eyes, but she persisted breathlessly, "I wish you'd put it on my finger again."

"Dee!"

The two tense figures merged, and there was silence in the room except for the clock on the mantel ticking off a minute, and then another.

"Sweetheart," Bill whispered at last, "you really mean that you're going to stay with me?"

She moved her head from his shoulder just enough to peer up at his radiant face. There was a tinge of laughter in her muffled voice.

"It's this house, Bill! I love it so. I can't bear to leave it for a mere man to look after."

"I go with the house, pal!" He checked his grin and put a finger under her chin to tilt her face to his. Gravely he warned, "There's one piece of unfinished business still, unfortunately. How about the fiancé who gave you the diamond ring? The man you toasted at the Bentleys'."

"*Himself?*" She giggled. "A confession, Bill. The diamonds came from Mother's estate, they were camouflage. That night when Babbling Bertha put me on the spot and I was forced to conjure up *someone* for a fiancé—suddenly I saw you standing there, as clearly as I see you now. I guess, *himself* was Lieutenant William Hamilton Mason. Always you, Bill, just *you!*"

Mason's arms tightened as though they would never let her go.

"Why didn't you admit it sooner, for goodness' sake? Think of the days we've lost—together."

Her eyes were bright with laughter, but very close to tears, as she leaned back to look him full in the face.

"I refuse to think of them—I'm thinking of the days we'll *have* together. My sable cloud has turned its silver lining, Bill!"